I0773315

I'll Be Seeing You

JOANNE KUKANZA EASLEY

RED BOOTS PRESS

Copyright © 2022 by Joanne Kukanza Easley

All rights reserved.

No portion of this book may be reproduced in any form, stored in a retrieval system or transmitted in any form or by any means without written permission from the publisher or author, except by a reviewer who may quote brief passages in a review to be printed in a newspaper, magazine, or journal.

This is a work of fiction, Names, characters, businesses, places, events, and incidents are either the product of the author's imagination or used in a fictitious manner. Any resemblance to actual persons, either living or dead, is purely coincidental.

Publisher-Red Boots Press

Cover Design-Erin Cronin Pearson

Author Photo-Spunky Cloud Photography

ISBN: 979-8-9867133-0-4

LCCN: 2022914329

Contents

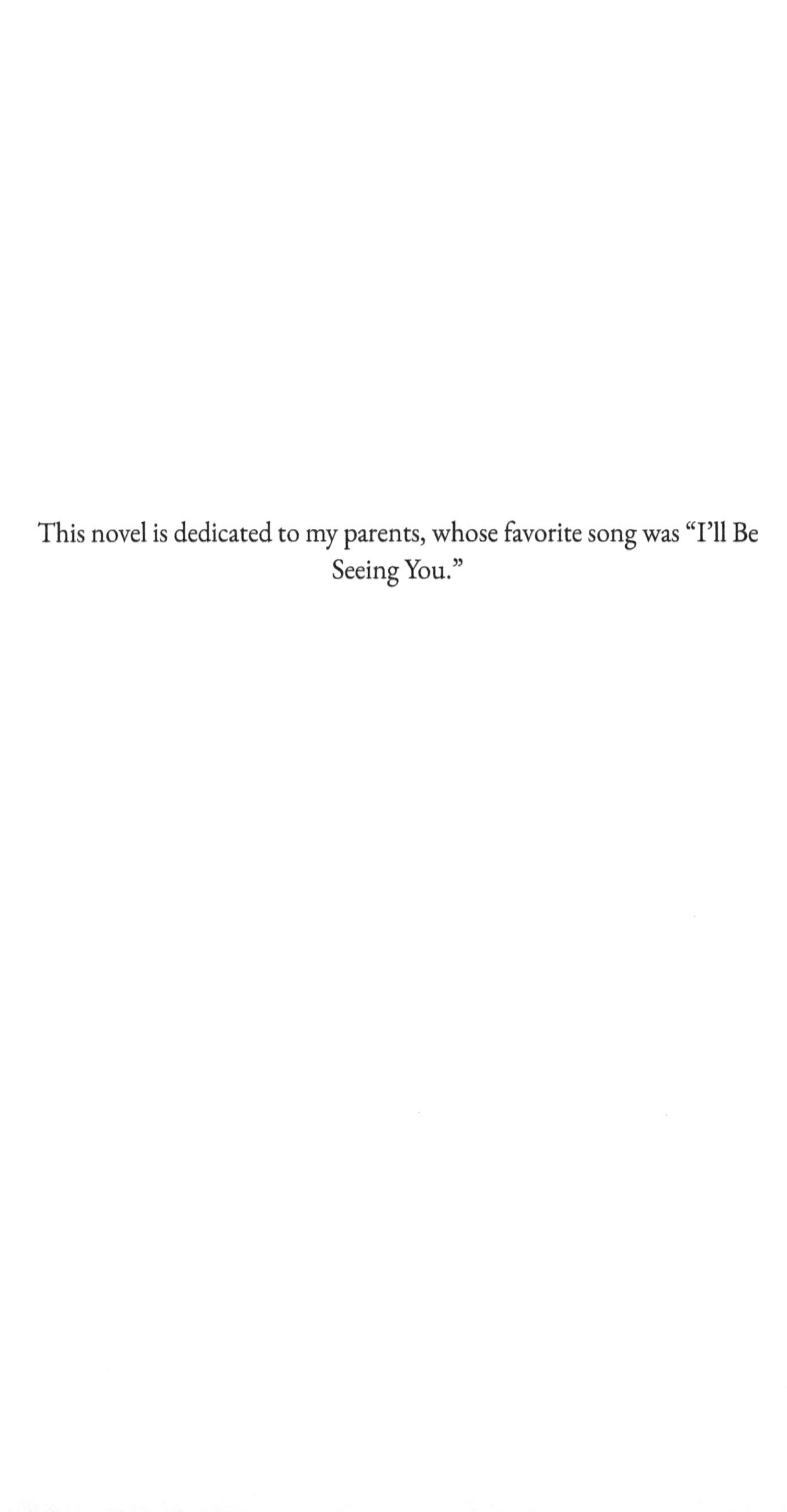

This novel is dedicated to my parents, whose favorite song was "I'll Be Seeing You."

Chapter One

A SEED IS PLANTED-1938

The first fourteen years of my life were about what you'd expect for the only girl in the family on a Texas cattle ranch. I was the middle child, bookended by my four brothers, two on each side.

My outdoor chores ended the day I found blood in my unmentionables. Terrified and thinking I was dying, I ran to Mama and blubbered the news. She stopped hanging laundry on the clothesline, walked me inside, and sat me down at the kitchen table.

"Well, Ruby, today you became a woman." She bit her lip and looked everywhere but at me.

"What's that have to do with the bleeding?"

Mama explained what she called "the facts of life." While she talked, I thought about the heifers and cows I'd watched in heat and being bred. I shuddered, telling myself people were different and anyway, I didn't have any plans to get bred, leastways not for a good, long time.

"Things are going to change for you now. No more working the cattle. You can still feed the chickens. And of course, you'll be helping me in the house."

Far as I was concerned, the whole thing seemed like a raw deal for girls, and my heart broke a little. No, a lot. Being demoted to household chores—woman's work—chapped my hide. Cooking, cleaning, and baking were not my idea of fun. My protests made no difference at all. Even appealing to my daddy didn't help, although I was the apple of his eye, and that had nothing to do with my red hair. Not just any red hair, but mahogany, I was told.

Mama told me to face up to reality. "I'm preparing you for the future."

I couldn't tell her I wanted no part of that future.

The summer after I finished eighth grade, a reprieve from the drudgery came in the form of Mama's half-sister, Imogene. She descended on our peaceful life, landing like a tornado. We'd heard stories—eye-popping stories of her days as a flapper and her "affairs of the heart" gone bad—so my brothers and I couldn't wait to get a gander. We were not disappointed.

Mama was tight-lipped about her New York City past. I knew she left there in 1919 to marry Daddy, giving up city life for the ranch, but that was about it. Couldn't figure why there was so much secrecy about her family.

Being what Daddy called a "natural beauty," Mama didn't usually fuss over her appearance. But the day Imogene came to visit, Mama asked me to finish up the baking so she could "freshen up." When she came back to the kitchen, I had to look twice at her transformation. Gone was her housedress and apron. She wore her Sunday-best dress and had fashioned her strawberry-blond hair into a pageboy. Her eyes and lips were painted, like she was fixing to go out on the town. That wasn't the only surprise I got that day.

Aunt Imogene arrived in a Cadillac car, a brand new 1938 model. The shiny black paint and whitewall tires were coated with dust, but that didn't stop my younger brothers Dylan and Jace from admiring every detail, from the running boards to the checkerboard-looking grill to the hood ornament.

The car door opened, and a tall woman stepped out, looking like a model on the cover of *Photoplay*, the magazine my friend Clare subscribed to. She wore a cream and royal blue dress with a cape! Her hat, shoes, gloves, and handbag all matched the blue color. When I saw how the road dust covered those shoes, I cringed. Imogene took off her hat and gloves and ran her hands through her curly mahogany tresses, the exact same color as my own hair, and just as wavy.

Mama noticed my reaction and said, "Shut your mouth, Ruby. Flies and all that."

I turned to her. "You never said she has the same hair as me."

Mama twisted her lips. Under her breath she muttered, "Imogene always threatened to come visit, but I never thought I'd see the day."

Why did Mama see Aunt Imogene's visit as a threat?

My aunt set one elegant foot in front of the other, carefully keeping her balance on the rutted dirt road as she approached us.

Knowing she'd taken the train to Fort Worth, I wondered how she got the car. With hands on hips, Mama came right out and asked.

"Well, if you must know, I stopped at the Cadillac dealer and said I wanted to take a test drive."

Mama rolled her eyes. "An overnight test drive to Mineral Wells?"

Imogene waved off the remark. "Details, details."

"Par for the course." Mama spoke low, so only I could hear.

Imogene stopped two feet from Mama. "Aren't you glad to see me?" Her smile lit up her face.

Mama's smile didn't reach her eyes. "Imogene. Wasn't sure what time to expect you, but I've got supper cooking. This is my daughter Ruby." She called the boys over and introduced them.

Words stuck in my throat. Like a fool, I just nodded and gave a little wave.

To my surprise, Dylan stepped forward and offered his hand. "Howdy, Aunt Imogene. Welcome to the Eaton spread. That Cadillac car sure is something." Jace peeked out from behind him. "This here is Jace. He's eight and kinda shy."

"Rose, those boys are the spitting image of Leland. By the way, where's your hubby and the two older boys? I think you said you have *five* children." Her astonished tone left no doubt how she felt about a large family.

"Bringing in the cattle. Ought to be along any minute. They can fetch in your luggage. Let's head inside."

Imogene grinned and put her arm around my shoulder. "Look at you. You surely favor your mother, although you were blessed with the Babcock hair."

Awestruck by my glamorous aunt, I almost swooned when I caught a whiff of her perfume. I'd bet a nickel it came from France. How would she react to staying in my room and sharing a bathroom with seven other people?

"This is quite the place you have here, Rose. So scenic. Seems like a going concern, but what do I know of cattle ranches?" Imogene strode toward the front porch with purpose, and we followed her like a line of ducklings.

Supper that night was one to remember and not because of the food. Mama made a pot roast with potatoes and root vegetables. Tuesday was baking day, so we had fresh bread. And blueberry pie for dessert.

After our blessing, we settled in to eat. Aunt Imogene took tiny little portions and refused Mama's homemade gravy. She even scraped off what was on the meat. That raised eyebrows. With their usual enthusiasm, my daddy and brothers filled their plates and dug in.

"Have to say, Imogene, never thought you'd grace our ranch with your presence." As he sopped up gravy with his bread, Daddy smiled, which sort of took the sting out of the words.

Even so, I held my breath, waiting for Imogene to respond.

"Well, it's about time I came to see my sister's family, right, Rose?"

Mama had frown lines between her eyes, and I sensed tension and a whole lot of history between the half-sisters. After a bit, she answered, "We're glad to have you, Imogene." A sort of non-answer. I could almost hear Mama wondering why she was here.

All four boys ate in silence. No one seemed much for talking tonight, which I thought was odd, since we had company. I searched around for something to say and finally just asked, "Why are you here, Aunt Imogene?"

Forks clattered onto plates, throats were cleared, and all eyes turned to my aunt. I regretted my question. Would Mama think I was too forward?

Imogene threw back her head and laughed. "So glad you asked, my dear. I've come to take you to New York for a visit. Call it a graduation present."

My jaw dropped, and a tingle ran up my spine. "Really? Oh my goodness! Mama, did you know?"

Mama's frown was bigger now and her cheeks glowed red. "No, I did not."

"That's mighty generous of you, Imogene," Daddy said. Then he got a look at Mama's face and backtracked. "We'll discuss this later. Without the kids."

After dessert, the grown-ups sat in the parlor and had their discussion. I couldn't hear a darn thing and had a hard time concentrating on washing the dishes. The song "Lullaby of Broadway" played in my head. Would Mama and Daddy allow me to go? Would I see the Empire State Building, go to a Broadway play, eat in a restaurant? My mind spun with the glamourous images I'd seen at the picture show and in Clare's magazines.

Just as I was wrapping the leftover pie, Mama and Daddy stepped into the kitchen. While I waited for them to speak, I held my breath.

Daddy smiled, and I knew. Mama came to my side and put her arm around me. "You're going to see New York City." She didn't look real happy about it, but boy, I sure was.

I raced to my room to start packing.

Early the next morning, Aunt Imogene and I skipped breakfast and piled in the Cadillac. Everyone stood on the porch watching us drive away.

Two hours later, we drove up to the car dealer. Aunt Imogene pulled out her gold compact and checked her image. "Wait in the car, kiddo. I'll get someone to drive us to the train station."

As soon as my aunt opened the car door, a red-faced man approached, waving his arms. "I thought you were just going around the block!"

Imogene strode right up to him. "Why the fuss? I've returned the car, although it needs a wash. And a fill-up."

"I didn't know you'd be gone overnight," the man fairly shouted.

Imogene smiled and handed him the keys. "You didn't ask."

The man opened and closed his mouth, like a catfish on a hook gasping for air.

Mesmerized by the drama, I couldn't wait to see how this would end. Imogene stood her ground and looked the man right in the eye.

He cleared his throat. "Quite right, Miss Babcock."

Seemed to me, Aunt Imogene had used the family name and her connections when she borrowed the car. Did the Babcock name carry weight even in Texas? I had to hand it to my aunt—she knew how to get what she wanted.

"One more thing," she said, placing her hand on his arm. "We'll need a ride to the train station." Her eyelashes fluttered, and from his reaction, she may have hypnotized the man.

He smiled and patted her hand. "Let me have the pleasure of driving you myself."

At the station, we boarded the train and found our accommodations. When this train arrived in Chicago, we'd switch to the New York Central for the last leg of the journey. I never thought the traveling part would take so long, and by the time we arrived at Grand Central Station, I was plumb wore out.

My first sight of the Manhattan skyline took my breath away. How many people lived and worked in those skyscrapers? Hundreds of people, maybe more than lived in all of Palo Pinto County, in a single building. Back in Mineral Wells, the Baker Hotel, with its fourteen stories, towered over the rest of the town, but it would be dwarfed in New York. There was no mistaking the Empire State Building, the tallest of them all. It was lit up like a Christmas tree. I couldn't imagine the electric bill.

As our taxi made its way down the streets, I gazed in wonder, my senses overwhelmed by the traffic noise, the neon lights, and the teeming crowds.

Aunt Imogene puffed on a cigarette in a long, black holder. "When we get home, I'm sure Vandine will have a little dinner for us."

The smoke made me scrunch up my nose, so I rolled down the window. "I'm not very hungry." I didn't tell her the smoke was making me sick.

"Suit yourself. I'm famished."

"Mama said Vandine taught her how to cook."

"Yes, she did. I suppose it came in handy for Rose, given the number of meals she must cook each day." Imogene blew out perfect circles of smoke. "I was never interested in such things."

Can't say her answer surprised me.

The taxi pulled up to the Babcock residence—what Mama called a veritable mansion. I confess I had to look up "veritable." After the driver brought our luggage to the porch, Imogene handed him a five-dollar bill. "Keep the change."

The smiling driver whistled as he stuck the bill in his pocket and hustled down the steps.

When a Negro lady opened the door, I about dropped my teeth. Mama never said Vandine was a Negro. What else hadn't she told me?

Imogene threw her arms around Vandine. "So good to be home and back to civilization." Urging me forward, she said, "Meet Rose's daughter, Ruby. Although we decided she'll go by her middle name from now on. Lauren suits her so much better. Don't you agree?"

Vandine raised an eyebrow. "Rose might could have a little somethin' to say 'bout that." She put her hands on the hips of her full-skirted shirtwaist dress and looked me up and down. "My, you sure are the picture of your mama. Exceptin' the hair. Ya know, I kinda like the name 'Ruby,' but I'll call you which one you say."

"I'd like if you'd call me 'Lauren.'"

"Pleased to meet you, Lauren." Vandine chuckled and said, "Let's get these bags in the house." We did, then the three of us headed straight to the kitchen.

The delicious aroma of hot apple pie brought back my appetite. After eating two pieces of Vandine's fried chicken and a biscuit slathered with butter, I only had room for one slice of pie.

"Thank you, Vandine. That was yummy."

I tried to clear the table, but Vandine waved me off. "Shoo, now. Time you settled in."

Aunt Imogene rose and stretched. "Let me show you around, kiddo."

Mama was right—the house was a veritable mansion—grand, with tall ceilings and gleaming walnut-paneled walls in the downstairs rooms. Crystal chandeliers hung in the foyer and dining room. Gold brocade furniture, colorful patterned rugs on the marble floors, gilt-framed oil paintings of my ancestors, fresh flowers in vases. Nothing like our ranch house. I felt like I had to tiptoe and whisper in such a place.

During the ten days I spent with my aunt, I lived in a state of jubilation and admiration. Too many times to count, the words "incredible" and "magnificent" came out of my mouth. We visited the Museum of Natural

History, and I had to be dragged away from the exhibits in the Hall of Ocean Life. Living in Texas, I'd never seen the ocean, and the size of the giant clam and whale skeletons amazed me. Aunt Imogene took me to the picture show to see *The Adventures of Robin Hood* with Errol Flynn. My first Broadway play at the Shubert Theatre, *I Married an Angel*, made me wonder if I could ever be on stage. Not likely, but it was fun to think about.

And the shopping! Aunt Imogene flounced through the perfumed air of Bloomingdale's, followed by eager salesclerks. The aisles loaded with merchandise, the elegant customers, and the escalator dazzled me. Uncertain about stepping on those moving stairs, Aunt Imogene had to take my hand before I'd set foot on them. I didn't know where to look first. The mannequins all wore hats. When I mentioned to Aunt Imogene I felt naked without one, she bought me a straw boater, and I wore it everywhere.

We ate in fancy restaurants with cloth napkins and waiters dressed up in suits—not once, but four times. I'd never imagined a life like the one Imogene lived.

I dreaded going back to the ranch. Why couldn't I stay? But I didn't have the backbone to ask my aunt. As we waited for the taxi for our return trip, I choked back tears as I hugged Vandine goodbye.

"You be sure to remember me to your mama, now."

All I could do was nod. In the taxi, I pondered the bits of family history I gleaned from listening to Imogene and Vandine talk. Mama's mother had died in childbirth, and she was raised by a string of nannies until Vandine arrived on the scene after Imogene's mother ran off. I couldn't imagine not having a mama, or even someone who cared, until the age of ten. Why hadn't Mama told me these things?

The trip back to Texas took even longer than the trip to New York, or maybe it just felt that way. Aunt Imogene seemed to have lost interest in me and spent her time in the lounge car. When my folks picked us up at the Fort Worth train depot, Imogene flat refused to get on the train to return to New York.

"Leland, take me to the nearest airport. I've had enough of travel by rail."

On the silent ride to Meacham field, I wondered if I'd ever see Aunt Imogene—or Manhattan—again. All I had to commemorate the trip was my straw boater and a collection of postcards. At the airfield, Mama stayed in the car while Daddy unloaded Imogene's bags, and a porter whisked them away. I hugged her goodbye and thanked her for the wonderful time.

"When you're a little older, come and see me again." Aunt Imogene blew me a kiss and followed the porter inside the terminal.

"I will!" Out of the corner of my eye, I saw Mama with her lips in a tight line, shaking her head.

As we drove back home, I marveled Mama was raised in the same house as Imogene. How did they turn out so different? Mama was as straitlaced as they come, while my aunt was what I'd call "jaunty."

Mama met Daddy when he visited New York City after the Great War. He stayed only a few days because he was needed on the family ranch. But Cupid's arrow had hit its mark. Two weeks later, he got the surprise of his life when Mama called from the Fort Worth train station. "And the rest is history," she always said. I figured there was more to the story but doubted I'd ever hear it.

Why in the world would Mama give up such a glamourous life for the dreariness of cooking, cleaning, and plucking chickens? Did the love of a man make you forget everything else but him? The whirlwind visit left me convinced that someday I would find a way to escape my fate as a ranch wife in Palo Pinto County, Texas.

Chapter Two

BACK AT THE RANCH-1940

Two years later, after a tough competition with the local girls, I was crowned Miss Mineral Wells. The title came with the chance to ride on the town float in the Fort Worth Stock Show Parade. While I was over the moon, Mama wasn't. "Don't let this go to your head."

At the dress shop, I chose a dreamy powder blue gown. When Mama first saw me in it, she had kittens. I didn't care because I felt like a princess. The plunging neckline wasn't really daring because a lace insert covered my upper chest, what the owner of the dress shop called an "illusion neckline to cover your décolletage." The fitted bodice flared into yards and yards of tulle. If it was strapless, Mama would have forbidden me to wear it, but it had the sweetest little cap sleeves.

The March wind chilled my arms, bare above my white gloves, forcing me to drape my midnight blue velvet cape over my shoulders, although I hated to do so. Seemed like it took forever to line up the floats, bands, riders, and livestock for the parade, and while I waited, I thought back to my trip to Manhattan. If I ignored the odor of the cattle and looked past the cow pies, I could pretend I was riding in the Macy's parade to Herald Square. As the procession lined up, the electricity and anticipation in the air reminded me of the excitement of New York—and my vow to escape from Mineral Wells. Maybe Mama liked the ranch life, but Aunt Imogene showed me what life could be like in the big city. At last, the parade got a move on, and we made our way through downtown Fort Worth.

That day, I waved and smiled until my face froze in place and my right arm was about to fall off. Then I got smart and used my left arm. Thousands of people lined the street. Newspapermen dashed up to my float, and my eyes saw spots after the flashbulbs all but blinded me. Through it all, I kept my best smile on my face.

The parade lasted a good deal longer than I thought it would. When we got to the end of the line at the Northside Coliseum, I stepped off the float, almost turning my ankle in my high heels, and hobbled to the restroom. As I washed my hands, I assessed myself in the mirror. The cold air lent color to my cheeks. I had been allowed to use a light touch of eye shadow, mascara, and lipstick. If you asked me, I looked quite a bit older than sixteen. My unruly wavy hair was escaping from my updo. I felt a little like Cinderella returning to normal after the ball, although my beautiful gown and blue satin slippers were intact.

I found my way to the participants' tent and met up with my family. Daddy smiled and looked right proud of me, but Mama just glanced at her watch. My brothers ignored me. Dylan had entered his first market steer in the junior division, and Jace was showing a breeding heifer later that afternoon. My older brothers, Travis and Mason, were competing in the cutting competition. They bragged on their Quarter horses' cow sense and agility, each certain of a ribbon in the amateur category. None of them had the slightest interest in my success. Up until three years ago, I would have been showing my own heifer, but my focus was on a whole new world.

"Daddy, we're fixin' to go see the exhibits before our events," Travis said. "That all right?" He spoke for all the boys, who squirmed and jostled each other as they waited for approval. With a nod, Daddy patted Travis on the shoulder, and the four boys scooted without saying a word to me.

A gaggle of reporters shoved their way up to us. "You the girl was on the Mineral Wells float?" I'd never had such attention focused on me. The commotion was startling but kind of nice.

Daddy kissed Mama on her forehead. "Rose, you stay with Lauren. I'm gonna catch up with the boys. We'll meet up later at the food tent. About three." Without a backward look, he shouldered his way past the crowd surrounding Mama and me.

I posed for more pictures and answered questions about Mineral Wells to the best of my ability. It was easy to spot who was from out of town by the questions. Anyone who asked about Crazy Water wasn't a local. After a while, Mama started looking around and fidgeting, like she wanted to get away, but I was energized and excited. Emboldened, I got more creative with my poses and smiled like there was no tomorrow. I could have vamped all day.

Firmly taking hold of my elbow, Mama shoved me behind her. She addressed the crowd. "I think we've answered all your questions. We'd like to view the competitions, and I have to get my daughter out of that dress."

A few groans, mostly good-natured, a few more blinding light bulb flashes, and my moment of fame was over. All of a sudden, I was tired, deflated, and my feet hurt in the new shoes. Felt like I had blisters on my left big toe and right heel. As I trailed behind Mama to the dressing room, I was fairly limping.

The rest of the day, dressed in my ranch clothes, I wandered in a daze, looking at the Appaloosa, Paints, and Quarter horses, but not really seeing them.

My best friend from school, Clare, came running up with two other girls from our crowd. "You sure looked great on that float, like a Hollywood movie star!" Clare gushed at me. She was my best friend for a reason.

Kate echoed Clare's assessment. "You still got your makeup on. Boy, you look real grownup, like you're about twenty years old!"

Donna patted her hair, an unfortunate carrot red and just as curly as mine. "Love the hairdo, but it's starting to come down. Here, let me try to fix it." She stood on her tiptoes to reach my head. I was five-foot-nine, and she was five-foot-even if she was lucky, but she was good with hair, I had to admit.

"Ruby, I'm going to go chat with Mrs. Fowler." Mama handed me a dollar. "Be at the food tent at three."

I yelled after her. "My name is *Lauren*!"

Mama just continued walking, didn't even turn around. She insisted on calling me by my given name, and I insisted on being called by my middle name, like Aunt Imogene had suggested. Mama and I hadn't agreed to disagree, just continued to argue the point. I was determined to win. All the kids at school and most of the teachers called me "Lauren." So did Daddy.

Three days later, when opportunity came knocking, I was helping Mama in the kitchen. Every Tuesday after school, my life revolved around making bread for the week. I had mixed feelings about it. Sometimes I yearned to be outside. Or in Manhattan.

My youngest brother, Jace, burst through the kitchen door. "There's a big fancy car comin' up the lane. Boy howdy, he's really movin' fast. C'mon and see."

Mama wiped her hands on a towel and patted Jace's shoulder. "Honey, I'm right in the middle of baking. Take Ruby with you to meet the car." She turned to me. "I can manage the rest. Let me know who it is. Can't imagine who'd show up here in a big fancy car."

"I told you not to call me Ruby. I go by Lauren."

Mama frowned. "Watch your tone. Ruby is your given name. I birthed you, so I'll call you by the name I gave you."

Turning to follow Jace, I shot back over my shoulder, "I hate the name Ruby!"

"That's too bad!"

The battle of wills continued, with neither of us willing to surrender.

My brother slammed through the screen door and called to me from the porch. "C'mon, sis."

The huge black car braked in a plume of dust. "Those whitewalls ain't so white anymore," I said.

"It's a La Salle Coupe. Don't make 'em with running boards no more, I guess." At ten, Jace was a car enthusiast.

The driver's door opened, and to our amazement, a woman stepped out. She was dressed in finery like I'd only ever seen in Manhattan and could have stepped right out of the pages of a fashion magazine. Like that new one, *Glamour in Hollywood,* or *Vogue.* Her red and black checkered suit had a peplum, the height of fashion.

She took off her smart beret and fluffed her tawny blond hair. "I'm looking for the girl who rode on the Mineral Wells float at the rodeo, and I think I just found her." When she smiled, her eyes crinkled in the corners. I guessed she was at least twenty-five, a very confident twenty-five. She stepped forward, taking off her leather driving gloves and holding out her hand. The divine scent of her spicy perfume arrived before she did. "I'm Jessica Tarkington, representing the John Robert Powers modeling agency of New York City, and I want *you* to be a Powers Girl."

"Holy Smoke," Jace said, eyes wide. "Wait 'til Mama hears this!" He turned tail and ran back to the house.

Being raised polite, I shook her hand. "I'm Lauren. What's a Powers Girl?" Inside, my mind swirled with the possibility of seeing New York again. Was this my chance? How would Mama react?

"I'll be delighted to tell you all about our agency." Then she peered past me at my mother, who was descending on us at a good clip. Jace was nowhere in sight.

Mama stopped short of us and said, "I'm Mrs. Eaton, and who are you, ma'am?"

Extending her hand, the visitor introduced herself, just as she did with me. "I would like to talk to you about your daughter's future."

Mama's eyebrows rose. "What do you mean?"

"Shall we go inside where I can explain?"

"I don't mean to be rude, but I don't know you. We don't get many strangers out here."

The big-city woman lost her confidence and seemed to shrink a little. Then in a flash, she recovered and stood tall. "I hope you'll consider me a friend after you hear what I have to say."

Mama took a step back and thought for a moment. "All right, ma'am. Come on in. Ruby, put on a pot of coffee."

Miss Tarkington cocked her head at me. "Ruby? Didn't you say your name is Lauren?"

"It is!" Before Mama could correct me, I took off for the house.

On the kitchen table, still dusted with flour, the dough was rising in the bread pans. I cleaned up the mess right quick and shoved the loaves to one end. Oops! I peeked under the towels and sighed in relief the dough hadn't fallen. In the dining room cupboard, I gathered three cups and saucers and the sugar and creamer set from Mama's company china. Then I grabbed some dessert plates. While I bustled around, I wondered why a lady from a New York modeling agency would attend the rodeo. She didn't seem the type to enjoy bronc riding and calf roping. I knew some folks came from Dallas and other big Texas cities but never heard tell of any East Coast people there. Maybe I just never noticed. I had to pinch myself to make sure this was happening. Had she really tracked me down and driven all the way out to the ranch to see me?

The water in the percolator cap just started to show brown when Mama and Miss Tarkington entered the room. Why the delay? Had Mama been giving her the third degree?

With a smile, I said, "Coffee's ready."

They sat at the table across from each other. I brought the percolator over and set it on a hot pad.

"Ruby, can you please bring us the cookie jar? And some napkins?"

With a puzzled frown, the modeling lady said, "I have to confess, I'm confused. Which is it? Ruby or Lauren?"

"Lauren," I answered at the same time Mama said, "Ruby." She gave me the look for talking over her. "Enough said. We don't need to air our differences in front of a guest."

Silence fell along with my stomach. Miss Tarkington rescued the situation, helping herself to a cookie from the jar. "These look homemade."

With pride, I said, "They are. Oatmeal raisin, my specialty. Coffee?" After I filled three cups, I took a seat.

"Let me give you my card." The modeling lady opened her black patent leather handbag and took out a slim case. She popped it open and presented my mother with a calling card printed with fancy writing.

"Who is this John Robert Powers?" Mama asked.

After a sip of coffee, our visitor set her cup on the saucer. "Do you read any fashion magazines, Mrs. Eaton?"

Mama's brow creased. "What's that have to do with Ruby?"

Even though she kept her face serene, I thought Miss Tarkington must be getting frustrated with Mama's resistance. "Let me start over. If you follow fashion, you have probably seen some of the lovely models who work for us."

"I do take McCall's," Mama admitted.

"Wonderful! Can you see Ru—Lau—your daughter on the cover? I can!"

Mama turned to me, looked me up and down, then said, "Not sure I want to."

Keeping my mouth shut and my ears open, I listened to the spiel about the John Robert Powers agency. I couldn't believe what I was hearing. Me on the cover of a high-fashion magazine? Could it happen? Mama would never allow it, I was sure, but Daddy might if I asked him right.

"Our models are versatile. They do catalog work for Sears, Roebuck, as well as print ads in all the women's magazines. Powers Girls represent both high fashion and more prosaic household products."

With her lips pursed, Mama shook her head. "I can't let my daughter leave school and move to Manhattan."

"Why not? Don't you want her to expand her horizons, have a successful career?"

"Of course I do, but Ruby's future is here."

I couldn't keep my mouth shut a minute longer. "Mama, please, hear her out. I think I'd like to try modeling."

Mama shrugged. "Doesn't cost anything to listen."

Miss Tarkington reached for another cookie, her flashy colored-gem-stone bracelet catching the light. "There's no cost for anything. On the contrary, the money will flow to your daughter."

Too nervous and excited to sit still, I got up, took the towels off the bread pans, and put the loaves in the oven. We had forgotten to bake the bread because of the novelty of a visitor.

"Oh, thanks," Mama said. "I plumb forgot."

The agency woman was nothing if not sharp. She must have realized we had dinner to prepare because she got right down to business. "I have a contract and brochure in the car. Let me get them for you, Mrs. Eaton. You and Mr. Eaton can read both documents and discuss them at your leisure. May I come back tomorrow evening to answer any questions?"

Before Mama could open her mouth, I blurted, "Yes! Please. Come by at seven and have dessert with us."

"That's lovely! Thanks so much, Miss Eaton."

"Miss Eaton" was a good move on the modeling lady's part, and she didn't give my mother a chance to protest my invitation. No flies on her.

A series of expressions passed over Mama's face: surprise, distrust, annoyance, and finally she produced a smile, albeit a small one. I think she knew it would look discourteous if she objected.

Dylan burst through the back door and stopped short when he saw the visitor. Younger than me by two years, he was at that awkward age of fourteen, when the sight of a pretty girl or woman made him blush. He stood at the door, gaping at the modeling lady.

"I can see you're busy." Miss Tarkington rose from the table and picked up her bag. "Thank you for the coffee and oatmeal cookies. Absolutely divine. It was a pleasure to meet you, Mrs. Eaton."

"Call me Rose. We'll see you tomorrow evening. I must start dinner. Ruby, please see our guest to her car and get those papers for your daddy."

"Yes, Mama."

Since reading the John Robert Powers modeling school brochure, my mind hadn't stopped spinning. The sights of Manhattan and the memory of the room I stayed in at Aunt Imogene's, a room with my own bathroom, played like a movie reel. I prayed I'd be allowed to go. This might be my only chance to change my fate. I doubted I'd finish high school, even though my English teacher gave me high marks and hinted I should become a schoolteacher like her, something I had no interest in. More than half the ranch kids didn't finish anyway. Of course, Mama had different plans for me.

While I mashed the potatoes, I snuck peeks at the pictures of the models in the pamphlet. It made me doubt myself. They were so confident, so self-assured. I read the list of classes I hoped to take: deportment, makeup, posture, walking, turning, hair and nail care. My nails were worn to a nub by my chores. I had never used makeup until this week when I rode on the float, and Darla at the salon had helped me apply it. And I knew I sometimes slouched since I was taller than a goodly number of my male classmates. The girls in the photographs wore high heels. When I was twelve, I tried Mama's church heels and turned my ankle. Limped for a week. At the rodeo, I hadn't done much better. If I was truthful, I'd waddled like a duck in my blue satin pumps.

When Daddy got in from feeding the cattle, I rushed to him with a big smile and a hug. He chuckled. "Whoa! What's all this about, sunshine?"

Mama rolled her eyes and shook her head. "Leland, watch out. Ruby is on a mission. This afternoon, we had a visitor from New York City, and she made a proposal about our girl we need to discuss."

Daddy raised an eyebrow. "That right?"

My fists clenched, and I felt sweat on my upper lip. "Yes, sir. I want to be a model."

"A model what?" He put his hands on his hips. Not a good sign.

I gulped. "I'll get the brochure."

With his mouth twisted in disapproval, Daddy studied the pamphlet. He handed it back. "I don't know, pumpkin. We'll talk about it. Don't go gettin' your heart set on this."

My hopes faded. Unable to speak, I nodded, then slumped over to the counter to slice bread.

That night, as usual, we gathered around the dining room table for a prayer and our meal. The atmosphere was tense, or maybe it was just me with my dry mouth and pounding heart.

Jace couldn't stop talking about the LaSalle coupe the lady drove to the house. "You shoulda seen it, black as night, and it sure moved!"

Stammering and blushing, Dylan described the beautiful Miss Tarkington. My older brothers were more interested in hearing about the visitor than eating the pork chops. They encouraged Dylan's tale and told Jace to clam up.

For once, I didn't have to endure the usual talk about the war in Europe. Mama and I worried that Travis and Mason were way too interested in war. We hoped the United States would stay out of the conflict.

Daddy passed Mama the mashed potatoes. "Whatcha think about that modeling agency woman?"

"She was a fashion plate, for sure. Said she spotted Ruby at the parade and thought she could be a Powers girl. You read that brochure, right?"

"Yeah, Rose, I looked at it. Don't know what to make of it."

It was hard for me to figure how Mama felt about me becoming a model in New York. Her voice and facial expression gave nothing away. She might as well be talking about doing the wash.

Just about eaten up with nerves, I accidentally bit the inside of my cheek and yelped. Everybody stared at me. "I'm fine. Just fine."

With the topic of the elegant visitor exhausted, my brothers returned their attention to the meal, polishing off the potatoes and carrots. I wasn't hungry and pushed the food around my plate.

"Well, I think it's crazy to consider sending Ruby away to live in New York City," Mama said.

Daddy put down his fork and clasped his hands. That meant he was thinking hard. I realized I was holding my breath and let it out in a whoosh. Everybody stared at me. Again. My face felt warm, and my belly hurt.

I waited for Daddy to talk.

"What do *you* want, Lauren?" Daddy asked. He called me by my preferred name. That's how I knew I was the apple of his eye. Mama said he was too indulgent with me. I thought he was perfect.

When I answered, my lips stuck together because my mouth was so dry. "I want to go. I think I'd like it."

Mama grimaced. "And I think you're too young."

"Miss Tarkington said there's a ladies' boarding hotel, the Barbizon. They're very strict and only let women live there. Men who come to call have to stay in the lobby. It would be proper."

"Already planning on men coming to call? Well, I never. See what I mean, Leland?"

Daddy held up his hand like he was directing traffic. "Now, Rose, Lauren's concerned about propriety. That's a good thing. How's about having her board with Imogene?"

"Imogene?" Mama's voice rose.

My brothers tuned in to the conversation since we were discussing Aunt Imogene, always a gripping character. They didn't say anything, but I sensed their interest.

"Well, she lives right close to that model place. Maybe we can compromise and have Lauren stay with her."

Was it really going to happen?

"Leland, I don't know. We're jumping the gun here. I don't want to put the kibosh on Ruby's dreams, but I'll have to think about it."

"Mama, please. Please call her!" Aunt Imogene lived on the Upper East Side. She said those words like a good Methodist would say "heaven." My aunt had never married, and I'd heard Mama whisper to Daddy she was a bit of a bohemian. I had to look it up to understand that my aunt was not of Bohemian extraction, just unconventional. During my visit to Manhattan, Aunt Imogene went out to Harlem and the Village to hear race music. I begged to go with her, and I think she considered it but decided she couldn't take me because there was drinking. Those evenings I sat alone, listening to records on her Bendix phonograph, the same music I imagined Aunt Imogene heard as she danced the night away.

Mama didn't talk much about her past, but I had learned a little family history over the years. Neither Mama nor Imogene knew their mothers—but for different reasons. Mama's mother died in childbirth, so she was raised by a series of nannies, even after Grandfather Edmund married Anna, Imogene's mother. According to Mama, Anna didn't have a maternal bone in her body, and she proved it by running off with an Italian count when Imogene was two years old. It was a huge scandal, but the Babcocks were old money, and so the hubbub died down. Edmund held his head high and continued to run his bank and buy real estate. And he hired Vandine, who, from what I saw, filled more than the role of housekeeper in the sisters' lives.

Ever since my trip to New York, I had been dissatisfied with ranch life, and Mama knew it. I believed she regretted sending me for that visit. And from watching the sisters' interaction, I got the feeling Imogene enjoyed butting heads with Mama.

My attention was drawn back to the dinner table by Daddy. "That agency woman is comin' back tomorrow night. Do we have to decide by then?"

"Yes," I shouted at the same time Mama said, "No!"

Daddy shook his head. "What's for dessert?"

I got up to clear the table, and surprisingly, Travis picked up his plate and followed me to the kitchen.

"What the heck, sis? You really think they'll let you go?"

Travis was twenty, the picture of Daddy, tall and strong, with the same square jaw and blue eyes. His hair was honey brown, like Daddy's and all the boys. The girls in high school and at the church youth group mooned over Travis and Mason, who, although he was two years younger, could have been his twin.

"Sure hope so. I want more out of life than marrying some rancher, and this is a once-in-a-lifetime chance."

He put his hand on my shoulder and looked me square in the eye. "When did you start wanting to be a model?"

I glanced away. "This afternoon, to tell the truth. Well, maybe when I rode on the float in the parade. Getting my hair done and being fussed over was kinda nice."

Travis dropped his hand from my shoulder and put his hands in the back pockets of his dungarees. "Don't know nothing about that stuff. Sure you can handle being away from home?"

Shrugging, I said, "There's only one way to find out. Gotta get dessert on the table."

I fetched the big bowl of cherry gelatin from the icebox and brought it into the dining room. Daddy looked a little disappointed we didn't have any baked goods, but I told him I'd make a pound cake for the following night. He smiled. "My favorite."

After the pound cake finished baking, I dusted it with powdered sugar and climbed the stairs. The door to my parents' room was partly open, and light poured into the dim hall. It wasn't really eavesdropping. If they didn't want anyone to hear, they would have closed the door.

"Rose, why not? She really wants this."

"Darling, she's too young. Too young to leave home. Too young to know her own mind." Mama sounded weary, like she'd been working hard to make her side of the argument. Although it wasn't really an argument. I'd never once heard my parents raise their voices at each other.

"You knew your own mind when you weren't much older."

"That has nothing to do with Ruby!"

"Why can't you call her Lauren? Everybody else does." Daddy had a point.

"Oh, I suppose I'll have to call her Lauren when she's a high-fashion model in New York."

I clapped my hands over my mouth, so I didn't shout with joy. Tiptoeing to my room, I shut the door softly, then jitterbugged around the room until I collapsed exhausted onto the bed. I slept like a log.

At school the next day, I couldn't pay attention. My head was no longer in Texas; it was in Manhattan.

When English class was over, Clare took my arm. "What's goin' on, kiddo? Mrs. Hemple had to call your name three times before you answered. You ain't been yourself since you were picked for Miss Mineral Wells."

"You're right. I'm not myself. The most exciting thing happened yesterday." I told Clare about my surprise visitor from the modeling agency.

Clare squealed like a stuck pig, and everyone in the hallway turned to stare at us.

"That's so exciting. Jeepers! Is your mama really gonna allow it?"

"I think so. I heard my folks talkin' last night when I went to bed."

"You spied on them?" Clare's fashionably thin eyebrows climbed her forehead.

"It wasn't like that. Their door was open."

Clare's eyebrows returned to the usual spot. "Oh, okay."

"Anyway, Miss Tarkington's coming to the house after dinner. I baked a pound cake for dessert. So, I guess my folks will agree."

"How can you live on your own in New York City? Can you afford it? I hear it's mighty dear."

"There's a women's hotel where the models board. Or maybe I could stay with my Aunt Imogene. I'd rather do that than live with a bunch of strangers."

"Yeah. I remember you tellin' me about your aunt. She's a spinster and likes jive music. Well, that oughta be interesting."

"Hope so. At least it's more interesting than baking bread and slaving over the ironing board."

"Good point."

When the bus dropped me off after school, I ran home. Before I got to the house, I had to shrug off my jacket because I was starting to sweat. It was getting hot early this year. The sky was clouding up. It hadn't rained to speak of since January, and I felt a few drops on my arms. Shoot! All I needed was a downpour to turn the road into a mud pit. Would Miss Tarkington drive out here in a rainstorm? By the time I got to the kitchen door, the sun had come out again, and I breathed a sigh of relief. There was a pile of chores waiting for me, and I had to help with dinner.

Keeping an eye on the clock, I made sure we sat down to eat promptly at 5:30. Then time became elastic. I watched as Travis cut up his meat in slow motion, and then the next moment, the clock seemed to be ticking double-time. I couldn't eat a bite. When Daddy had seconds, I just about died.

At last, everyone swallowed their last mouthful, and I cleared the table fast and scooted upstairs to comb my hair. Squinting in the mirror, I tried to see a fashion model but failed. Could John Robert Powers really turn me into one?

When I came back downstairs, Mama and Daddy were greeting Miss Tarkington in the hallway. I stepped forward to catch the look on Daddy's face. He looked normal, straight-faced. Didn't crack a smile.

My parents led the modeling lady to the dining room, and I hurried into the kitchen. Since my brothers weren't invited to this confab, I dished up four slices for them. Travis, Mason, and Dylan ate their cake standing in the doorway so they could have a gander at our visitor. Jace had no interest in beautiful women, just dessert. He asked me to pour him a glass of milk, and I fumbled the bottle, almost dropping it, in my haste to get to the dining room. Mason whispered, "What a dish!" as I scooted past them with the dessert. He wasn't referring to the pound cake.

By the time I sat, Mama had already poured coffee. I placed a piece of cake on each dessert plate and passed them around.

After taking a bite of the cake, Miss Tarkington patted her lips with the napkin. "Delicious, Lauren."

Mama cleared her throat but didn't correct her about my name.

After a silence that seemed to go on for hours, Daddy asked, "Have you ever worked with girls as young as Lauren?"

Looked like Mama and Daddy had discussed a lot more things last night than what I heard.

"We work with young women starting at age sixteen, so Lauren would be one of our younger models. As I mentioned, we would provide lodging at the Barbizon Hotel for Women, a well-respected organization. We—"

"That place won't work for her," Mama interjected.

I struggled to keep my face blank, although my leg was jittering like crazy under the table. Last night, I was sure I heard Mama say I could go. Did she change her mind? I clamped my lips shut so I didn't moan out loud.

"Oh, I see." Miss Tarkington's face fell. "I'm sorry your daughter won't be joining our agency."

"Not so fast, ma'am," Daddy said. "We didn't say she couldn't go."

My heart beat double time, and I could barely breathe.

Mama broke off a chunk of pound cake with her fork but didn't eat it. "My half-sister lives in Manhattan. She's willing to have Lauren stay with her while she studies with Mr. Powers."

I couldn't believe Mama called me "Lauren." Thunderstruck, I swallowed my whoop of victory.

Clapping her hands, our guest brightened up right quick. "That's wonderful!"

As she picked up her coffee cup, Mama's hand shook. "Imogene lives on the Upper East Side. On East 71st. Where's the modeling agency located?"

"We're in midtown. It's not far."

At last, I was able to speak. "So, I can go? Really?"

Mama's lips twisted. "I always knew I couldn't keep you down on the farm—or ranch, to coin a phrase. After you got a taste of city living, I knew something like this was likely to happen someday. Looks like someday is here."

My mouth fell open. I snapped it shut, felt tears rising. "Mama, I didn't know. You never said…"

"No, I didn't."

With tight lips, like he was trying to control his emotions, Daddy patted Mama's hand. Then he said the words I wanted to hear. "Where do we sign?"

After promising to come by in two days' time to pick me up for the flight from Fort Worth to New York, Miss Tarkington left. My brothers swarmed into the hallway, shouting questions at me, all talking at the same time. I hadn't had their undivided attention since I took a header off my horse Miss Priss when I was eleven. They were acting like I was a celebrity or something.

Daddy put his fingers in his mouth and whistled. The boys came to attention and stopped their nonsense. "Family meeting. Kitchen table. Now."

We all filed into the kitchen and sat around the old, scarred table where I had rolled out bread dough for the last time. The reality hit me. It was all happening so fast. Was I having second thoughts? No, that couldn't be. The seed planted two years ago had sprouted and taken firm root in my heart. I wasn't meant to be a ranch wife.

Mama was worried about me finishing high school. I wasn't. A high school diploma wouldn't mean a darn thing for my modeling career.

The next morning, I phoned my friend Clare to tell her the news. She yelped and dropped the phone receiver, and from the racket, it must have bounced all over the floor. I heard her whooping it up, and then she got on the line. "Hot diggity dog! I wish I could go with you. When you're rich and famous, send for me."

"I don't know about the rich and famous part. But maybe you can come visit over the summer."

"How are you getting there? Who's taking you?"

"No one's *taking* me. That's another thing. I'm going on an airplane! Miss Tarkington is picking me up tomorrow and driving me to the airport in Fort Worth."

"You going to school today?"

"Nope. Why should I? That's history."

"This afternoon, I'm coming over to say goodbye."

"Sure thing. I'll be here packing."

"I'm taking the bus out to your place. Maybe one of your handsome brothers can give me a ride home."

Clare pounded up the stairs and raced into my room. She rocketed into me and almost knocked me off my feet with her exuberant hug.

"Good Lord, Clare." I pulled away and continued folding my underwear.

She laughed and sat on the floor. "I told everybody at school. No one could believe it, but I said since you weren't there and won't be there tomorrow, they'll see."

Sinking to the bed, I stopped folding my clothes. "It still seems like a dream. Even while I'm packing, my mind wanders, and then, boom, it hits me all over again."

Clare rose from the floor and plopped down next to me. "I can't believe your mama is letting you go."

"If it was up to her, I don't think she would. But Daddy makes the decisions, and he wants me to have this opportunity. They both know I don't want to live on the ranch forever."

"Forever? Well, you could stay through high school."

"Sure, I could, but I don't want to. This is the best thing that ever happened to me."

"Tom Miller's face was hangin' down to his shoes when he heard the news."

I glanced up. "Really? Since when does he care?" I'd had a crush on Tom Miller since the seventh grade, but he was too busy with football, baseball, basketball, and working at his daddy's grocery store, to pay me any mind.

Clare patted my hand. "Everybody knows he's sweet on you."

"Everybody but me." I snorted. "And him. He never said a word. Now it's too late."

My friend stood and looked at her reflection in the mirror over my dresser. She pinched her cheeks, bit her lip, and fiddled with her already-perfect hair. "Travis is giving me a lift home. I guess this is goodbye."

I walked her downstairs, where Travis was waiting.

"Let's go, kid. I gotta be back to pen the cattle."

Clare smiled up at my brother and batted her eyelashes. "I'm ready."

I stood at the door watching them drive away in Daddy's pickup. Would I ever see her again?

The next morning, I was up with the chickens. Hardly slept a wink. My stomach was in knots. I drew a bath, soaked for a bit, then dried off. Last night, I had laid out my traveling clothes, so I was ready in a jiffy. My navy faille jacket-dress had white cuffs. I'd have to take care not to soil them. Pulling on cotton gloves, I rolled on my silk stockings and attached them to my garter belt.

To my surprise, last fall Mama let me buy navy pumps with a peg heel, not as sophisticated as high heels, but still better than flats. Aunt Imogene had sent me a lovely navy envelope bag for Christmas. Mama had rolled her eyes and said it was way too old for me. Carefully, I unwrapped it from the tissue I stored it in. This was the first time I had an occasion to use it. I put my white cotton gloves inside and wished I had black leather driving gloves like Jessica. Since we would be colleagues, I decided to call her by her first name.

I'd stashed the rose-colored lipstick from the day of the rodeo under my mattress. On my first try, I got the lipstick smeared over half my face, so I wiped it off and tried again. I blotted a perfect kiss on the tissue and smiled at my image in the mirror.

Last night, Mama had packed a box of my treasures to send to New York. She said, "A touch of home will be a comfort if you get homesick." Keeping a straight face, I laughed inside. Homesick? Not a chance. She filled the carton with my Bible, a few books, keepsakes from school and church, and my favorite quilt.

"It might take a couple of weeks to arrive. Be patient."

I wasn't known for my patience.

Once I'd styled my hair, I followed my nose to the kitchen, where Mama was making breakfast. The smell of bacon perfumed the room, but I couldn't eat anything heavy. I poured a cup of coffee and added plenty of cream. There was one dried-out piece of pound cake left, so I nibbled at that.

Mama came up behind my chair and kissed my head. Tears sprang to my eyes. Even though we had our differences, I would miss her. "Lauren. I suppose you'll go by Lauren from now on. I expect you to write to me every week, girl. Promise me."

I turned in my chair and took her hand. "Promise."

She sighed and sat down beside me. "Imogene is a bit of a character. I'm sure you got a hint of that when you stayed with her. Her heart is in the right place, but her views of the world are a little...different. Don't forget your Sunday school lessons. Live by our Christian values, the Ten Commandments, and the Golden Rule, and you'll be fine."

"Will you come visit, Mama?"

Mama blinked and glanced at the stove and got up to turn the bacon. With her back to me, she said, "I don't know. It's always one season or another at the ranch. If we're not calving, we're branding or getting ready for market. And my garden...I just don't know."

It sounded like a litany of excuses, and I doubted she would make the trip. What did she have against Manhattan?

The bleat of a car horn dragged me from my speculation, and I jumped up from my chair. "She's here!"

Daddy and my brothers came clomping down the stairs, ready for breakfast.

I raced past them like they weren't even there and threw open the door. Jessica stood there in another stunning fashion statement. Her violet, cape-shouldered suit showcased her narrow waist. A matching cloche with a tiny veil finished the look.

Aware of my bare head, I regretted not having a suitable hat. My church hats were all I had, and neither the summer straw Aunt Imogene had bought me, nor the black felt derby, went with my navy faille.

Daddy said, "Take care of my little girl, now."

"Yes, sir!" Jessica turned to my brothers. "Gentlemen." Three of them turned red.

Mama rushed in from the kitchen, wiping her hands on a towel. "You be sure to call us when you get there." She hugged me so tight, I squealed.

Daddy carried out my luggage and put it in the trunk of the car. I threw my arms around him, then broke away and hopped in the LaSalle, without a backward glance. My eyes focused straight ahead on the future.

Chapter Three

NEW YORK DAZE-1940

Jessica drove with confidence. As far as I could tell, she did everything with confidence.

"How long does it take to drive to Fort Worth?"

Jessica glanced sideways at me and answered, "As quick as I can make it. Once we hit pavement, hold on to your hat. Oh, you're not wearing one!" She chuckled. "Is this your first flight? Or should I say, flights?"

"Flights?" I thought my eyes might pop out of my head.

"We have to change planes. There isn't a non-stop flight."

"What are you gonna do about this car?"

"I'll take it back to the guy I borrowed it from. He doesn't live too far from Meacham Field. He'll give us a lift to the airport."

I didn't say a thing. Maybe I was in shock. Some guy casually lent his fancy car to Jessica? Figured there was a story there but wasn't sure I wanted to know it. So, I kept my lip zipped. If I hadn't realized my previous life was over, I did now.

When we got to Fort Worth, the car squealed to a stop at an office building. A tall, blond man pushed through the door and helped Jessica out of the driver's seat. With his arm around her, he walked her to the passenger side and gave me a look. I realized he wanted Jessica to sit in the front seat, so I got out and climbed in the back. The man drew her close and gave her a big smooch. She pulled away and said, "Down, boy!" but laughed. He did, too. He leaned in for another kiss and then ran around the front of the car.

"Lauren, this is Jeb Hudson, a friend of mine. Jeb, meet Lauren, the newest Powers Girl."

Jeb met my eyes briefly in the rearview mirror. "Howdy, miss." He only had eyes for Jessica. I was so much excess baggage. Anyway, he was really old, probably at least twenty-seven.

"How did ya like Mineral Wells, sugar? Where did ya stay?"

"Well, I couldn't afford the Baker, so the next best place in town, the Crazy Hotel!"

Jeb threw back his head and laughed. "Yeah, Crazy Hotel, Crazy water, Crazy radio. Mineral Wells is one crazy town."

That got my dander up. Even though I was leaving, Mineral Wells was my hometown, and unlike some places, lived up to its name. For goodness' sakes, they actually *had* wells that produced mineral water that didn't make you crazy but made you sane! Sure, the Great Depression led to many of the hotels and wells closing, but Crazy Crystals were still sold all over the country. In fact, Mama kept a green box in the medicine cabinet.

Jessica and Jeb were chatting away in the front seat, keeping their voices low. Fine with me. When I closed my eyes, a picture show of my family and friends played on my inner eyelids. Mama, Daddy, my brothers, Clare, and yes, Tom Miller. I sighed, then my eyes flew open as the car made a sharp turn. We were at Meacham, and I was about to have my first airplane ride.

The lovebirds got out of the car and fell into another clinch—straight out of a Hollywood romance, like Rhett Butler and Scarlett O'Hara, or Cathy and Heathcliff. I made myself busy getting my luggage, so I didn't have to watch.

Jeb raised an arm and called, "Porter!" A uniformed man rushed up to help with our bags. One more kiss, and Jeb drove away. Jessica and I followed the porter inside the terminal with its tall glassed-in tower. We joined a line of people at the American Airlines counter, where we learned our flight would leave in an hour. Our luggage disappeared down a conveyer belt, and we got claim checks to pick it up in New York. I hoped our luggage changed planes when we did, but how could we even know until we got there? I kept my thoughts to myself because I didn't want to seem like a rube to Jessica.

We waited in the lobby until our flight number was called, then walked outside to the airplane and climbed up the metal stairs. The propeller noise roared louder than the high school football stadium on Friday night, and the breeze blew my hair out of the clips. I must have looked a wreck. Following my mentor, I absorbed every last detail. In my mind, I was already composing my letters home to Mama and Clare. I had a little notebook and a pen in my purse, so I figured I could make a start on the trip.

Since it was my first flight, Jessica insisted I take the window seat. My nerves were on high alert, and I gratefully sank into the wide seat. The stewardess in her smart navy uniform and cap strolled by offering magazines. Jessica took a copy of *Vogue* and handed it to me. "This will be your Bible. I expect one day you'll be pictured inside, if not on the cover." Flattered, I accepted the glossy magazine.

The roar of the engines and the vibration of the airplane set my teeth on edge. We were instructed to prepare for take-off. Just when I thought the plane was about to disintegrate, it began to roll, slowly at first, then faster and faster. My stomach sank, and I realized we were airborne. The plane tilted as it climbed, and I just about fainted. Then the sight of the ground below with neat little grids of streets, long curving roads, and green fields made me forget my nerves and marvel at the sight.

After a while, the stewardess came by to offer beverages. Jessica asked for coffee, and I asked for a coke. The blond stewardess didn't ask me what kind, and I was too shy to ask for a Dr Pepper. She handed me a Coca-Cola, which was okay.

Jessica leaned back in her seat and chatted about her stint as a Powers Girl. She had done a lot of print work for the Sears Roebuck catalog as well as fashion shows. Sadly, her time as a model came to an end when she turned twenty-four, but a job as a recruiter became available, and she jumped on it. "Some of my colleagues took jobs at Bergdorf Goodman or Henri Bendel." She shuddered and made a face. "Retail work just didn't appeal to me. I guess I wanted to stay in the modeling business, even though I'd have a different role."

She told me startling stories about the nightclubs and restaurants like the elegant Stork Club, El Morocco—with its blue zebra booths—and Sardi's. Powers Girls were frequent guests at these venues. The more adventurous traveled to Greenwich Village, where the Negroes played the blues. When Jessica mentioned Café Society, I about dropped my teeth. Aunt Imogene raved about the place when I visited her two years ago. Now I knew what Mama meant when she said Imogene marched to the beat of a different drum. The only Negroes I knew were the Washingtons. They lived in town, and the whole family worked at the Crazy Hotel. My head spun with the sheer number of new experiences coming my way.

The stewardess came by, bearing a tray with a sandwich. Too wound up to eat much, I only choked down a bite or two. Then the sound of the engines changed, and my stomach felt like it was rising up to my throat. Jessica put down her coffee. "Not to worry, kiddo. We're probably on approach to Memphis. We'll be on the ground soon. Pray that our luggage makes the connection too."

"Believe me, I am. What happens if our bags don't make it?"

"They'll find them and deliver them to your address. But let's look on the bright side and think happy thoughts."

"Okay."

The plane landed with a jolt and a couple of bounces. To my surprise, the passengers clapped and cheered.

We got off the plane and beelined for the terminal. Our next flight would depart in two hours, so I had time to use the restroom and freshen up.

The second flight was a little bumpy. I gripped the seat arms and felt my underarms get sweaty. But I couldn't help it; my nerves were getting the best of me. When the plane began to descend, the lights of New York were visible miles away. It was dazzling, like Christmas. We landed at the New York Municipal Airport. Jessica said that was in Queens, not Manhattan, and gave me a quick lesson in the geography of the boroughs that made up the city.

We waited twenty long minutes for our luggage to be brought to the baggage reclaim area. When I saw my suitcase, I perked up. A porter helped with our bags and hailed a taxi. The ride to Manhattan was slow due to the heavy traffic, but eventually we arrived at Aunt Imogene's house on East

71st. Jessica told the driver to wait while she walked me to the door. She looked at me and said, "Swanky! Your aunt must be loaded."

"I guess." I shrugged.

The door opened, and Vandine let us in. She was wearing her usual shirtwaist dress and pearls. As she helped haul my luggage over the doorsill, her brown face creased in a welcoming smile.

Jessica introduced herself and asked, "Is Miss Babcock in? I'd like to say hello."

"No ma'am. Miss Imogene is out," Vandine replied. She was all stiff and formal, not knowing Jessica.

I'd bet she was at a blues club. "Thanks so much for getting me here, Jessica. I'll be at the school on Monday to start."

"My pleasure." Jessica turned to the door, then looked over her shoulder and said, "Over the weekend, you might want to look through the brochure and make a list of questions. You have my card. Call me if you need anything. Otherwise, I'll see you Monday at nine a.m. sharp."

Vandine closed the door after Jessica and turned to me. "You get you any supper, young lady?"

"No. My stomach was too upset to eat. I hadn't ever been on an airplane before."

"Well, come on in the kitchen, and I'll set you right."

I followed Vandine into the kitchen and found my appetite. A meatloaf sandwich, apple pie, and a glass of milk filled me up.

"Say, isn't it late for you to be working?"

"Honey, I knew you was coming, and I wasn't about to turn in for the night 'til I got you settled. You know your aunt. She's a gay one. Loves her music."

"I remember." A huge yawn caught me by surprise, and I felt my eyes getting heavy. "Guess I better get to bed. Same room?"

"Yep. Let me help you carry your bags up."

"Thank you."

"You still goin' by 'Lauren.'"

I grinned. "Yes, I am."

"What your mama have to say 'bout that?"

"It took her two years to agree."

Vandine placed my suitcase on the bed. "Put fresh linens on the bed this morning. Plenty of towels in the bathroom too. Now get you some rest."

"Good night. Thank you for everything."

My second-floor room looked out on the street. The bed was already turned down, and I couldn't wait to dive into the butter-soft linens. I unpacked my toothbrush and entered the private bathroom, remembering how hard it was after my visit to go back to sharing one bathroom with six people. Well, those days were over. Again, it hit me—I had a new life. Too tired to run a tub, I washed my face with rich, lavender-scented soap, put on my pajamas, and got under the covers. Lying in bed, I thought about my mother growing up in this house and the contrast with the ranch. While contemplating the romance of the girl from Manhattan marrying the cattleman from Palo Pinto County, I drifted off to sleep.

The next morning, I showered, dressed, and followed the aroma of frying sausage to the kitchen. Vandine asked how I wanted my eggs.

"Two eggs over easy comin' right up! Sit you down."

I sat at the round table in the bay window overlooking the small yard where the trees were starting to leaf out and daffodils showed yellow buds. A glass of orange juice and a coffee cup were waiting for me, and I poured a cup from the carafe, adding plenty of cream and sugar.

Vandine brought my plate, and I dug in. She was a great cook, and I realized I'd been the beneficiary of her talents all my life. Vandine had cared for Mama from the age of eleven until she left home to marry Daddy. Immediately, I slammed the door on memories of home. Waste of time.

"Is Aunt Imogene going to have breakfast?"

"It's only seven. She don't rise this early. Maybe see her closer to eleven."

"Oh, that's right." I finished the eggs, sausage, and biscuit. Stuffed to the gills, I shoved my plate aside, picked up the newspaper, and skimmed the headlines. Subway fares remained at five cents, same price as two years ago. I browsed the ads. Bloomingdale's was having a sale. I sighed, not in my budget. Several bargain basement shops, more in line with my means, had sales too.

After downing my coffee, I brought my plate and mug to the sink and returned to my room to unpack. With that done, I read and re-read the John Robert Powers brochure about fifty times. Just as I was beginning to wonder if I'd ever see Aunt Imogene, she knocked on my door and entered before I could say a word.

"Darling! You've arrived and settled in. Let me be the first one to welcome you to Manhattan. You'll love it. I had a feeling you'd be back after our last visit. I'll lay out the ground rules for you."

Startled, I jumped to my feet and stared at her. She wore a rose-colored negligée with a matching robe, slippers, and a jeweled turban from which peeked a few mahogany curls. Ground rules? This I had to hear.

"Surprise! There are no ground rules." Imogene threw out her arms and laughed a rich, hearty laugh that seemed too big for her slender body. Once again, it was hard for me to believe this woman was my austere mother's half-sister.

"I was raised with great latitude and laissez-faire and look how I turned out!" She bowed. "No applause, please. It's way too early in the day for me to blush."

I didn't know what to say. What was "lay zay fair"?

"You'll have a key, of course. Comings and goings are your business. Just let me know if you'll be gone for an extended period so Vandine can plan. How old are you, Lauren?"

At first, I was surprised she didn't know how old I was, then realized that was par for the course with my aunt. "Sixteen."

"What is it you'll be doing here in Manhattan? Your mother mentioned some sort of schooling if I recall. Tell me more." She swept to my unmade bed and sat right down, patting the spot beside her. "Sit. And talk."

Imogene was a steamroller of a woman, so I obeyed. My aunt was quite familiar with the concept of Powers girls and modeling. "Yes, most of them live at the Barbizon. How dreary for them! Rules from here to Sunday. There are no men allowed beyond the lobby if you can believe it. I can't, and I couldn't live that way." She placed her hands as if in prayer and gazed at the ceiling. "Thank you, father dear, for this lovely home and my financial independence."

My mind flitted to the stories about Imogene's exploits I'd overheard at home before her one and only visit to our ranch. *"Leland, she was a flapper, for goodness' sake. Sixteen years old and caught in a raid at a speakeasy. Father was in Chicago on business, and our brother Clark had to travel from Boston to bail her out. After Father died, she went wild. And the affairs."*

"Now, now, Rose. That's none of our concern. I'm certain she's outgrown that sort of thing."

"I'm not so sure she ever did. But at least I haven't heard of any antics lately."

From what I'd already seen, the late nights continued. Had she outgrown her wild ways? Maybe I would have been better off at the women's hotel. Frankly, I was apprehensive about being on my own in this city.

Aunt Imogene had browsed through my wardrobe, pursed her lips, and shook her head. "Darling, these duds are straight from Sears, Roebuck and Company. No offense, I suppose it's all a cattle rancher can afford. Later this week, I'll take you to Bloomingdale's and find you some stylish dresses. No niece of mine can be seen around town in those deadly dull rags."

Although slightly offended by her comment, I knew she was right. The frocks I'd packed were the best I had, but they couldn't compare to the fashions at Saks or Bloomingdale's. I had a twinge of guilt—quickly ignored—at Imogene spending money on me and looked forward to our shopping trip.

Monday morning, I dressed in my navy faille and set out for the John Robert Powers modeling agency. On the subway, I paid close attention, so I didn't miss my stop. I marched up the stairs to the street and studied the addresses on the buildings. Apparently, I was moving too slow because I was jostled by all the businessmen rushing along the sidewalk. I guess I was the only person in Manhattan who didn't know where they were going. At last, I spotted the address I was searching for and pushed through the revolving door into the lobby of the midtown office building on Park Avenue. The directory was posted, and I found the Powers Agency in the Ps, right where it belonged. In the elevator, my stomach stayed in the lobby as the rest of me went upwards. What a sensation! I'd have to get used to it since I was now a resident of Manhattan.

A bit apprehensive, I peered down the long hallway. The glass door of the agency lobby gave me a view of several young women seated in straight chairs. They all wore some version of my outfit. Jacket-dresses were the ticket this season. I entered and approached the receptionist, who took my name and directed me to wait with the other girls.

A self-assured blonde, who looked to be about my age, held out her gloved hand. "Hi, my name is Mildred, but I go by Milly. Pleased to meet you."

"I'm Lauren. Is this your first day, too?"

Mildred smiled, and her dimples were stunning. I didn't have dimples, and I didn't have Milly's self-assurance, either. "Yes, it is, buttercup." She glanced around at the other girls. "I think we're all in the same boat here. My folks drove me here from Nebraska. I was Miss Omaha, and someone from the Powers agency saw my picture in the newspaper. The next thing I knew, I was heading to the Big Apple."

"Oh! I had a similar experience. At the Fort Worth rodeo. I was on the Mineral Wells float, and my picture was in the paper, and now I'm here. Are you staying at the Barbizon?"

"Why, yes. Are you too?"

"No, I'm living with my aunt."

"Whereabouts?"

"On East 71st."

"I'm at 63rd and Lexington. Not far at all."

I was so happy I'd made a friend. Milly was eighteen but looked younger. I also met Francine, Fiona, Katherine, and Eleanor. Not a one of them was from the Big Apple. To my relief, Milly, Katherine, and Eleanor were friendly, all three down to earth. Then there were the "fillies from Philly" as I came to think of them: Francine and Fiona. They stuck together like Siamese twins. Something was off about them, but I couldn't put my finger on it.

Promptly at nine o'clock, a door opened, and two tall, elegant women entered the lobby. They introduced themselves as Vivian and Sally, our instructors. I had expected Mr. John Robert Powers himself, but they told us we wouldn't meet him for a couple of weeks.

We all stood and followed the two women down a corridor tiled in ugly green linoleum. Vivian, a brunette, and Sally, a freckled ginger, ushered us into a chilly, dark space. Not very impressive. Sally flicked on the overhead lights and pulled the Venetian blinds open, which helped.

Jessica waltzed into the room. "I can't stay, just wanted to drop in to welcome you. Some of you were recruited by me, so we are acquainted." She flashed a smile at me, nodded at someone behind me. "Toodles. Off to a catalog shoot." She left the room as breezily as she entered.

Vivian and Sally gazed after her with wistful looks on their faces. I was beginning to see the hierarchy.

"Ladies, please take a seat at a desk, and we'll begin." Vivian clapped her hands. At the blackboard, Sally wrote down our schedule for the day.

I sat next to Milly. The six of us paid rapt attention to the duo, who welcomed us and explained the curriculum for the next two weeks. Standing, walking, turning class might sound easy, but it was exhausting. Posture was so important. Being taller than most boys my age, I tended to slouch. That would have to stop.

At noon, we were given an hour for lunch. Milly had been in town for a week and suggested we try the Automat.

I'd never heard of such a thing and said, "I thought you said laundromat. What's an Automat?"

"You're in for a treat. It's really keen. They have rows and rows of windows with food behind each one. You get change from the cashier, nickels only, and select your items, then just pull up the window and vwala, you got lunch." Milly waxed enthusiastic about the experience.

Too embarrassed to ask what "vwala" meant, I agreed to try it because all that standing, walking, and turning made me hungry. The other girls tagged along.

Over our sandwiches, soup, and pie, we chatted about our hometowns. Francine and Fiona, both brunettes, were city girls, from Philadelphia, and not in the least intimidated by the noise and bustle of the New York streets and avenues. Katherine, with hair as black as night, was from Memphis, and Eleanor, a honey blond, hailed from Savannah, Georgia. We were all recruited by women who used to be Powers girls.

Eleanor drawled, "Powers girls who get a little long in the tooth become recruiters or instructors. I think it's real nice they offer those jobs."

Even though the food wasn't up to Vandine's standards, I ate every crumb of my sandwich and pie. Then I noticed the other girls had picked at their meals, leaving most of it. Francine and Fiona looked at my empty plate, then at each other, and smirked. They were holding hands under the table—how odd. In class, they had acted so confident. Why did they need to reassure each other? I decided they weren't friend material.

Back at the Powers modeling school, our teachers awaited us with folded arms and frowns. "You're five minutes late," said Vivian. Sally chimed in. "Don't let it happen again. Promptness is a hallmark of Powers Girls."

Chastened, we took our seats and endured a lecture about the standards expected of us. The rest of the afternoon flew by, chocked full of new experiences and information. We were measured, weighed, and evaluated from every angle. Then, Vivian handed out a list from Mr. Powers himself, that had the minimum wardrobe requirements for every model

One good tailored suit

One dark dress with long sleeves and one with short sleeves

One light dress with long sleeves and one with short sleeves

One dark and one light evening dress

A fur jacket

Shoes for all occasions

Hats and hatboxes

Vivian enthused, "Just as a doctor carries his black bag and an attorney his briefcase, models have their own signature: the hatbox."

Taking over from there, Sally named all the things a model must carry in her hatbox besides her hat. Makeup, gloves, hairbrush, and accessories, the list seemed to go on for minutes. My head was spinning with the number of things I had to buy. How could I afford it all? Daddy had given me one hundred dollars as a stake, and I had my pin money from selling eggs, about twenty-two dollars.

The afternoon concluded with a talk on potential earnings. Powers girls started at five dollars an hour and could earn up to ten dollars for print work if their look was popular. Fashion shows paid even higher rates.

Vivian spoke of girls who landed contracts for five thousand dollars annually with cosmetics firms. Sally mentioned the publicity stunts where several Powers girls were used as an enthusiastic crowd for public events, like speeches.

As our instructors spoke, Milly and I looked at each other with wide eyes. If what they said was true, we were in the money.

At four-thirty, we were dismissed for the day and reminded to return promptly at nine the next morning.

The fillies, Francine and Fiona, were both at the Barbizon with Milly, but they charged on ahead, not waiting to walk with us. Milly and I proceeded north. Katherine and Eleanor were at the Webster Apartments on Thirty-fourth Street and headed south.

My friend and I could barely stay together in the hustle and rush of the after-work crowd. When we got to Lexington, the weight of day one left me, and I twirled in a circle with my arms raised. I bumped into several dark-suited businessmen and earned a couple of frowns, but also a few smiles. Milly laughed and grabbed my elbow. "Go easy there." I said goodbye to her at the entrance to the Barbizon and continued on the last mile to Aunt Imogene's home.

I let myself in and went straight to the kitchen. Vandine was busy with dinner preparations. "There you are, child. How'd it go?"

I went to the new Frigidaire and poured a glass of orange juice, then sat on a stool so I could watch Vandine as she shelled peas. Mama's fondest wish was to have a Frigidaire. Daddy promised one when they went on sale. How strange to be confiding to Vandine, instead of Mama, about my day. But I'd have to get used to it because my ranch days were over. Already, I knew Manhattan was home.

"It was interesting, I'll say that. There's so much to ponder and so much to learn. But I liked it. There are six of us in training. None are from New York, so we're all getting used to the city. Two of the girls are from Philadelphia, and they were kinda stuck up."

As I spoke, Vandine nodded and dredged chicken breasts in butter, then milk, then flour, then butter, then cornflakes. "Don't pay no mind to them. No accountin' for some folks."

"Yeah. I did make one friend. Milly."

"That's good. Now your aunt is having her a dinner party tonight. Go on and clean up. She be expectin' you in the lounge at seven."

"I thought I'd see more of her."

"You thought wrong." Vandine smiled and shook her head to soften the words.

Over the next weeks, what it meant to be a Powers Girl seeped into my marrow. The program had a class for everything: how to walk, how to sit, how to cross your legs, how to stand, how to turn, posture, hand placement, foot placement, the art of walking in high heels. Because the "fillies" had already mocked my Texas accent, I paid special attention to elocution class. Learning to speak proper was important. After hearing how well-spoken our instructors were, I made sure to study grammar and improve my vocabulary. I read Reader's Digest and devoured the New York Times.

Aunt Imogene made good on her promise to take me shopping. We went to Bloomingdale's, Saks, and Henri Bendel. One look at the price tags and I begged to leave and find one of those basement shopping places.

"You must be joking, darling. I'd never set foot in such a place."

"But my total budget is one hundred and twenty-two dollars. You saw my list."

"Forget the budget. You don't have one. You have me, and I have accounts at all these establishments. If you plan to succeed in the modeling business, you can't stint on your wardrobe. Surely, you can see that."

I left Henri Bendel with a spring skimmer in a black-and-white-striped hatbox. The rest of my new wardrobe from Saks and Bloomingdales would be delivered to the house. Aunt Imogene was energized after the shopping trip, but I was spent. She hailed a cab.

"I don't know how I can ever repay you, Aunt Imogene."

"I'll tell you how, drop the 'Aunt,' will you? It makes me feel ancient." She opened her compact and applied face powder, smiling at her reflection, then at me.

"Okay, I can do that. And I really, really appreciate this."

She waved away my thanks. "I'm happy to do it, darling."

Two weeks passed in a delirious blur. Each day, I learned more about my new profession. I especially loved the way the instructors ended the day, with stories of the latest success of different Powers girls, like who landed a contract with Revlon, who would appear on a magazine cover.

An introductory photo session was held the final day of training. When a tall young man with hair the same shade as mine strode through the door, I gasped. My gasp must have been audible because he glanced at me with the most amazing green eyes. His gaze nailed me to the floor. He nodded at me—in recognition of our mutual hair, I wondered. He smiled and introduced himself to the group.

"'Allo, ladies. I am Alain, and I will be your photographeur today." He started bringing in his equipment with the help of an assistant, another young man, who faded into the background. All eyes were on Alain, I noticed. At least four of us paid rapt attention. The fillies stood in the corner whispering, their heads close.

Eleanor broke the spell and sauntered to the front of the room, where Alain was setting up what looked like a gigantic umbrella. She dimpled and tossed her honey-blond hair behind her shoulder, then held out her hand.

"Ah'm Eleanor. Pleased to meet you, Alain." Her Southern accent apparently could be turned off and on like a switch. In our elocution and diction classes, she spoke without dripping sugar all over her words.

There was a murmur among the less bold girls. How I wished I had her nerve!

Milly sighed and whispered to me. "That girl has more guts than I do." This from the girl I had thought so self-assured. But she was right; Eleanor took poise to a whole other level.

Katherine drawled, "I guess she's staked her claim. We'll see about that!" She sniffed in disapproval.

Alain smiled slightly at Eleanor and said, "Mamselle, I am busy setting up. Please have a seat."

I bit my lip, so I didn't burst out laughing.

Eleanor tossed her head. "Very well," she said without a trace of her accent.

We took our seats, and after a minute, Vivian entered the room. "Today, we are doing headshots and full-body shots for your resumes. Take this opportunity to get comfortable working with the camera. And the photographer, of course. Let me introduce Alain Morseau. He comes to us from Paris."

Six voices, sweeter than honey, greeted him.

Vivian rolled her eyes and smirked. "I expect professionalism, ladies."

Glad I'd worn my prettiest frock, a cap-sleeved print, I smoothed the skirt over my hips. That day, I'd left my hair down, styled in a rolled pageboy with pompadour bangs. Did I look my best?

Vivian called us up one by one for our pictures. We were instructed to watch and learn when it wasn't our turn.

My name was called last. That gave me a chance to study the good and bad points of each of my classmates. Vivian made the same corrections to the other girls' poses over and over, and I vowed I wouldn't make the same errors. After my photos were taken, Vivian clapped and turned to the other girls. "Lauren was perfect. Take a lesson."

That earned me frowns from everyone but Milly. I was happy to have an ally.

Vivian announced we would return on Monday to accompany more established Powers girls to their jobs. This was an opportunity to make our faces known to those who hired models.

As soon as we were dismissed, the fillies flounced from the room. Four of us lingered, each trying to be the last to leave, to have a word with Alain. He and his assistant were busy putting their equipment in cases and appeared oblivious to our machinations—thoroughly professional, to our collective chagrin.

After several minutes of delay, we reluctantly began to file from the room. As I was passing the threshold, I felt a tap on my shoulder.

"Mamselle? Is zis yours?" He held out the lace-edged handkerchief I had surreptitiously dropped during my picture-taking session. Mama taught me a lady always carries a hankie.

I turned to face Alain and noticed his green eyes were shot with cinnamon, like rays from an otherworldly sun. He stood so close that I caught a hint of his spicy after-shave.

"Why, yes, thank you." I smiled and took the scrap of lace from him.

"*Mon plaisir.*"

The pleasure is all mine. No, I couldn't speak French, but I sure wanted to speak with this Frenchman. Would I ever see him again?

Chapter Four

A New York Education-1940-1941

A mere six weeks after stepping into the offices of John Robert Powers, I was working regularly as a Powers girl. Many of my assignments were humdrum: print ads for department store advertisements, catalog work for Sears, Roebuck. Then I found my calling as a runway model. When I strutted down the runway at Bloomingdale's, I wasn't a little girl from a North Texas cattle ranch; I was an elegant woman wearing the finest fashions the world had to offer. Later, I learned Imogene had whispered into a few ears in the fashion industry about me. Maybe she started my runway career, but I wouldn't have succeeded if I hadn't been up to snuff.

The only thing I didn't like about modeling was stripping down in the dressing area, practically in public, and having the hands of the dressers all over my body. Most contact was cold and professional because many of the dressers were swishes, but once in a while, there was a handsy jerk. I soon learned to put a stop to that sort of freshness.

In late May, I traveled to Chicago for a fashion show at Marshall Field's. As I boarded the plane, none other than Alain Morseau was sitting in the aisle seat. When I saw him, I almost dropped my straw handbag. He rose and gestured me to sit next to the window. I hadn't been in an airplane since my arrival and was happy this was a non-stop flight to Chicago Municipal Airport.

Alain and I shared a cab to the Palmer House. At last, I had a chance to get him interested in me. "How did you end up in New York? I thought Paris was the fashion capital of the world."

He sighed. "The war. The Nazis. Some of the fashion houses have closed business. Very little work. I have a mother and sister to provide for, so I came here."

"How do you like New York? Have you ever been to Chicago before?" I was nervously spewing questions, and while he spoke pretty good English, he might have trouble understanding.

"Big cities are much the same. Tall buildings. Everyone moves so fast. I miss French food." He told me that the Empire Room was not to be missed. It was very elegant, with good music and decent food.

"May I take you to dinner tonight?" He turned to face me as the cab raced through the city streets. His eyes captivated me. I struggled to find words to describe the color, seafoam, celadon, chartreuse. Then the rays of cinnamon. I'm afraid I stared.

When I recovered from my surprise at his invitation, I said, "That would be lovely." Although I wanted to squeal with joy, I remembered my elocution lessons and modulated my voice.

A porter scurried to take our bags. The Palmer House was gorgeous, rivaling anything I'd yet seen in Manhattan. I checked in and took my hatbox to my room. A bellboy brought up my luggage a few minutes later. I tipped him a dollar, which was apparently quite generous, given his reaction.

While I unpacked, I drew a bath. Thank goodness I had packed an evening gown. If I hadn't, I wouldn't have been able to accept Alain's invitation.

My emerald-green satin gown was cut on the bias and very flattering I'd been told. I brushed my hair for several minutes, then constructed an updo to the best of my ability. I'd gotten better working with my hair, but its length and waviness were a challenge. Powers girls soon became experts at applying makeup. I used a lighter touch than some of my fellow models. Imogene had given me a bottle of French perfume, Shalimar by Guerlain. Just a whiff of the scent made me think of faraway places and romance.

It was inspired by the fella who loved a woman so much he built the Taj Mahal for her.

Alain knocked on my door at seven. When I let him in, I was thrilled at the way he looked at me. I returned his gaze and gulped.

From the moment we entered the green and gold supper club, I was entranced. An orchestra played on the stage. The waiter bowed when he handed me a green leather-bound menu. The cuisine was French, and so was the man sitting across from me.

"Have you been to Chicago before?" Alain asked.

"No. First time." I took a sip of water.

Alain ordered Champagne, a vintage that was still available. He bemoaned the invasion of Paris by the Nazis and expressed disgust at the quick surrender of the French army.

"My mother has gone to live in the country. I am happy that she and my sister were able to do so. I feel so bad that I am here and cannot protect them."

"That's awful. Do you think the British will come to France's aid? They are supposed to be at war with the Germans."

"Nazis." The way Alain said the word made me shudder; it was spoken with utter disdain, as if he were speaking about vermin. In a way, he was.

"Your President Roosevelt wants to stay out of war. That is a shame."

I had hoped for a more romantic dinner, and maybe my dismay showed on my face. Alain took my hand. "Sorry, *ma chéri.*"

My whole body convulsed at his touch, and my face warmed with embarrassment at not being able to hide my reaction.

The waiter arrived with the Champagne, popped the cork, and poured. Alain clinked my glass with his. "To getting to know you, Lauren."

The way my name came off his lips made me shiver. His eyes met mine, and again, I was transfixed by the unique color. At first glance, his eyes appeared green, but on closer examination...I shouldn't have examined them closer because since I had, I was under their spell.

We sipped Champagne, and I accepted a second glass, hoping to appear worldly and sophisticated. I'd never tasted alcohol before that night. The bubbles tickled my nose, and I pretended I was sipping a sour coke. How old was Alain? Somewhere in his late twenties, I guessed.

He offered me a cigarette, and I shook my head. When he saw the look of distaste on my face, he put his cigarette case down and didn't light up. I glanced around the room and noticed we were the only two people not smoking. I'd tried a gasper or two with the girls at lunch and had coughed until I cried, and my head went shimmery. Smoking was not for me. I was flattered that Alain responded to my dislike of the habit.

I was famished, and the waiter appeared to take our order. Alain didn't ask me what I wanted, just ordered "caray danu avec fla-zho-lay" for two. How surprised I was when a dish of pale green pinto beans arrived topped with a hunk of lamb with the ribs sticking out. The beans were creamy and the lamb tender. Delicious. *Flageolets*, I'd have to remember that. I was eager to pick up a few words of French, but the pronunciation was nothing like one would think, given the spelling.

He ordered red wine, and I took tiny little sips from the crystal glass. The burgundy wine was bitter and made my head swim. Not wanting to become any more tipsy than I was, I refused a refill.

Alain insisted on ordering one of the flaming desserts, and I couldn't say no. I tasted alcohol in that, too, and wished for some plain old peach cobbler, like we had in Texas, but didn't say anything since that would be rude. For me, the highlight of the evening was the company, not the food.

The band began to play "Moonlight Serenade." Alain rose and came to my chair. "We must dance, *ma chéri*."

"Okay." *Okay?* I sounded like a twelve-year-old, but my body responded like a grown woman.

He held me close, and it felt wonderful, just like I imagined it would. Milly already had a steady beau, so she wasn't much for going out anymore. I relied on the Southern belles, as I'd come to call Katherine and Eleanor, when I wanted to see a movie. Other than that, I didn't lack for male companionship. Invitations to dinner and dancing were plentiful, but I never saw a man twice.

My heart had been stolen the minute I set eyes on Alain. One night in the Stork Club, I saw him leaning into a beautiful woman. I felt ill and asked my date to take me home. Another night, at El Morocco, he was with a different woman, and I didn't know if that was worse than if I'd seen him with the same one. Because I wasn't experienced in matters of the heart beyond my schoolgirl yearning for Tom Miller, I didn't know what to do. I supposed I could have tried to approach him, see if he remembered me, but I had too much pride. He knew I was a Powers girl and how to find me, if he cared to do so.

But that night, I was in his arms. Transported straight to heaven, over the rainbow, and over the moon.

When the song ended, he tilted my chin and brushed my lips with his. I staggered with the sensations—new sensations—below my navel. He took my elbow and led me back to the table. He signed for the check. "We have an early morning. Thank you for a wonderful evening."

Thank *me*? Thank *you*.

We stood and walked past the crowded tables, turning heads. In the elevator, I couldn't think of a thing to say. My mind wouldn't hold a thought. I pictured flour pouring through a sieve and almost laughed. A homespun memory at a time like this?

Our rooms were in the same corridor. Unable to fit the key in the lock, I handed it to Alain, who unlocked the door. For a moment, we stared at each other, then he cupped my chin and kissed me. I melted, and he seemed to know it. I took his hand and pulled him into my room, without thought, without reserve, without anything.

Kicking off my shoes, I stopped when I realized what was about to happen. We were going to make love, and I didn't know how. Sure, I'd seen the farm animals in their primal scene, but humans were different, weren't they?

Alain took off his jacket and loosened his tie. He smiled and took my hand, kissed my palm, and placed it on his cheek. "You want this?"

I nodded, unable to speak.

He picked me up, put me on the bed, and undressed me. Slowly. Lovingly. Stopping to kiss me again and again. Soon I wore only my silk stockings, and I shivered as I waited for him to remove them. Alain disrobed, and I kept my eyes on his face, unwilling to look at his lower body. I made to remove my stockings, but he stayed my hand.

"*Non*. Leave them."

He lay next to me, and I felt his manhood poke my belly. "Could you turn off the light? I'm a little shy."

"Oh, I so want to see you." Alain sounded disappointed, so I agreed to leave one of the bedside lamps on low. The mellow light provided enough illumination for me to watch his face as he traced my body with his hands.

His kisses grew deeper. He tasted wonderful. His caresses left me wanting more. I lost my shyness and took him in my hand.

"*Oui*? Now?" His whisper touched my neck, and I gasped.

"Yes!"

When he entered me, there was a brief stab of pain, soon forgotten. We moved together; it came naturally. Then his body convulsed, and he collapsed on me. After a moment, he rolled to the side. "Did you not come?"

"What do you mean?"

"Did you have an orgasm? You know this?"

"No. What is it?"

His face fell. "*Le petit mort*, the moment of ecstasy, the climax. You do not know these things?"

My face felt warm, and I looked away. "No, I don't. It's my first time."

"What!" Alain jumped up. Glimpsing his nakedness, I quickly averted my eyes. He turned up the lamp and exclaimed when he saw the blood on the sheet. He dropped to the bed and put his head in his hands. "What have I done? Lauren, I thought you were a worldly woman. Experienced in these matters."

"Like the other women I see you with?"

He raised his head and stared at me. "What is this?"

"I've seen you around town with several women."

"Forget them. I have. This is about you and me. Us. I'm afraid to ask your age."

"Sixteen."

Alain's jaw dropped. "A child. You are a child."

I sat up and pulled the sheet to cover my breasts. "Not any longer."

Alain stayed the night in my room. He was tender and apologetic, which confused me. Why was he sorry? Didn't he love me too? I hadn't said the words and didn't know if he had since he had spoken French while we were making love.

When I woke the next morning, Alain was gone. I read the note he left: *Cher*, I will see you in the lobby promptly at nine. We can walk to the Marshall Fields together.

I looked at the bedside clock and saw that it was already eight o'clock. I'd have to hurry. My private area was tender, but after bathing, there was no more bleeding. Still, I used a sanitary napkin so as not to soil my panties. Looking out the window, I saw the sun was shining, and people on the sidewalk were wearing lightweight clothing with no outerwear. I wore my summer suit, a lovely, checkered number Imogene had bought for me.

Alain waited in the lobby, and when he saw me, his face lit up. A wave of relief washed over me. I returned his smile, rushed to him, and fell into his embrace. "You are beautiful." Words I needed.

He took my arm, and we walked through the elegant Peacock doors onto State Street. Chicagoans called it "that great street," and I could see why. There seemed to be more people than on Fifth Avenue in Manhattan. After only two blocks, we reached our destination. The store rivaled those in New York and had a central courtyard that soared upward. The elevator operator nodded and asked for our floor number. When we arrived in the staging area for the fashion show, Alain went to find his assistant, who had the duty of hauling Alain's favorite camera. There were several photographers from Chicago as well, but Alain was there to capture the event for John Robert Powers.

During the show, my head was still in bed with Alain, and I missed my cue twice. Was this what love did to a woman? I needed to concentrate.

Several of the items I was given to model were exquisite, and I vowed to look for them when I returned home. That thought brought me up short. I now considered New York home. Three months away from the ranch, and I was a whole new person, especially now that I was no longer a virgin. I knew many of the other girls weren't either, but there was a contingent pledged to purity. I had considered myself one of them—until last night.

Back in Manhattan, Milly and I were booked for an ad for Bendel's. As soon as she saw me, she said, "Hmm. Something's different about you. And I can guess what it is. Alain?"

My smile and nod were the only answers I needed to give.

Milly grabbed my hands. "You're positively glowing. The rest of the girls will be so jealous! He's so handsome."

I spent every minute I could with Alain. We dined at the finest restaurants, saw Broadway shows, went dancing, and always ended up at his apartment. He taught me about making love and how to use protection against pregnancy. I came to understand he was very experienced in those matters and was grateful for that.

As a much-in-demand photographer, he worked long hours. I had much more free time and took to visiting him at his shoots. Alain was always glad to see me, but I sensed he was holding something back. He seemed distracted, worried. And I knew why.

One night in August, we returned to Alain's favorite place to eat, *Le Restaurant du Pavillon de France,* a highlight of the World's Fair, which would close when the fair did in October. The subway out to Queens and back was tiring, but he insisted the food was worth it. After we ordered, Alain huddled with Chef Soulé, a rotund and charming man who kept his staff hopping. I felt a little left out since they talked in mile-a-minute French. When our food arrived, the chef returned to the kitchen, and I had my lover to myself. The meal was delicious, but Alain was preoccupied and didn't share what he and the chef had discussed. I tried to get him to open up but received one-word answers and Gallic shrugs. My stomach sank because I had a feeling it was about the war and not the menu. France had surrendered to the Nazis with embarrassing quickness, and the shock of the Occupation lingered.

Later that night, after we made love, Alain sat on the edge of the bed, his back to me. "Lauren, there is something I have been considering and have made up my mind." Turning to me, his eyes filled with tears, and he hung his head. "I am returning to France to fight in the Resistance. Ever since de Gaulle's speech, I cannot refuse. My mother and my sister are with my uncle in the Free Zone. He lives in Toulouse, and they are safe for now."

Unbelieving, I sat up and exclaimed, "No, you can't! Don't leave me."

He didn't meet my eyes, just shook his head. "I must."

"Please, Alain."

He stood; his naked body now as familiar to me as my own. The ambient light from the living room cast shadows and sculpted him into a statue. As heartless and cold as marble, he told me to leave.

Sobbing, I gathered my clothing and ran into the bathroom to dress. When I came out, he was standing at the living room window, smoking.

"Alain?"

"Go. Do not make this harder than it is. I am sorry, but I have a duty."

When I got back to Imogene's, Vandine had retired for the night, and my aunt was nowhere to be found. Probably out at Café Society. Like a wounded animal, I scurried to my room and threw myself on the bed and wept.

The next morning, I bathed, dressed, and left the house on time for my modeling job, although I wanted to bury myself in the bedcovers. Determined to carry on, I carried on, but my heart wasn't in it, and I couldn't dredge up a smile as I held the jar of mayonnaise I was hired to promote.

"Something eating you, miss?" The producer's voice was gentle, and his expression concerned, but the last thing I wanted was to spill my story to a man.

"Maybe a summer cold coming on. I'll be okay." I had to perk up, or I'd get a bad reputation, and that would be the end of my career.

Giving it my all, I smiled and gazed with rapt fascination and adoration at a slice of bread as I slathered it with mayonnaise.

"That'll do it, miss."

Thankful I'd made it through the shoot, I hurried home to have another cry.

The following week, I had a runway show at Bloomingdale's, one of my favorite jobs. This was a big event to showcase the new fall fashions, and it was like old home week. The old gang was reunited: Milly, Francine, Fiona, Katherine, and Eleanor. The others chatted and laughed as we dressed in the first costume. I faked it, pasting on a phony smile.

Milly flashed her new engagement ring and was met with squeals of delight from the Southern Belles. The fillies smirked and remained silent. They never discussed their dating life, so unlike the rest of us. A few secret smiles and sidelong looks passed between them as Katherine and Eleanor raved about their social activities.

All eyes turned to me. "You haven't said a word, honey," Milly said. "How's Alain?"

I blinked and sniffed. "Alain left for France. He's worried about his mother and sister. He plans to join the Resistance."

The girls voiced sympathy. I put on a brave front, but inside I was dying.

In September, I missed my period but didn't panic because I wasn't very regular. Then I started throwing up every morning, and by the time October came and I missed again, I knew I was in trouble. There was nothing to do but confess to Imogene.

That evening, she and I sat down to dinner, a rare occurrence. Imogene raved about the sole amandine while I pushed mine around my plate.

Imogene lit a cigarette and studied me. "Not a fan of fish?"

"I'm pregnant." Burying my face in my hands, I bawled like a newborn calf.

She took it in stride. "Darling, what a pity. Who and where is the putative father? Flown the coop? They often do."

"It's Alain, the photographer I've been seeing. He returned to France to fight in the Resistance."

Imogene puffed on the cigarette and blew out the smoke in a string of perfect little Os. "Hmm. Good for him. *Someone* has to defeat those dastardly Nazis. As I'm sure you've heard, most of the fashion houses have closed due to the unfortunate occupation of Paris by those heinous bastards. It's impossible to travel to Europe these days. How can I help?"

"I can't tell my mother."

"Of course not! Rose will have my head. Do you want to end the pregnancy? I have a doctor I can recommend."

"No! I couldn't do that. I will have to bear the child, but I'm not prepared to raise a baby. Will I have to go to a home for unwed mothers?"

"No, darling. I'll see you through. There are childless couples who are desperate for a baby, although I can't imagine why. In fact, my half-brother Clark and his wife Evelyn are trying to adopt. They live in Boston, so no one in Manhattan need ever know."

"Oh, people will know when they see my big pregnant belly. I can hardly model in that condition, so I can't support myself. What will I do for seven months, hide in the house?"

"Lauren, I said I'll see you through, and I will. Rose would have my hide if she found out, and I'm sure she'd blame me. We'll just take things a day at a time."

"Wait! Won't Uncle Clark tell Mama?"

Imogene rolled her eyes. "Don't be naïve. They would do anything for a child, so they'll keep it quiet."

If I hadn't felt shame enough about having sex outside of marriage and getting pregnant, add the guilt about keeping Mama in the dark. How would she react to this disaster? Would she make me go back to the ranch and raise the baby? That's what I figured. And Daddy would be so disappointed in me. I would no longer be the apple of his eye, and that was a prospect I couldn't face.

Trying to envision such a life, the phrase "withering on the vine" came to mind. Endless days of diapers, cooking, and cleaning. Scandal and disapproval, knowing stares at church. Tom Miller wouldn't look at me. Neither would anyone of any repute in Palo Pinto County.

To my relief, the morning sickness stopped in November. I continued to model and carried a supply of safety pins and rubber bands to make skirts and pants fit my expanding waistline. Although I wasn't showing yet—just had a thicker waist—it was only a matter of time before my condition was obvious. The holiday season was prime time for fashion shows, and the money was good, so I wanted to continue working as long as possible. My last show was the week before Christmas. I barely got through the event because the clothes selected for me didn't fit. I had to exchange outfits with Milly and Katherine. Their skeptical looks and meaningful glances at my belly led to my confession.

"Yes. I'm pregnant."

They seemed genuinely concerned for me and had a million questions about my plans.

"Good Lord, kid, I wouldn't want to be in your shoes," Katherine said. "I suppose your career is over. Too bad!"

Milly hugged me. "Honey, you're gonna have to tell the agency. You can't wear anything fitted. Maybe they'll have some catalog work for you. You know, shoes, handbags, maybe even maternity wear."

Katherine brightened. "Gee, I didn't think of that. That would be swell, wouldn't it?"

Touched by their support, I burst into tears, an all-too-common occurrence lately. "Alain never knew. I wonder if it would have changed anything if he had." I wiped my eyes. "Probably not."

Milly's idea was genius. The agency was very understanding and did find me some catalog work. It was boring but kept me busy and in pin money. Shopping for maternity clothes was embarrassing. Imogene had no interest in that type of clothing, so I was on my own.

In the evenings, I stayed in and listened to jazz and blues records from Imogene's vast collection of race music. Billie Holiday reached into my chest and ripped out my heart as she sang "Ghost of Yesterday" and "Body and Soul." Reduced to tears by the lyrics, I shut off the Bendix and trudged upstairs to my lonely bed.

Since I didn't know much about pregnancy in humans, I visited the library to see what I could learn. There was a small branch in Lenox Hill, but I chose to visit Patience and Fortitude, the famous pair of marble lions that lie proudly before the majestic Beaux-Arts main library building at Fifth Avenue and 42nd Street. In my current condition, I would need patience and fortitude.

By the end of January, I was just too bulky to work and spent more and more time at the library's main branch. With my huge abdomen, I couldn't hoof it the entire way as I would have in the past, so I took the Lexington line subway.

I scoured the card catalog for the books I needed, but the Dewey decimal system had fled my memory banks. Asking a forbidding elderly gray-haired woman at the desk, she glanced at my middle, pursed her lips, and led me to the section I needed. As I struggled with the enormous books, a man of indeterminate age hurried over to help me.

"Here, let me take those off your hands." He was shorter than me and slight. "I'm Harold. What's your name, honey?"

"Lauren. Thanks so much for your help. Do you work here?"

"Yes, I do. At your service."

With surprising arm strength, he lugged my books to a table in the reading room. "Couldn't help but notice you are with child *and* without wedding ring. You might want to stop by Woolworths and fix that."

I felt my face get warm. "Gee, thanks, I think."

"Honey, believe me, I know a thing or two about camouflage." He walked away with an exaggerated wriggle and tossed a wink over his shoulder. When he saw me grin, he blew me a kiss, then walked on without the theatrics.

I realized he was queer, but he was also thoughtful and kind, and I decided I liked him quite well.

Harold's advice was brilliant. I stopped at Woolworth's on the way home and bought a two-dollar ring. Soon it became a habit to wear it when I ventured outdoors. I received a lot more nods and smiles than before my sham marriage. Harold was astute. On my next visit to the library, I thanked him for his suggestion and told him how well it worked.

He waved my thanks away. "Happy to help."

"Let me buy you lunch."

"You gotta deal. Let me tell the warden." Harold swished over to the woman at the desk. Now that I thought about it, she did have the look of a warden.

With a big grin, he hurried back. "I'm yours for an hour. I know a little Italian place right around the corner. Let's make tracks!" With a balletic turn, he set off through the Rose Reading Room.

Harold and I grew close over the next two months. With Milly working full time and her preoccupation with her beau, I needed a friend. We were an unlikely pair. I towered over him. Harold seemed ageless, and when he told me he was forty-four, I was stunned. He had a young-at-heart attitude and always had a good word. He was quick with the one-liners and kept me laughing when my situation was anything but funny.

I read dense, arcane medical books with gory drawings that depicted what was happening inside my body. The chapter on the birth process set my teeth on edge. How could a woman survive that? How could a woman do it over and over, like my mother had?

Once a week, usually on Friday, the warden allowed Harold a little extra time for lunch. He knew all the best restaurants and which places had lunch specials. He ate with relish, and I wondered how he stayed so trim. My belly was growing to a ridiculous extent. My arms and legs looked like toothpicks in comparison to my body. Back pain and frequent urination were my new reality. Why did any woman willingly subject herself to this?

I turned seventeen. Harold brought me a cupcake and sang "Happy Birthday" to me on the library steps. People nearby stopped and joined in. I was so embarrassed.

When I mentioned to Vandine that my birthday had passed, she threw up her hands in dismay. "Honey, you shoulda told me. Well, we'll just have us a celebration tonight. Your aunt will be here. I'm gonna bake you a cake. Chocolate?"

"Thanks, that will be lovely."

I dreaded my obstetrician appointments. The stirrups, cold table, clinical disinterest, and discomfort made me shudder. While I mourned the loss of my figure, Doctor Evans was pleased with my progress. He told me I could deliver anytime, but first-time mothers often were late. Cheery news. I wanted it over with. I wanted my body back.

That Friday, Harold and I ate at our favorite Italian place, the site of our first lunch.

"I probably won't be around for a few weeks. The doctor said I could deliver at any time."

Harold wiped his mouth delicately. "Looking at that belly and the way you waddle, I'd agree."

"Gee, thanks."

"You know I mean that in the nicest way possible." He patted my hand. His blue eyes were merry behind the lenses of his wire-rimmed glasses.

"I'll miss these lunches." Tears sprung to my eyes.

"Well, we can pick up when you're ready. Are you having second thoughts about adoption?"

Stunned, I said, "Heck, no! If I know anything, I know that I'm not capable of taking care of a baby. I can't even take care of myself."

Harold tilted his head and pursed his lips. "You're young, honey. You'll learn."

He walked me to the subway and hugged me.

Chapter Five

NEW YORK COMEUPPANCE-1941

Imogene made arrangements for her Boston relatives to come to New York as soon as the baby was born. I told her I didn't want to meet them. She insisted that I do. Not only didn't I want to meet them, but I also didn't want to see the baby. Just wanted the whole tragedy over and done.

One April morning, two weeks past my due date, I trudged into the kitchen at six a.m., feeling like my back was caught in a medieval torture device. I gasped when I saw a young Negro man leaving through the back door. He glanced back at me, grinned and put a finger to his lips, and left. I swore I'd seen him before but couldn't remember where. A few minutes later, Vandine entered the kitchen, and I asked her about the man. She got flustered. "Oh, that Imogene. You don't want to let on you saw him to your auntie." Shaking her head, she left the kitchen.

I felt the strangest sensation between my legs, then a splash. Looking down, I saw a puddle on the floor. I screamed. Vandine came running, took one look, and sat me on a chair. "I'll get Imogene!"

They rushed back to me. With her hair in disarray, Imogene tied a robe over her negligée. "We better get you over to Lenox Hill. Your baby has announced its intention to debut." Despite her appearance, Imogene's voice was calm, which I needed at the moment. "I'll grab your bag and bring your coat. Vandine dear, stay with Lauren." She dashed from the room. A massive, deep pain made me bend forward and moan.

Vandine grabbed towels and mopped the floor. She went to the sink, wet a soft cloth, and handed it to me. "Put this on the back of your neck."

I opened my mouth to thank her, but a yelp came out instead. The pain was getting worse.

A few agony-filled moments later, Imogene breezed into the room, fully dressed, her hair contained by a stylish turban. She'd taken the time to apply lipstick. "Let's get you in the car." She took my elbow and helped me out of the chair.

My legs were wobbly, and I wasn't sure I could walk out to the garage at the rear of the property. Vandine took my other arm, and the three of us made it out the door and to the car. That brought to mind the man I'd seen leaving.

"Who was that Negro man in the kitchen?"

Imogene stumbled but recovered her balance. "I'll tell you later. Right now, we've got to concentrate on you and your baby."

Vandine's lips tightened, and she shook her head.

Another pain hit, and my attention centered on my body that felt like it was splitting in half.

Imogene pulled up to the curb at Lenox Hill, honking her horn like a madwoman, and a nurse ran out with a wheelchair. The last thing I remembered was putting on a hospital gown and getting a shot. My eyes blurred, and my head swam...and then, nothing.

When I woke, my body felt like I'd been beaten. My wrists were chafed, and my privates stung and burned. A nurse came in with another shot, and I drowsed.

The next time I woke up, Imogene was there with a bouquet of tulips and a fake smile. "There you are! How are you feeling, darling?"

My lips were glued together. With my throat parched, I croaked, "Horrible."

"By the time you go home next week, you'll be fit as a fiddle. Doctor Evans is the best."

"What did I have?"

"You sure you want to know? You're not changing your mind about adoption, are you?" Imogene looked horrified.

"No. Just curious."

"A girl. And she has the Babcock hair. Clark and Evelyn are here to take her home. They want to meet you."

"How did they get here so fast?"

"Fast? It's Friday. You had the baby on Tuesday."

"What? I don't remember anything."

Imogene clapped her hands. "*Brava*! Exactly as Dr. Evans promised. No pain and no memory. It's called Twilight sleep. You're welcome. Freshen up, dear. Clark and Evelyn are waiting anxiously in the hall."

I asked for a mirror, and when I saw my image, I almost flung the mirror across the room. My face was pale and drawn. "I can't face them looking like this!"

Imogene brushed my hair, pinched my cheeks for color, and applied a touch of coral lipstick. I felt a little more human.

Bearing gifts, Evelyn and Clark hesitantly entered my private room. They presented me with a two-pound box of Li-Lac chocolates, a bouquet of roses, and a wrapped box from Bloomingdale's.

Evelyn looked about my mother's age. She wore a beautifully tailored spring suit in dusty pink with a stylish hat. Her tremulous smile couldn't hide her trepidation at meeting me. Why did a woman her age want a baby? Clark's gray hair pegged him as even older. His horn-rimmed glasses and gray flannel suit confirmed he was as advertised, a stodgy old banker. I tried to picture him with a baby and just couldn't. Of course, I couldn't picture myself with a baby, which was why they were here. After an awkward introduction and expressions of gratitude, they left to claim their prize.

My mind was fuzzy. I wasn't having second thoughts about my decision because I wasn't having thoughts. The twilight sleep lingered on. My body still ached, and I wanted a coke more than anything but was too enervated to ask for one.

A week later, pale, flabby, and weak, I left Lenox Hill. My appetite hadn't returned, so I gave the chocolates to the nurse. The tulips and roses were dead. I still hadn't opened the Bloomingdale's box, just didn't care enough.

Back at Imogene's, I retreated to my room. At my follow-up appointment with Dr. Evans, he told me my body was healing. My brain wasn't. Even Imogene noticed. When I'd been home a week, she stopped in my room before she left for the evening.

"Kid, you're just sitting here moping around. Something's got to give. When I was your age, I was out dancing every night."

"I've heard the stories. What on earth is the Black Bottom?"

Imogene threw back her head and laughed. "That went out of style with rolled stockings and fringed dresses. I'll never forget when they banned the Shimmy. Bunch of party poopers!"

I grew serious. "You never did tell me who that Negro man was I saw leaving the morning...I-the baby came."

Imogene pursed her lips. "I was hoping you'd forgotten."

"No." I closed my magazine and sat up. "Tell me. Vandine ran from the kitchen when I asked her."

"Joe is...a friend of mine."

"What kind of friend?"

"You know what kind."

Wow! Imogene was nothing if not blunt. I realized my mouth was hanging open. "No wonder Vandine wouldn't talk. What does she think about it?"

"It doesn't matter what she thinks. But if you must know, she disapproves. Of course, Joe isn't my only lover. There are others."

My eyes widened, and I stifled a gasp. "I see."

"I doubt that. Don't be judgmental, darling."

I frowned. "Please don't think that. How could I be, after what I've done?"

She stepped to the side of the bed and patted my shoulder. "Kiddo, if you don't put this behind you and forgive yourself, I don't know what kind of life you're going to have. So snap out of it!" With that, she waved and left the room.

I thought long and hard about what Imogene said, but continued to be a lump, a listless shadow of my former self. Vandine was kind and cared for me like I was her own child, fixing fried chicken to tempt me into eating, bringing me magazines, encouraging me to call my friends. Still, I languished in self-imposed isolation and misery. How long could this continue?

Then, a month later, Mama showed up unannounced on Imogene's doorstep. I was lying in bed with a fashion magazine, dreaming about my past glory days as a model. Going by what I saw in the mirror, those days were over. My hair was lifeless and falling out. Dry flaky skin replaced my former creamy complexion, and I had dark circles under my eyes.

Drawn from my languor by a commotion, raised voices, and thundering footsteps on the stairs, I gasped when Mama stormed into my room. She stopped short and gaped at me. Rushing to the bed, she sank onto it, her hands covering her mouth.

I turned my face away.

When she spoke, her voice shook. "Oh Ruby, I never should have agreed to let you come to this city. I can't believe what's happened. Here I was about to chastise you, but I see you've been sufficiently punished."

Punished? So, my mother felt I deserved punishment. At least I knew where I stood. In a way, I wished she could save me from what had already happened, but that was foolish, wishful thinking.

Imogene appeared in the doorway. "A word, Rose?"

Mama joined Imogene in the hall. I couldn't hear their conversation, but their heated voices left no doubt in my mind that things were ugly.

"We'll finish this later," Mama told Imogene, who stalked off down the hall. With a fake smile, Mama came back and sat on the bed.

"I hope you're not angry with Imogene. This isn't her fault. She helped me."

Mama frowned. "That's beside the point. You're underage. She had no right to keep your pregnancy from me."

"What would you have done?"

She stood and paced, wringing her hands. "Oh, Lord, I don't know. I suppose I would have found you a place in a home for unwed mothers. In that condition, I wouldn't want you to come home and have your brothers see you."

"I see." Chills ran down my spine.

She faced me. "Ruby, watch your tone."

I jumped to my feet. Hadn't felt so energized in months. "My tone? I'm not a child to be chided about my tone." My voice rose.

"Let's not fight. I'm just sorry I had to learn of your dilemma in a letter from the Boston Babcocks."

"Is that what you call your brother and his wife, the Boston Babcocks?" I was flabbergasted.

"Yes, that's exactly what I call them. Clark is so strait-laced, and Evelyn is a wishy-washy shadow of a woman. My father always regretted sending him to Harvard."

The idea of Mama calling anyone "strait-laced" was ridiculous. "Evelyn didn't seem so bad."

"Oh, she's not. Just dominated by Clark. To look at him, you'd think he was a mouse, but he wears the pants for sure."

I moved to the window seat overlooking Park Avenue. The trees were in full leaf, and geraniums bloomed in the flower boxes. According to the newspaper, it was June 12th, so I'd missed two months of 1941.

"Why don't you start packing?" Mama made it sound like an order, not a question.

My head swiveled so quickly that I got a crick in my neck. "Are you serious? No! How could you even imagine I would go back to the ranch? I'm a city girl. No, a woman."

Mama sank onto the seat at my vanity table. "What are you going to do? Model?"

"I'm not sure, but I need to get back to life. No more lounging around in bed feeling sorry for myself."

"Tell you what, let's take a walk, get some fresh air." Mama stood and headed to the door. "We can find a nice place for lunch. You can freshen up. Meet you downstairs in half an hour."

I never learned what transpired between my aunt and my mother, but the two avoided each other for the rest of Mama's stay. As I carried her bag to the taxi, I asked the question that had been on my mind since her arrival.

"Does Daddy know?"

Not meeting my eyes, Mama said, "How could I keep something like this from him?"

Crushed and barely able to speak, I said goodbye and promised to visit soon but had no intention of doing so. My relationship with her would never be the same.

Spurred to action by my anger and disappointment in the woman who birthed me, I emerged from the cocoon of despair, determined to face the world again. Each day, I took long walks and tended to my appearance. A haircut and conditioning treatment and long-overdue manicure and pedicure energized me.

Imogene told me about a type of exercise program that was all the rage. The Pilates, Joe and Clare, had a studio on Eighth Avenue, and I decided to give it a try. Not wanting to invest much money in exercise costumes, I shopped for shorts, athletic shirts, and footwear at the basement shop at Gimbels.

I entered the studio hesitantly, removing the trench coat I'd covered myself with. On the linoleum floor were several low tables that looked like torture devices. Joe Pilates, an older man wearing shorts and a t-shirt, showed me around the space. Posters on the wall showed proper body alignment, prompting me to correct my sloppy posture. A young woman lay on one of the torture devices, pushing her feet against the edge. Doubtful about the program, I remembered Imogene said the top Broadway dancers swore by his method. After the birth, my body had lost tone, and even though I'd lost weight, I was flabby. It was embarrassing, and so I decided to give Joe's Contrology a chance.

To my amazement, the exercises were difficult, but they sure yielded results. I was hooked and haunted the studio Monday through Friday. One afternoon, Joe's wife Clare offered me a job as a trainer. Flattered, I accepted. Since I was going to the studio five days a week, I might as well get paid to do so. My body became long and lean again, and I fit into my pre-baby wardrobe. But I never considered returning to modeling.

Harold and I met for lunch once a week. He refrained from mentioning my scandal, and I wasn't about to. As we strolled to our favorite Italian place, he entertained me with the latest escapades of his subtle war with the warden. Soon, he had me laughing.

"When will she retire? She's older than Methuselah."

"Don't insult Methuselah, honey."

Our friendship picked up right where we left off.

Memories of Alain haunted me. I hadn't heard from him and had no way of knowing if he was dead or alive. All I knew was that he had intended to go to Toulouse. Each day the newspaper headlines screamed news of the horrific war in Europe. Great Britain was being bombed with heavy damage. The Germans became outright aggressive against the United States, sinking one of our ships with a submarine, Uboat-69. Although the crew was allowed to evacuate to lifeboats, people were shocked, and President Roosevelt announced an "unlimited national emergency," whatever that meant. The Germans occupied France and instituted rationing. Jews were persona non grata, and there was talk of people being shipped in trains to camps in Germany. It didn't bear thinking about, so I didn't.

I got in touch with Katherine and Eleanor. They were still modeling for Powers and living at the Webster. An invitation to join them at El Morocco, where a date eagerly awaited proved irresistible.

When I told Imogene about my plans, she led me to her room-sized closet. "So glad you've returned to the land of the living." She gestured at the racks of evening dresses. "Take your pick, anything you'd like."

I selected a very daring fitted silver satin gown for my reemergence into Manhattan nightlife. Matching heels and a marabou boa completed my look. My hair had regained its luster, and I fashioned it into a coronet. On my head, a little satin frou-frou bijou of a hat with the tiniest veil. I felt like a million bucks and apparently looked it. When I got out of the cab in front of the club, the doorman rushed to assist me. Someone important must be inside or expected; reporters and photographers six-deep lined the walkway. Bulbs flashed, blinding me. I smiled. They weren't there to see me, but for a few seconds, I pretended they were.

Inside, I gave the hostess Katherine's name, and she ushered me to a corner booth, with its signature blue zebra upholstery. Katherine and Eleanor scooted out of the bench to hug me and exclaim over my gown. I waved away their compliments and studied the three men who stood and nodded. Who belonged to whom?

I heard my name called and turned to see Milly rushing toward me, towing her beau. She waved her left hand, sporting that impressive diamond solitaire ring. We squealed with delight and hugged.

"We've set a date! Martin and I are getting married in September. You must come!"

I glanced at Martin, who looked amused and a little befuddled. He would have to get used to being dragged around by my friend. "Of course, I will! Wouldn't miss it for the world."

Martin whispered in Milly's ear. She nodded and said, "Have to run. Toodles!"

The three of us scooted into the booth with our dates. My fella was the dark blond man in a pin-striped suit. Of course, he was tall—my friends knew I preferred tall men—and square-jawed with the most darling dimple in his chin. A dazzling smile.

"Pleased to meet you, Lauren. I'm Theodore Cullen." With another brilliant smile, he offered me a cigarette which I refused. "Do you mind if I smoke?"

I did but didn't say so. "Not at all." Gave him my own smile.

A waitress approached and asked me what I was drinking. "A Manhattan. What else?" I laughed, not knowing what that little joke would cost me. Why hadn't I ordered my usual Pink Lady—a drink I could make last all evening?

Theodore and I danced several numbers. He was a superb dancer and quite attentive, murmuring compliments into my ear. When we returned to the table, I was so thirsty I downed the Manhattan. To my surprise, it went down quite smoothly. The drink went straight to my head and made me feel like I was floating. Reminiscent of the feeling I had after the shots I was given in the hospital. I liked the sensation.

"Steady there, Lauren."

I laughed and ordered another. Theodore didn't comment, although he did raise his eyebrows. "Are you a model too?" He was on his third Manhattan. Who was he to judge?

"Used to be."

"No longer? Why not? Such a gorgeous girl."

"I had...some health issues. But I'm fully recovered." Funny thing, I couldn't remember having a baby, just had vague recollections of toting around my big belly for what seemed like eons. Did he pick up on my uneasiness?

Theodore's eyes devoured me. "I can see that." He leaned forward and took my hand. "Let's get out of here. What do you say?"

I said "yes."

In the cab on the way to Theodore's apartment, he told me a little family history. His people were wealthy, high-society New Yorkers for generations, and he worked at his father's Wall Street firm. "The Cullens weathered the Depression without any undue discomfort."

Even in my tipsy state, I was put off by his arrogance. If I were thinking clearly, I might have changed my mind about his invitation.

The taxi dropped us off at his penthouse, only a few blocks north of Imogene's home. With a little salute and a "good evening, Miss," the liveried doorman hustled to open the door for us.

The elevator ride was smooth, and so was Theodore as he took me in his arms and bent me backward for a breath-taking kiss. My body melted, and he picked me up and carried me into his bedroom.

I spent the night. Early the next morning, sober and aghast at my actions, I grabbed my clothes, softly closing the door, and dressed in the hallway outside his room. I was about to sneak out when Theodore appeared, stark naked and erect, and pulled me back into the bedroom. "Where do you think you're going?"

I gulped. "Home."

"Can I change your mind?"

He did, and I left two hours later. Walking home in my silver satin gown at ten in the morning, I held my head high despite my shame and aching head. Since Alain left almost a year ago, I hadn't had sexual relations. Wincing a little, I strode past churchgoers, not making eye-contact, full of regret.

At Imogene's, I poked my head in the kitchen and received a raised eyebrow from Vandine and a smirk from Imogene, who was eating an early—for her—breakfast. I didn't say anything. Upstairs, I tried to remember if Theodore had used protection, and I couldn't.

When I got my period three weeks later, I was relieved, to put it mildly. Why hadn't I heard from Theodore? Not that I wanted to see him again. Our night together was a foolish mistake. Then I saw him one afternoon on the Lexington line as I was returning from a late lunch with Harold. He met my eyes, then looked away.

What on earth?

To my surprise, he then stalked up to me. "If you're wondering why I didn't call, it's because I learned you had a child out of wedlock. And given how easily you slept with me, you're not the kind of girl I care to associate with."

His words rocked me, and I was too stunned to reply. He strode away with his smug face and smug attitude, the damn hypocrite. I got off at the next stop, several blocks from home, needing the air and time to think. One of my friends had betrayed me. Who?

When I arrived home, I glimpsed Imogene in the lounge with another woman. Locked in a passionate clinch, they didn't see me. I backed away and tiptoed up the stairs. Right then, I decided I needed to leave. Even at seventeen years old, I knew I was in over my head and needed to regroup. With my shattered relationship with Mama, I'd never return to the ranch, so I decided on Greenwich Village, where Harold lived, far away from the Upper East Side.

A few days later, I met Harold for lunch at a new Indian restaurant and, over blisteringly hot lamb curry, asked if he knew of any apartments in the Village. He did but warned me it was rough, small, and overpriced.

"Not like the lap of luxury you're used to on the Upper East Side, sweetie."

"I need a change." I relayed the Theodore incident.

"The cad!"

Then I told him about Imogene and her many lovers of both sexes.

"No judgment here!"

After looking at two dreary, dingy walk-ups, I decided to remain in the lap of luxury. But I never went back to El Morocco and avoided the Lexington line during business hours.

The war news out of Europe was confusing. I bought the *Daily News* on September 2nd. The Reds were fighting the Nazis, which I hoped meant the United States wouldn't have to enter the war. But Roosevelt's world-wide radio broadcast the night before indicated otherwise. The President threw aside "any technical neutrality" and pledged that the US would crush the Nazis. He would have a fight on his hands in Congress. Would they vote to get in a shooting war with the Axis powers? Seemed to me we were already in the war, with the Navy stepping up the delivery of munitions to Great Britain.

The Resistance in Paris was active, assassinating Nazis when they could. There were severe reprisals. I couldn't find a thing in the paper about Toulouse. Where was Alain? Was he even alive?

Mama's last letter, which I hadn't bothered to answer, informed me Travis and Mason had enlisted and were in basic training at Fort Wolters. Their departure left Daddy in the lurch, so Dylan and Jace, at fifteen and eleven, had to leave school to help on the ranch. With that news, the war became real to me.

In November, to my horror, I encountered Theodore again when walking home from the Pilates studio. His sneer and disdain cut me to the quick, making it clear I had to leave the city. After I related the incident to Imogene, she commiserated and said, "A change of scene might be just the ticket. Why not try Dallas?"

I couldn't figure out why until she mentioned Neiman Marcus. She knew people there and assured me I'd love the store.

"Retail? I'm not sure I'm suited for that."

"Oh, heavens, I'm not talking about sales. They have marvelous weekly fashion shows, and, with your experience, you'd be an asset to them. Let me whisper in a few ears. But remember, you're always welcome here."

I said goodbye to only four people. For old time's sake, I met Milly for lunch at the Automat. I remembered, when I first arrived in Manhattan, how awed and intimidated I was by the restaurant and the fast pace of New York. Now I felt as jaded as a fifty-year-old barfly. Milly looked radiant, married only two months and already pregnant. She was enamored with the new home they were building in Scarsdale.

"It's huge! A Tudor with half-timbering. Quite popular right now. Five bedrooms, and Martin says we'll fill them all. Three full bathrooms, with a private bath just for us. A powder room for guests. And the kitchen! So modern. Martin says he won't mind the commute at all. It's a wonderful place to raise children, they say."

While my friend prattled on about her preparations for the nursery, I wondered why she thought I'd be interested in that sort of thing. I hoped she'd be happy with her choices. We parted with assurances of undying friendship and promises to write, but I wondered if we'd keep in touch.

Harold insisted on one last night at Café Society after a dinner of Chinese food. I would miss him and told him I'd write when I got settled in Dallas.

"You'd better, sunshine. I don't want to lose touch."

"Will you visit me?"

"Maybe. Do you know any cowboys?"

Saying farewell to Imogene and Vandine was harder. I picked up Italian food from Tony's, and we dined at the kitchen table. The eggplant parmigiana was divine. Imogene opened a bottle of Chianti, bemoaning the fact there wouldn't be any more for a while with the war. Even Vandine accepted a glass, but I don't think she took a single drop, being a lifelong God-fearing Baptist.

During the year-and-a-half I'd lived on East 71st, I'd learned how close my aunt and her housekeeper were. After Anna ran off leaving two-year-old Imogene, Grandfather Edmund hired recently widowed Vandine, whose husband died in the Triangle Factory fire. She moved into the third floor with her daughter Pearl, and provided the stability neither Imogene, nor Mama, had known. Free-spirited Imogene had been a handful from the day she was born. She never had fit in at school, and Edmund was forced to hire private tutors and teachers to instill the basics in her busy mind. Vandine's daughter, Pearl, benefited from the same education. I hadn't met Pearl, but I hoped to, someday. My aunt's teenage years as a flapper were painful for Edmund, but being the stoic he was, he survived. He was pleased when his daughter demonstrated a love of music, although her preference for jazz and race music over opera and the symphony had frustrated him to no end.

When Edmund died eight years ago, Vandine comforted Imogene, who was only twenty-two, and unequipped to function as an adult. Because of society's expectations, there were boundaries between them, but those limits melted away in private. Vandine, a very conservative Christian woman, was leery of race-mixing. I supposed that had to do with her childhood in the South, which her family fled at the turn of the century. Although Vandine disapproved of Imogene's unconventional ways, that didn't stand in the way of their mutual love, which I witnessed first-hand. A stark contrast to my relationship with Mama.

As I helped Vandine clear the table, Imogene said, "I'm going to miss you, darling. But I'll visit. After all, Dallas does have one redeeming feature—Neiman Marcus. I'm sure you'll shine there."

"If I get the job."

"You'll get the job."

Chapter Six

LIFE IN BIG D-1941-1946

After arriving in Dallas, I checked into the Baker Hotel with three trunks and settled into my well-appointed room. I didn't know how long I'd be there, but the huge bed was so comfortable, a long-term stay wouldn't be hard to take. My nest egg from modeling would see me through for several months, so I had no immediate financial worries.

In two days, I had an interview at Neiman Marcus. Once I secured the position, there would be plenty of time to find a place to live. Imogene had mailed the director of marketing a letter of introduction, so I figured the job was mine. Wished I'd been able to sneak a peek at it, but I hadn't. I'd seen the store's ad campaign in *Vogue*, and the photos were stunning, a stark contrast to my childhood memories of the department stores in Fort Worth, or Cowtown, as it was known. How would it compare to Bloomingdales, Bendel's, or Saks? The downtown flagship dominated Main Street. I knew Neiman Marcus held weekly fashion shows, and all the oil tycoons shopped there, as did the ranching money. It was the headquarters for the debutante scene, and their bridal department was legendary.

I stepped out of the hotel to a cool and sunny December day, which confirmed my decision to walk the three blocks to my interview. When I entered through the doors, I was greeted by an atmosphere of perfumed opulence. The salesclerks could have doubled as models, well-dressed and coifed, with gracious smiles. Everywhere I gazed, the finest fashions were on display. Quite impressive, and I wasn't easily impressed.

A young woman approached. "May I help you, Miss?"

"I have an appointment with Mr. Rudy McManus."

"Of course! Please follow me."

Just as I suspected, my perfunctory interview was a mere formality. Mr. Rudy McManus asked few questions and was rather sycophantic. Imogene must have really talked me up in her letter. He rose from his desk, indicating the questioning was over. "Miss Eaton, welcome aboard. Our personnel department will conduct your orientation on Monday at nine a.m."

"Thank you, Mr. McManus."

"Rudy." He smiled, revealing a chipped tooth, which gave him a devil-may-care look. He was a little too old to worry about the draft and too young to have fought in the Great War. He offered refreshments, which I declined, then escorted me on a personalized tour of the store. I was impressed with the displays and selection, even after my experience with Manhattan's finest retailers.

On Saturday, I signed the lease for a one-bedroom apartment in an elevator building not far from work. The flat was available on the fifteenth, so I'd be enjoying the amenities at the Adolphus for a while longer. When the weather permitted, I'd be able to walk. Otherwise, the streetcar was an option.

On Sunday, December 7th, the world we knew ended. That afternoon, I clicked on the radio, dialed in a station playing Harry James, and gathered supplies for a manicure when an announcer broke into "You Made Me Love You" with the horrific news that the Japanese bombed Pearl Harbor, a naval base in Hawaii. I couldn't believe my ears. How dare they attack the United States of America?

Shaken, I rushed to the telephone to call the ranch, but stopped, remembering the shattered relationship with my family. I knew the war declaration sealed the fate of my brothers Travis and Mason and figured they'd be shipping out to the Pacific very soon.

Monday morning, I arrived on time for my orientation, wondering what the day would bring both for me and for the country. The ambiance in the store was subdued, with not as many smiles. I sat through two hours of presentations about the mission and philosophy of Neiman Marcus. I hadn't known that stores had missions and philosophies, but I learned.

At eleven, a clerk carried a radio into the room. President Roosevelt made a speech to Congress and the nation. It didn't last long. His words, "a day that will live in infamy," sent chills down my spine. Congress declared war on Japan.

We were dismissed for lunch, but I had no appetite, so I took a walk instead of eating. A sense of unreality was in the air. Shell-shocked people filled the streets. I stopped short at the sight of a line of men extending the entire block and continuing around the corner. Glancing at the sign on the building, I saw it was an army recruiting office. I thought about Alain. Was he still alive? Would the United States enter the war in Europe too?

Returning to Neiman Marcus, I rejoined the others in orientation. There were tiresome forms to be filled out. A policy manual to read: time and attendance, dress code, hair, and makeup. A big yawn.

At the end of the day, my boss came to the conference room and introduced herself. A woman boss! With the war, women in charge would become more common, I hoped. As a career-minded woman, I was eager to see how far I could rise.

Ava Grimley, the head of womenswear, was anything but grim. She looked like a million bucks, with her shiny brunette hair and porcelain skin, almost as translucent as my own. Her smile was well-practiced. A shade less than sincere? I'd watch my step with her.

"Welcome to Neiman Marcus, Lauren. We're happy to have you join us."

"Thank you. I'm happy to be here." I hoped my earnestness came through to her.

Ava turned out to be a great mentor; my first impression of her was wrong. She really was happy I'd joined her department and soon had me hopping. And I loved it.

There were only two things I lacked: a friend and confidant—and a man. Alice Munoz filled the friend vacancy on my second day of work. She was a tiny little thing, with an olive complexion and black hair, but had a big personality and a big heart. As assistant head of merchandising for women's clothing—quite the accomplishment at twenty-five—she was my immediate supervisor, although she never acted like it. Originally from Houston, she adored big D and showed me around town.

Every day, we sought out the diners with the best lunch specials. As we walked together along Main Street, we must have looked like Mutt and Jeff, given the difference in our height. Heads turned, but we just giggled and carried on.

On the weekends, I explored Dallas and its jazz clubs. The hottest clubs were downtown. The Baker Hotel, my former residence, was the place to be seen. When I asked Alice where I could hear some race music, I thought she was going to faint.

"Lauren, Dallas is strictly segregated. No race-mixing here. What kind of place is New York City that you would ask such a thing?"

I told her about Café Society, where I spent many evenings listening to great music. I should have known Manhattan would be more tolerant and advanced than Texas.

"Well, we don't have anything like that Village place here in Dallas. But some of the Negro jazz players do come downtown to play. Maybe you can find someone to go with you."

I did find someone. One night when Tommy Dorsey was in town, I met Benjamin Worth at the Baker Hotel's rooftop Peacock Terrace.

"Hey, sugar, wanna dance?"

A good-looking man smiled at me. Although he was only a little taller than me in my heels, he carried himself with confidence. His wavy dark blond hair fell over his eyes, and he brushed it back. He held out his hand. Poised—and certain I wouldn't refuse.

I didn't.

During a slow number, he murmured, "Name's Benjamin Worth. But you can call me Ben, and you can call me anytime."

We danced for an hour without a break, and when I shook my head in refusal at another, he placed his hand on my back and ushered me to a table. He pulled out my chair, sat beside me, and took a brown paper bag out of his pocket.

"Drink?" He offered me the pint of gin.

"Tonic water, please." When I first learned one had to bring their own liquor to night clubs and buy a set-up—mixer and ice, I was floored. So different from Manhattan.

"Teetotaler? Baptist?" His grin was charming.

"Just don't care for the taste of liquor," I lied. "But you go ahead."

"Tell me, will your lips kiss those that have touched alcohol?" He grinned again and ducked his head.

I liked this man. Not my usual type, but he charmed my socks off, and we chatted like old friends for hours. After another turn on the dance floor, I glanced at my watch. "Good gracious, it's after twelve. Have to run."

"Let me see you home."

I thought for a moment. Until that night, I had never let a man see where I lived. Should I make an exception for Ben?

He rode the streetcar with me and held the door to the lobby of my building. Not pushy like so many of the men I'd dated in New York City, but respectful, even with the flirting.

"Good night, Ben." I stepped into the elevator and pushed the button.

"Wait! Aren't you going to give me your number?"

I laughed and blocked the door from closing while reciting the number. Darned if he didn't take a pen out of his jacket pocket and write the number on his hand. That right there was the cutest thing I'd ever seen.

We saw each other every weekend. Ben was the best boyfriend, taking me out to dinner, bringing me flowers, dancing until we couldn't any longer. Each time we met, I learned more about his life and dreams. I played it coy, painting a colorful picture of my upbringing on the ranch and my time as a model, but omitting the lurid details of past mistakes.

Leaning across the table at El Fenix, I asked, "What do you do for a living, Ben?"

"I'm in the rail business. I joined my father's firm straight out of high school, learning from the ground up, as my old man likes to say."

After Pearl Harbor, whenever I met a man, the conversation pretty quickly got around to draft status and plans. Ben told me he was only twenty when they started the draft in 1940 and didn't have to register. When Roosevelt declared war on Japan, he wanted to enlist the next day, but his father prevailed on him to stay. Because of the nature of his job,

Ben qualified for a legitimate deferment because of wartime needs to keep the men and munitions moving.

I really fell for Ben. Just the thought of him with his jacket off, sleeves rolled up as he arranged for a rail shipment, made me shiver. Everything about him made me shiver.

One balmy night in late April, I invited him up after an especially scorching kiss at the elevator. I drew him inside the elevator, then into my apartment. We were grinning at each other like fools—until we got to my bedroom. Then it got serious. Seriously good.

As we lay there satisfied and happy, he asked me to marry him.

I said "yes."

A week later, we tied the knot at City Hall. Ben's parents took us out to dinner afterward. I didn't invite my family. Rationalizing my behavior was easy. After Mama had damaged our relationship, our communication was reduced to infrequent, terse, and formal letters. With Travis and Mason deployed to the Pacific, my parents were working harder than ever. With gas rationing, I doubted they could make the trip, not that I'd give them the chance to refuse.

After the ceremony, I felt a little guilty and called the ranch. When Mama picked up, I said, "I've got some news! You're talking to Mrs. Benjamin Worth."

Silence.

"Mama, are you there?"

"Good gracious. I didn't know you had a beau."

"Well, now you do."

"How impertinent."

"Sorry."

"I am too, Lauren. Our relationship needs mending, and that's hard to do long distance."

Did she expect me to visit? I put the kibosh on that idea real fast. "We're both busy with work. My job is quite demanding, and Ben's work at the railroad is vital. I don't see how we can drive down to the ranch."

"That's a shame." After a brief silence, she said, "You haven't asked about your brothers."

A slap in the face couldn't have hurt more. But I deserved it, being so full of myself. "Have you heard anything from them?"

"A letter from Travis. Nothing from Mason. Not since the surrender at Corregidor."

"Oh." I didn't know what to say. If I told her I had no idea where Corregidor was, it would expose my ignorance.

"Well, Lauren, I don't have any more time to talk right now. I've got to feed the chickens and start supper."

"Don't Dylan and Jace take care of the chickens?"

"Not anymore. They have to help with the cattle. It's impossible to hire help these days."

She sounded tired and resigned. And worried.

Since Ben still lived with his parents, the obvious plan was to have him move in with me. As he carried in his suitcases, I realized I had never lived with a man before. There would be a shaving kit in my bathroom and an extra toothbrush. With only one closet stacked to the ceiling with my things, Ben had to make do with a clothing rack set against the wall in the small bedroom. Despite those minor adjustments, my heart was full and my happiness off the charts.

A month later, my blissful married life came to an abrupt halt. When Ben got home from work, he slumped into the kitchen with a haunted look on his face. Addressing the air over my shoulder, he announced. "Lauren honey, I'll just come right out with it. I enlisted today."

Stunned, I dropped the dishes I was about to carry to the dining table. "No! You have a deferment. Wait, you're joking, right? Please tell me you're joking."

His tight lips and head shake told me he wasn't.

"Why? How can you leave me? We just got married." Tears tracked down my face.

He came to me and drew me close. "Sugar, I gotta do it. It's my patriotic duty."

"What changed? Why now?" I shrugged out of his embrace and stepped back.

His voice cracked and tears sprang to his eyes. "A buddy of mine was killed at the Battle of Midway. My best friend." He grabbed my shoulders and looked into my eyes. "Don't you see, honey? I have to go."

"Do you?" My voice shook. "What did your father say when you told him?"

"He doesn't want me to go, but he understands. He signed up in the last war."

By then, I was sobbing like a lost child. "I guess I can't change your mind."

"I enlisted. Signed on the dotted line. There's no goin' back."

"Well, you just broke my heart. We're newlyweds. And never even had a honeymoon trip."

"When I get back, we'll do it up right. A big reception at the Baker and a real honeymoon. I'd kinda like to visit Hawaii, pay my respects at Pearl Harbor, but we'll go wherever your little heart desires."

Not answering, I knelt on the floor and began to pick up the shattered dishes. Ben pulled me to my feet. "Let me do that."

I turned away. "I'm not hungry, but dinner is on the stove."

"Won't you sit with me?"

"No. I'm going to lie down." Without glancing back, I entered the bedroom, closed the door, and secured the lock, something I never thought I'd do. Sinking to the bed, the dam broke, and I stifled my howls with a pillow. I'd already lost one man to the war. Letting my mind wander to forbidden territory, I wondered what my life would be like if Alain had stayed. Would we be married and raising our baby? Appalled at the direction of my thinking, I sobbed even harder. I had sworn never to think about the baby. In that alternate reality, I wouldn't have moved to Dallas, married Ben, and be facing another loss. At eighteen, I figured I'd already lost enough to last a lifetime.

Ben passed his physical and within days, was sent to Fort Wolter. Those last hours together were tense. We didn't talk much, avoided eye contact, and when he approached me wanting to make love, I agreed but lay there like a stone. Who was I punishing? Me or Ben?

When his departure day arrived, I said goodbye outside our building, where his father waited in his Cadillac. I just couldn't bear to watch him get on a train and chug away. He should be scheduling those trains, not riding off to war on one.

As soon as Ben got in the car, I ran back inside, pounding up the stairs instead of taking the elevator. I threw myself on the bed and cried. Cried for hours, until I was dry. Clutching his pillow as if I could conjure his body in its place, my grief consumed me.

The following morning, I stared at my puffy face in the mirror and broke down again. Sickened by the way I'd treated Ben before he left, self-disgust rose in my throat like vomit. And I looked hideous. No amount of makeup could hide the effects of my crying jag. I scrubbed my face vigorously and did the best I could to camouflage the damage. Halfheartedly, I dragged a comb through my hair and dressed for work.

When I arrived at the office, Alice took one look at me and rushed to my side. "Oh, Lauren. He's left then?"

"Nothing I can do about it. So, here I am."

With the war effort, all resources were channeled to the military, and rationing became a fact of life on the home front. Every household received coupon books with firm limits on meat, dairy, and sugar. For women, one of the most painful restrictions was on nylon. With the lack of hosiery, women painted their legs, going so far as to draw black lines to imitate seams. Imogene sent me a huge package with hose in all shades. She had cornered the Manhattan market on nylons, so I never had to resort to makeup or—shudder—painting that ridiculous black line. The war had little effect on my personal life. I felt guilty about how little the rationing affected me. But then, I ran in circles that had ways to get around the system.

During the long, lonely months that followed, I channeled what energy I had into my work. The fashion industry faced real challenges with the rationing and all the new rules, testing our collective ingenuity. Funnily enough, Stanley Marcus, my boss's boss's boss, was recruited to head the textiles division of the War Production Board, and he did his patriotic duty, by God. He held many meetings with his top buyers and clothing department heads to brainstorm how to remain fashionable, given the restrictions necessitated by war. Conserving resources was foremost, so restricting the amount of fabric used to construct a garment to the tough standards was inevitable.

If I heard the phrase L85 one more time, my head might explode. But those limitation orders were the Bible for manufacturers. Potential jail time or stiff fines were the penalties if the rules weren't followed. I wasn't looking forward to dull fashion for however many years the war lasted.

There were mandates for manufacturing every item of clothing, from blouses, coats, skirts, dresses, to evening gowns. For blouses, if tucking or pleating were used, ruffling couldn't be and vice versa. Dullsville. No hoods. No more than one pocket, inside or out, and patch pockets with over twenty-five square inches of material were forbidden.

Hairstyling products were in short supply. I chose to wear my hair a la Veronica Lake, with a deep side part and waves down to my shoulders. Many women adopted the style of Victory Rolls, using rags to curl their hair. Then the snood appeared. I refused to wear a snood. Hiding my crowning glory in a hunk of fabric or netting would not happen.

Civilians were limited to only three pairs of leather footwear per year. Rightly so, soldiers' boots were the higher priority. Innovative materials like cork and hemp were used for summer shoes.

On another dreary workday, Alice and I left one more interminable meeting about the allowed shoe colors: Black, white, town brown, army russet. Two-toned shoes were prohibited. Boot height was restricted. Stitching and bows were banned. So depressing.

"If I hear the words prohibited, restricted, conserved, or limited one more time, I might scream," I said through gritted teeth.

Alice showed her dimples and replied, "I agree. But on the bright side, Mr. Marcus started the Hosiery-of-the-Month club for his charge customers. That was real swell."

"Yeah, he's a peach."

She elbowed me in the side. "Don't be a snot."

My friend had a way of chasing away my grumpiness. "We've got to find a way to wow our customers with the so-called new fall fashions. I'm out of ideas."

"Come on, chica, let's grab a coke and put our heads together."

The days passed, each much like the last. Often, I stayed late at work, fussing with details, not eager to return to my lonely apartment. Ben's clothes on the rack in our bedroom were a sad reminder. I slept in one of his pale blue dress shirts. Each night, I ran my hands over his jackets, wishing he was inside. His scent slowly faded from his suits. Then the day came when I inhaled deeply and there was nothing. I cried.

Alice and the other girls from work invited me out in the evening, and although I missed going out to clubs, and especially missed dancing, it would be unseemly to go out on the town. Heck, it was unseemly to even think about it. On the weekends, I shopped with Alice or went to a movie or museum. In a way, I was serving a prison sentence while Ben was serving our country overseas.

I wrote to him every day. His letters came in no discernable pattern. Some weeks nothing; other weeks, a treasure trove of several would arrive. I couldn't glean much about the peril he faced from his censored words; for that, I relied on the radio and newspapers. Where the hell was Tunisia?

In December, I clenched my teeth and reluctantly dialed the ranch to wish my family Merry Christmas and Happy New Year. To my relief, Daddy answered the phone.

"Sure do wish you'd come home for the holidays."

Guilt's sneaky fingers poked the back of my neck. "Daddy, I don't have a car, not to mention gas coupons."

He sighed. "I know, honey. Wishful thinkin'." His voice became upbeat. "Hey, this week, we finally heard from Travis. His unit's in New Guinea, fightin' the Japs alongside the Aussies."

"What about Mason?"

Silence.

After a long minute, he said, "Ain't heard nothin'. Things went real bad for us in the Philippines."

My heart fluttered in my chest. "Oh. I sure hope you hear soon."

"Me too." His voice thickened. "Excuse me. Let me get your mother."

I heard the receiver being set down. Closing my eyes, I pictured the ranch kitchen with its scarred wooden table, and an unexpected pang of longing pierced me.

My mother came on the line. "Lauren. How are you?" Her voice lacked warmth. Not unexpected.

"Fine." Did I sound as stilted as she did? One of these days, I supposed we'd have to fix our relationship, but I was singularly unmotivated to do so. With the war, we were each locked in our own private wretchedness of waiting. Like two strangers making small talk, we chatted for a few minutes, then said goodbye.

After I hung up, I wandered to the Philco console, Ben's parents wedding gift. The top-of-the-line model cost almost one hundred dollars and gave us so much pleasure. Opening the front panel, I put on some Tommy Dorsey, remembered my first dance with Ben, and sank to the floor in tears as Jo Stafford sang "Embraceable You."

In January 1943, the Office of Price Administration announced that ration coupons were no longer needed in restaurants. I could resume lunch dates with Alice and not have to bother making an evening meal.

Despite my work, I felt untethered, like a lost soul. My job filled fifty hours a week and maintaining my wardrobe and fabulous New York pre-war shoes occupied a chunk of time, but there were vast wastelands of emptiness when all I did was worry about Ben. Everywhere I looked, the lurid posters plastered with slogans for the war effort reminded me of the danger he faced. "Buy war bonds!" "Loose Lips Sink Ships!" "Do Your Share for Freedom!"

Uninspired at work, I persevered. Watching the pathetic excuse of the weekly fashion shows I produced, I dreamed of the pre-war glamour of New York, even considered modeling again, but soon dismissed the idea as fantasy.

The war news out of the Pacific theater was improving for the Allies. I hoped that meant Travis would stay safe. Mason's unknown fate caused me to have palpitations about him and my husband. I hadn't received any V-mail in weeks. The news from North Africa seemed positive, with the Allies pushing the Germans out of Tunisia and bombing Italy. Ben was in Tunisia. Would he be part of the invasion of Italy? The not-knowing was unbearable at times.

When I looked in the mirror, I saw a drawn face and weight loss. I'd lost my spark and my pep. At loose ends, I decided to take more walks and do the Pilates floor exercises at home. It helped pass the time.

On September 8th, General Eisenhower announced the surrender of Italy. I was ecstatic, not realizing what that meant: the Germans were in charge. Then, on September 9th, the Allies invaded Italy at Salerno. The fierce fighting resulted in many casualties.

Ben died there, far away from me.

When I got the telegram, the first person I called was Harold. I waited until the evening when I knew he'd be home. The phone rang several times, and I was about to hang up when he answered. "It's your nickel." His familiar voice filled me with warmth.

"It's Lauren."

"Oh my, how wonderful to hear your voice. I got your last letter but haven't had a chance to answer. To what do I owe the very great pleasure of hearing your voice?"

I started sobbing.

"Oh, no!"

"B-b-ben was killed in Italy."

"Oh, honey. I'm devastated for you. This is the worst. Is someone with you?"

I lied. "My friend Alice is on her way." The truth was, I didn't want to see anyone.

Picturing Harold's furrowed brow, I could almost feel him patting my hand. "That's good. Wish I could be there."

"I-I do too." I dissolved into tears again. "I miss you terribly."

For hours, I wept, and the next morning called work to tell them I couldn't come in. I kept reliving the day Ben left and the scene when he told me he enlisted. And the way I acted on our last days together. I didn't want those memories to embed themselves in my mind, but they corkscrewed their way deep inside. Lying in bed, I tried to picture dancing with him at the Peacock Terrace, the first time we made love, the day he moved into my apartment, the first meal I burned for him.

The malevolent war had taken two men from me.

A week later, I telephoned the ranch. When my mother answered, she sounded exhausted. I imagined she and Daddy had every right to be with the burdens of running the ranch, with no help besides Dylan and Jace.

I blurted the news. How else to deliver word of utter devastation? "Ben is dead. He was killed in the Battle of Salerno, in Italy."

Given the thud and clatter, she must have dropped the receiver. I heard her telling my father, then he came on the line. "Lauren, we're real sorry to hear that. You comin' home, girl?"

Stunned by the question, I fumbled for an answer. "Um, no, Daddy. I'm staying here."

"Sure wish you would. Maybe think on it. Will ya at least do that?"

I whispered, "Okay, I'll think about it." Of course, I wouldn't, but I couldn't hurt him again. He'd never said a word to me about my mistake, but the mere fact he knew turned my stomach.

"Hang on, I'll get your mother."

Mama's voice was subdued. "Lauren, you need to come home. We could use a hand around here."

Astonished at her response, I ignored the remark and continued with what I had planned to say. "The worst thing is, Ben was buried there. He won't be coming home."

"That's a shame. Will there be a memorial service?"

"Yes. His parents are planning one."

"I'd be there if I could, but you know I can't get away."

I didn't say she wasn't invited. "Talk to you soon. Goodbye."

The service was as sad as any event I ever hoped to attend. Ben's parents, whom I'd only met twice, seemed shrunken, mere husks of themselves. Grateful to my friend Alice for driving to the cemetery and staying at my side, I struggled through the service. After the ceremonial burial of an empty casket, an officer placed the folded flag in my hands. I stared at it, willing it to transform into Ben.

When we returned to their home for the reception, Mr. Worth pulled me aside and asked me to give him the flag. "Look, you only knew him a few months. Don't you think that memento rightfully belongs to his parents?"

Stunned and intimidated, I handed it over, then found Alice at the buffet table. When I told her about the flag, she frowned. "That was wrong of them. Do you want to leave?"

"I do, but it would look bad all around if I did." We stayed for twenty minutes, twenty excruciating minutes. The mourners were all acquaintances of the Worths. Me, I was worthless. His parents were devastated and had no room in their broken hearts to include me in the circle of grief. Maybe the guests thought I was a distant cousin, not Ben's widow. I believed his father blamed himself, but what could he have done in the face of Ben's determination—lock him in his room? I too felt guilty. I'd begged him to stay with me to no avail.

Alice tried to engage me in conversation as she drove me home. I had nothing to say. I wanted to die. There I was, a widow at nineteen with a romantic history full of tragedy. Never again, I vowed.

After a week, I returned to my job and threw myself into the work with determination. It wasn't easy to be enthusiastic about the current fashions for women. Hemlines hadn't changed in ages, and so many items had an air of the military with button-through shoulder pockets and other trimming. Trousers for women became popular. Why would a woman hide her legs? But, to coin a phrase I soldiered on.

For a full year, I refused all offers of male companionship, but due to the shortage of men, there weren't many. In patriotic Texas, most men who weren't drafted chose to enlist. I avoided the news from Europe not only because that was where Ben died, but because I couldn't bear to ponder

Alain's fate. Would I ever know, given the state of communication in what they called "the fog of war?" The Nazis had invaded the south of France once the Allies made gains in Africa. In my heart, I believed Alain was dead too. But he'd been dead to me since that night when he threw me away like a used tissue.

Somehow, two years passed. On May 8, 1945, VE day, Dallas broke out in celebration. We all hoped victory in Japan would follow shortly. I decided it was time to rejoin life. The men came home, and I was more than ready to welcome them. Resolutely shutting out thoughts of Ben, I dated. A lot.

And I drank. A lot. My first taste of alcohol as a sixteen-year-old with Alain led me to a huge mistake. Would I have been seduced if I hadn't indulged? Then, after the ordeal of twilight sleep, the very first drink I had—that dastardly Manhattan, pure liquor—ignited something in me, and my tolerance for the harsh taste increased. When I moved to Dallas, I avoided alcohol at first, which was easy to do because of the liquor laws. I even lied to Ben about not caring for it. Now I was pouring liquor down my throat like I was born to it.

One morning, I came to work in yesterday's clothes, with the stench of gin oozing from my pores, and Alice, ever a good friend, took me aside. "Go home and sober up. This is your only warning. If you come in like this again, you're finished here. And I'll drop you as my friend." Her eyes blazed, and I knew she meant every word.

So, for a month or two, I followed the straight and narrow.

Then, in September, just weeks after the war in the Pacific ended, Imogene swooped into town for a visit, reminding me of the allure of Manhattan. On my recommendation, she booked a room at the Adolphus. I didn't see much of her since she spent much of her time with a former beau who moved to Dallas to work with Trammel Crow. We met for dinner twice, and she never mentioned my widowhood. On her last night in town, we attended the Dot Franey Ice Show at the Century Room, with Herman Waldman and his Orchestra providing the musical backdrop. "For God's sake, you can't even buy a drink in this town. So déclassé to carry one's liquor bottles like a porter."

"You get used to it."

"I wouldn't. Don't you miss the sophistication of Manhattan? The variety, and I mean in men, as well as shopping venues. Neiman Marcus is a lovely store, but we have Henri Bendel, Saks, Bloomingdales, and Bergdorf Goodman. To me, it appears that the returning men are getting all the good jobs and promotions. Think about it. That's all I ask. I can talk to my connections at Bergdorf Goodman. Just say the word."

Although I dismissed Imogene's idea, six months later I had an epiphany: she was right. Ava Grimley was given "other duties," and her job was handed to a veteran. I saw my future and didn't like it.

While I took care never to show up at work with a hangover, the return of men from the war was like a buffet at which I stuffed myself. One-night stands—and plenty of gin—drove Ben's memory to a deep place in my brain. I so wanted him to stay buried. One bitter morning, I woke up in a strange room with no memory of how I got there, next to a man I didn't recognize, my face planted in his hairy back. The recklessness of my actions hit me. My standards had slipped, and I had to stop. Deciding to take Imogene's offer of a job at Bergdorf Goodman, I resigned from my now-tenuous position at Neiman Marcus and moved back to Manhattan in March 1946.

Chapter Seven

ANOTHER BITE OF THE BIG APPLE-1946-1947

As I left my Dallas apartment for the last time, I ticked off my mental checklist: radio returned to Ben's parents, Ben's clothing donated—including his shirt I used to sleep in, apartment cleaned, key given back to the super. I was done with Dallas and headed back to Manhattan. Why didn't I feel anything? No anticipation, no nothing.

As a last favor, Alice had agreed to drive me to Love Field for my flight to New York. Things hadn't been the same in our friendship since that incident when I came to work in yesterday's clothes. Ashamed of my behavior and acutely aware of how I'd lost favor in her eyes, I stowed my bag, climbed in the front seat, and stared out the window. Our goodbyes were hasty and polite, nothing more.

A porter rushed to load my three suitcases onto his cart. Two weeks ago, I'd shipped my trunks ahead to Imogene's and wondered if they'd arrived safely.

While I waited for the flight to be announced, I recalled my first departure out of Texas in 1940, from Meacham Field in Fort Worth. It seemed so long ago, a lifetime ago, but it was only six years in the past. At twenty-two, I believed my wretched life experience made me much wiser than my years.

I would soon prove that to be a delusion.

During the flight, I flipped through a magazine and wondered if I was making the right decision. How would I fit in at Bergdorf Goodman? It was so important to make a good first impression. Alice's lukewarm letter of recommendation burned a hole in my new suede clutch. Imogene's referral carried more weight; she was one of their best customers. Would anyone in the women's department remember me from my modeling days? I sure hoped not. Kind of late to be second guessing myself.

My inheritance from Ben, a check for $20,000, was my top priority. Whenever I thought about carrying the enormous sum on my person, my heart galloped. I must open a new bank account as soon as possible. This gift would remain untouched. Like a grown-up, I'd let the interest accumulate for my retirement.

Nestled next to Ben's bequest was the "death gratuity" check for $300.00 from the government. My blood boiled at the terminology. Was I given a *tip* for sacrificing my husband to the war? I would cash the check for that inadequate amount and donate it to charity.

The thing I anticipated most was my reunion with Harold. I couldn't wait to see him in person and buy him lunch. Maybe I could bribe the warden so we could make an afternoon of it.

During my time in Dallas, Milly and I had kept in touch through occasional letters. When she learned I was moving back to Manhattan, she called me long-distance. During the entire conversation, children were wailing and screaming, "Mommy!"

"Got your letter. Killer-diller! We must do lunch. Got a pen? 11 Stonehaven Road, a hop, skip, and a jump from the station. Can't talk long. Martin will flip his wig when he sees a long-distance charge on the phone bill. Toodles." I hung up, trying to imagine the chaos of her life. I'd have to trek out to Scarsdale to visit her. She was up to her eyeballs with children and seemed desperate to go out to a grown-up lunch.

Brought up short at the thought of a five-year-old girl being raised on Beacon Hill by the Boston Babcocks, I wondered if she had my eyes or Alain's. Resolutely pushing that thought from my mind, I knew I'd have to steel myself when meeting Milly's children.

The plane landed with scarcely a bump. After alighting, I waited half an hour for my luggage. A porter helped me out to the taxi line. Within minutes, the cabbie pulled up to Imogene's place on East 71st.

My homecoming must have slipped Imogene's mind. Once again, she was out for the evening. and Vandine let me in. Her rich Southern voice with her Carolina accent was music to my ears. "Oh, honey, I was so sorry to hear about your husband passing." She enveloped me in a hug and patted my back.

"I appreciate it, Vandine. It's been almost three years, but it still hurts thinking about what our future would have been like."

"I hear that. It's been thirty-five years since my Lincoln died in that dreadful fire." She pulled a handkerchief from her dress pocket and dabbed her eyes. "Now, I got your room all made up and some chicken and dumplings for supper. Tomorrow is my daughter Pearl's birthday. You never did meet my girl, did you?"

"No, but I'd sure like to."

Vandine beamed. "Good. We're having a luncheon for her tomorrow."

"I can't wait!"

"Here, let's tote your bags upstairs. You go freshen up. Dinner will be ready in a jiffy."

"Did my trunks arrive?"

"Sure did. The delivery man hauled them up to your room."

With a belly full of chicken and dumplings, I slept like a log in the comfortable bed. When I woke early to the smell of coffee and bacon, I wondered how I'd keep my figure with Vandine's cooking. Throwing on my robe, I raced down the stairs.

To my surprise, Imogene was in the kitchen. She and Vandine were going over the menu for lunch.

My aunt floated over to me in her powder blue negligee and threw her arms around me. "I knew you'd be back! You'll love it at Bergdorf Goodman. But you have two weeks before you start, so enjoy."

Still not a word about my widowhood, but that was Imogene. "I will. Tomorrow will be fun. I'm excited to meet Pearl."

"Not only is it her birthday, but we're also celebrating the opening of her first dress shop," Imogene said.

"That's wonderful."

"Runs in the family," Vandine said. "My mama was a seamstress of some repute in Harlem, so it comes natural."

"What time do the festivities start?"

"Twelve-thirty," said Vandine with a smile.

"I'll be back from the bank in plenty of time." I turned to Imogene. "Later this week, I'm taking the train to Scarsdale to catch up with my friend Milly. She's housebound."

"Your modeling friend? Is she ill?"

I chuckled. "No, she has three children under the age of five."

"Dear God. Wear something washable. And good luck. I'd like to be a fly on the wall, but I can't imagine traveling to the hinterlands." To emphasize the point, Imogene shuddered dramatically.

"Next week, I'm taking my friend Harold out to lunch."

"Oh yes, the man from the library. Give him my best."

When I returned from my errand, laughter and happy voices from the kitchen floated on the roast-beef-scented air. I raced to my room to freshen up. When the bell rang, I'd just finished applying lipstick. Time to meet Pearl.

Descending the stairs, I heard the affectionate greetings exchanged between Imogene and Pearl. They grew up together in this house, and the feeling of closeness and family was unmistakable. As I entered the foyer, Imogene performed introductions.

Pearl's smile lit up her face. The resemblance to her mother was startling; they both had that beautiful mocha skin and large eyes. Her periwinkle suit was the epitome of elegance, and the belted jacket showed off her tiny waist. To my surprise, she pulled me into an enthusiastic hug. "I've heard so much about you, Lauren."

My cheeks burned. What had Imogene confided to her? Thinking fast, I asked, "Is that suit one of your designs? I just love it!"

"Why, thank you. Yes, it is. I'm offering it in several pastel shades."

"I bet it sells out in days," I enthused.

Vandine appeared in the hall. "Lunch is just about ready. Five minutes, no more."

"Let's have a cocktail first." Imogene directed us to the dining room where a bottle of chilled Champagne awaited and popped the cork.

I gulped. The frosty bottle and sparkling bubbles called to me, but I resisted. "Vandine, do you need any help?"

"I sure could use a hand getting it all on the table."

As I left the room, Imogene made a toast. "Happy Birthday, Pearl! Thirty-eight. Have you started lying about your age yet?"

Pearl laughed and said, "Look at me, darling. No need."

While Vandine put the finishing touches on the gravy, I scooped the side dishes into serving bowls and pondered Imogene and Pearl's close relationship, almost as if they were sisters. What would it have been like to grow up with a sister, a close confidant who would always be supportive?

Vandine's signature mashed potatoes were perfect. The collard greens were tender and sweet. And her homemade buttermilk biscuits melted in my mouth. During the delicious meal, we discussed Pearl's plans for the grand opening. "How did you come to choose retail?"

With a smile, Pearl said, "After I studied business, I wasn't sure what I wanted to do, so I got a job with Ester Parham at the National Beauty Supply Company. Ester was a wonderful mentor and taught me all about the business. She opened the first woman-owned establishment on 125th Street. That woman is dynamic! She had grand plans to expand into hair products and believed Harlem needed more Negro women-owned stores, especially clothing. And since I inherited my skill with a sewing needle from Grandma Ida, I decided to open a women's apparel store." She picked up her champagne glass. "The rest is about to become history."

As I listened to Vandine and Pearl talking about the difficulty Negroes in Harlem faced in getting loans and finding housing outside their crowded neighborhood, I realized New York was just as segregated as Dallas. When I landed in Manhattan at sixteen, such things didn't register. Now I understood that the warmth and closeness of my relationship with Vandine, and Imogene's race-mixing ways were far from the norm. Hearing about the struggles Negroes faced made me uncomfortable, and Pearl noticed. She patted my hand. "It won't be like this forever. With people like Ester

Parham and Rose Morgan, things will change. On a happier note, they're building a fabulous new housing complex in Harlem, the Riverton. I'm on the waiting list for a flat."

"Remember, only three years ago, there were riots in Harlem." Vandine shook her head. "Race relations have a long way to go."

"But Mama, now we got some of our people on the City Council and even in the United States Congress. And the Urban League is getting strong community support."

"Honey, I do send them a little something from time to time, but change will take years."

Imogene stood and raised a glass to make a toast. "Here's to 'Pearl's Divine Creations.' We wish you all the success in the world."

While Imogene opened a second bottle of Champagne, Vandine and I sipped water.

After the hot fudge pudding cake, I could barely stagger from the table. Vandine's cooking would be the end of me. Excusing myself, I plodded upstairs to change into looser clothing and dredge up my canvas sneakers from one of my trunks. That done, I packed a satchel with my workout clothing and headed over the see the Pilates. But when I arrived at 939 Eighth Avenue, I didn't go in. With my face and abdomen still bloated from the drinking I'd done in Dallas, I couldn't bear the scrutiny of those slender, fit people.

Although I didn't return to the Pilates studio, I did the floor exercises in my room, at least those I could remember. I had to counteract the effects of drinking, so I added a daily walk to my regimen.

To tell the truth, I was apprehensive about my trip to Scarsdale, and it had nothing to do with Milly. How would I react to her children? I reviewed the details of her brood: her eldest, Martin Junior, was four. Milly had been pregnant with him when I fled to Dallas. Priscilla came shortly after, then Teddy, who had just started walking. The enormous difference between Milly's pre-marriage life and her current reality struck me. I didn't want to exchange places with her, but I hoped she was happy.

I got off the train at Scarsdale and noted the Tudor style of the station. Milly had gone into rhapsodies about the Tudor architecture of her Scarsdale home. As I followed the directions to Milly's—it was only a short walk—I had more than my fill of the style. Strolling up the drive, I saw a tricycle on its side among assorted playthings. I glanced at the door and noticed three little faces and six pudgy hands pressed against the sidelights. Good grief. The children disappeared, and moments later, a flustered Milly, dressed in a chenille bathrobe, opened the door. Her face was shiny with cold cream, and her hair was in rollers.

"Oh Lauren, you look like you just stepped off the runway. I love your suit. Lilac is the color this spring! Those purple suede pumps and hat are to die for! Come on in."

I did so gingerly. As three tots circled me like I was prey, I forced a smile and stated the obvious. "You're not ready. What about lunch? Did you make a reservation?"

"Yes. No. It's a long story. My sitter canceled."

"Find another one."

"Easier said than done. Come into the kitchen. I'll give the kids a snack and try to scare up someone."

As soon as the snack was consumed, sibling rivalry—at least that's what I think it was—reared its head. Two minutes of the screaming, crying, and fighting children was enough. I quickly hatched a plan to give Milly some quiet to make her calls.

"Children, I've got a marvelous idea. Why don't you show me your rooms?"

As if someone had put a cork in their mouths, they stopped yelling. I walked to the stairs, and they followed me like a pack of jackals.

After a bout of "me first, me first," we agreed it was only fair to tour their domains in the order of age. Martin's nautical room, with a bed shaped like a boat, was first. Next, we toured Priscilla's princess-inspired space, with its canopied bed and pink carpet littered with pink toys. Teddy's cowboy-themed room included bunk beds made from rustic timber, shelves holding a collection of horse figurines, and featured a wall mural depicting a fantasy version of the West. As we progressed down the hall to each chamber, I relaxed a little and complimented each child's charming and no doubt expensive room.

With the children pacified and quiet, we descended the stairs just as Milly came charging out of the kitchen. "I found someone! Marge, my next-door neighbor, agreed to bring her baby over for a couple of hours. Willya take the kids to the playroom while I get ready?"

Five minutes later, she came back in a too-tight matronly suit in an awful maroon shade and crooked lipstick. She reeked of Chantilly, which clashed with my Shalimar, and made my eyes water. I didn't say a word, but I felt bad for her. Recalling her beauty at age eighteen, I gasped when I realized she was only twenty-four. She looked at least thirty, a tired and pudgy thirty.

"Something wrong, Lauren?"

"Oh, no. I was just thinking about how hungry I am."

The front door opened. "Yoo-hoo! Where are you, Milly?" Marge had arrived, and during quick introductions, we helped with her stroller and a gigantic bag of baby things. She had packed like she was staying a week.

"You're a lifesaver, Marge." Milly hugged her and promised to sit for the baby in return. She turned to me and practically shoved me through the door. "Let's go! It's only a couple of blocks."

As we strolled to the lunch spot, Milly gave me the lowdown on her neighbors and their palatial homes, how many bedrooms and baths—and how many children. I struggled not to cross my eyes with boredom. Couldn't she see I had no interest in that kind of life? I hoped we'd share some girl talk in the restaurant. On arrival, the maître d' seated us in a sumptuous leather booth where we had a splendid view of all the Scarsdale matrons.

First things first, we ordered Martinis with extra olives and a dozen oysters on the half shell.

Milly took a dainty sip of her drink and said, "I've got some juicy gossip about our former colleagues, the gals you call the Philly fillies."

"Do tell." I had always thought there was something a little hinky about Francine and Fiona.

"They were kicked out of the Barbizon for 'unholy relations.'"

"What?" My eyes almost popped out of my head.

"Yeah, they've been that way for years."

"But they dated men."

"So what?" Milly pursed her lips. "Did you ever hear them rave about how much in love they were with whomever? Did either of them ever have a serious beau?"

"Now that you mention it, I don't think they ever dated the same man twice."

In a conspiratorial whisper, Milly asked, "Ever hear of a beard?

I didn't think she meant a man's facial hair. "Beard?"

"It's a term for someone to hide behind when one has an illicit relationship."

"Oh."

"Yeah." Milly drained her Martini and ordered another. When I raised my eyebrows, she frowned and said, "Don't judge me. I'm not driving."

"No judgment." After having an illegitimate child, and my own misadventures with men and drinking, who was I to criticize? Determined to cut back on my alcoholic consumption, I restricted myself to one drink. While Milly wasn't driving, I wasn't sure she'd be capable of walking if she kept up her intake of gin and vermouth.

The oysters arrived, along with Milly's second drink. "Ooh, they're so fresh!" Before I could serve myself, she slurped her way through three. Between sips, she continued to catch me up on our former colleagues. "Katherine and Eleanor are still modeling, although they're looking to get jobs as instructors either at Powers or the new Ford agency. John Robert Powers isn't the only name in modeling any longer. He's got serious competition. Ford is advancing money to their models based on their *bookings*. Let me tell you, they're cutting a swath through the scene." Milly held up her empty glass to signal for a refill.

"Interesting." It hadn't occurred to me to become an instructor at an agency. Maybe I should look into it since I wasn't certain how I'd like my new position at Bergdorf Goodman.

On the waiter's recommendation, we ordered shrimp salad and returned to our Martinis. The olives made a delightful contrast to the oysters. While Milly chatted away about her children and a recipe for gingerbread cookies, I tuned out. Sadly, my friend and I no longer had anything in common.

Relieved to see our waiter approaching with our salads, I suppressed the urge to bolt my food and run back to the train. The shrimp salad, served in avocado halves, and spiced with a hint of curry, was outstanding. By the time we finished, Milly had drained her third Martini and plucked out the olive, which she popped into her mouth, nearly missing. I was starting to wonder if her storybook, happily-ever-after life hadn't turned out quite the way she had imagined.

Milly bit her lip, then blurted, "Martin is having an affair. At least, I'm pretty sure he is. I'm mortified." Milly rummaged through her bag, then looked up, with tears streaming down her cheeks. "Do you have a handkerchief?"

I handed her mine. "Are you sure, hon? As I recall, Martin seemed totally in the palm of your hand, enamored like I've seldom seen."

Milly sniffed and patted her nose. "Maybe three kids and fifteen pounds ago." Her face crumpled, and the tears returned.

I ordered two coffees and listened to Milly's tale of woe: late nights at the office, detecting a perfume other than her Chantilly on his clothing, moving his expense account records to the office. It seemed she had plenty of reason to be worried, but I didn't want to fan her fears.

When the waiter came with the check, I asked for more coffee and insisted on paying. How could I help her? I racked my brain for ideas and finally hit on Joe Pilates' Contrology.

Setting down my coffee cup, I said, "I've been thinking about going back to see Joe and Clara at their studio."

Milly wore a puzzled frown. "Who're they?"

"The Pilates. Before I moved to Dallas, I studied Contrology with them, even taught a few classes."

"When was this?"

"After, you know...the baby." My face warmed. Would I ever get over the shame?

Light dawned in her eyes. "Yeah, I remember now. You really whipped yourself into shape. Maybe I'll give it a try."

"I recommend it. In fact, I've been doing the floor exercises at home."

Milly smiled, and I caught a glimpse of the fresh girl I met six years ago. Since she was a little unsteady, I kept a death grip on her elbow as we walked back to her home. At the door, I declined an invitation to stay awhile. "Got a train to catch. It was so good to see you." After a quick hug, I turned and hustled away from Milly, her troubles, and suburbia.

I spotted Harold waiting for me on the library steps on Fifth Avenue and barreled into his arms, smack between the famed lion statues, Patience and Fortitude, ignoring the curious stares of the visitors and patrons.

"Oof! Don't knock over an old man. I turned fifty in January, you know."

"Harold, you haven't aged a day in six years!"

"So sweet of you to notice. Come on, let's make tracks. The warden gave me the rest of the afternoon off."

Arm-in-arm, we descended to street level. Harold suggested our favorite Italian place, and I agreed. When he didn't compliment my appearance as he usually did, it confirmed that I had more work to do.

While we waited for the antipasti, Harold bemoaned the fact he hadn't been able to come to Dallas to visit. "You left Manhattan at a very inopportune time. With that dreadful war, travel was impossible."

"I understand. The war took a toll on everyone in one way or another."

Harold reached for my hand. "It took a great big toll on you. You lost two men."

Tears sprang to my eyes.

"Oh honey, I didn't mean to ruin our luncheon."

Attempting a smile, I squeezed his hand and said, "Harold, you always lift my spirits. You couldn't ruin our time together even if you tried. Of course, I still hurt, but I have to live."

The waiter brought our first course, and we dug into the salami, pecorino, and roasted red peppers. Harold still had his outsized appetite.

We chatted about my upcoming new job and Harold's old one. After the main dish of seafood linguini, I refused dessert, but Harold ordered cannoli. I tasted a tiny portion, and it was divine, but I contented myself with an espresso.

Lingering until three, we took pity on the staff who were pointedly setting the rest of the tables for dinner. We parted on the sidewalk.

"Thank you for lunch, sweetie. I'm going to head back to the Village. Tom will expect dinner, and I need to pick up a few things."

"You're going to eat dinner?"

"Well, yes. You know I never miss a meal."

I laughed. "What's your secret? You never gain an ounce."

Harold put his finger to his lips. "That would be telling."

"I'll call you soon."

"You better!" He blew me a kiss and turned for Seventh Avenue while I headed to the Lexington line. Our destinations were more than the distance in city blocks; they were worlds apart.

As I came through the door, Vandine stood in the foyer. She reminded me that Imogene had a gala this evening, so she had prepared a cold supper for me.

"Thanks, but I stuffed myself on linguini this afternoon. Maybe I'll nibble something later. No need to wait on me."

"Oh, I'm not. Got choir practice this evening." With that, she retrieved her bag and wrap from the hall closet and made her way out the door. Vandine was devoted to the Metropolitan Baptist Church.

After my experience at Neiman Marcus, I strolled into Bergdorf Goodman full of confidence. The Babcock name cut the mustard, and I was welcomed with warmth and enthusiasm by my co-workers. However, my new boss was a different story. His oiled hair and pencil-thin moustache were as repulsive as his personality. Mr. Thomas Evermore.

"Miss Eaton, you will have to work as hard as the other girls. The Babcock name will have no influence on how I rate your performance."

"Lovely to meet you, Mr. Evermore. I wouldn't have it any other way." Already, I knew I wouldn't last long in this position.

The work was not fulfilling, and the days dragged. I had no say in merchandising, no input into the displays or event planning. Seemed to me, I was no more than a glorified salesclerk. Another downside, I had less time to spend with Harold. And the clientele was snooty, not down-to-earth like their counterparts in Dallas. Dreams of having my own establishment ran through my head. Pearl was doing it; why couldn't I? But I was getting sick of the rag game, burnt out as a model, bored beyond words by retail clothing. The seed had been planted and was sprouting roots. I couldn't envision a life spent following orders from a man.

Three long weeks after I began my tenure, as I was returning try-ons to the racks and plotting how to achieve my goal, I heard a woman call my name.

"Well, look what the cat dragged in. Lauren Eaton. Never thought I'd see you selling rags." The haughty tone and clipped speech grated on my nerves. Taking a moment to compose myself, I turned slowly to greet Fiona. Of course, her paramour Francine was right beside her.

"Hello, ladies. Lovely to see you again! How may I help you?" Maintaining a pleasant facial expression was difficult. I didn't believe for a minute this encounter was accidental.

Francine's insincere smile preceded her words. "We heard you were back in town. Whatever made you take this job? Are you in financial straits? And how is the little girl? She must be five years old by now."

I restrained myself from slapping her across her smug face. Now I was sure who had spread the news about my troubles to Theodore Cullen and anyone else who'd listen. "Are you here to shop, or is this a...rather odd social call?" My own insincere smile trumped hers.

Francine's eyes widened, and she took a step back, reflexively reaching for Fiona's hand. "How rude. Let's go, Fiona. Bloomingdales surely has more professional staff." With a snide look, the two lovers sashayed out of daytime dresses.

Twenty minutes later, I was summoned to the august presence of Mr. Thomas Evermore. Before entering his lair, I stiffened my spine and my resolve. "You wanted to see me, Mr. Evermore?"

"Yes. Don't bother taking a seat. This will be fast." He smoothed his moustache, and I repressed the urge to shudder. "Miss Eaton, you've only been here three weeks, and already a complaint has been lodged against you. This report will remain in your file. Permanently. Now, return to your post and remember, this is your only warning. If this happens again, you will be terminated."

"Mr. Evermore, may I ask the nature of the complaint?"

"No, you may not." He stood and pointed at the door. "Go!"

In a state of shock, I turned on my heel. Back in daytime dresses, I watched the clock tick off the long minutes remaining in my shift, itching to leave the sales floor and get home where I'd freshen up, put on an evening dress, and hit the Latin Quarter. Since my return to Manhattan, I frequented the same nightclubs I had in the past, except El Morocco, of course. I loved to dance and always found willing partners. Committed to curbing my drinking, I returned to my practice from more innocent days, when I made a daiquiri or pink lady last all night.

That evening, I was swept off my feet by one Michael Goldfein, a banker at Lehman Brothers. When he told me where he worked and I didn't faint at his feet, he doubled his efforts to impress me. He was quite forward and invited me up to his apartment, but I refused, remembering my debasement at the hands of Theodore Cullen and my embarrassing lack of discretion and chastity in Dallas. By God, I was turning over a new leaf.

Michael wined and dined me and begged me, but I held my knees together with a force of will I hadn't known I possessed. He told me he couldn't live without me and proposed after only three weeks of increasingly urgent wooing. We hadn't even had sexual relations. While it was odd that Michael never asked about my past, my family, or anything except my modeling career, I pushed those thoughts aside.

"You're gorgeous, baby. I think you could walk into any agency in town and be strutting down the runway the very next day."

"Michael, that's history. Anyway, I'm over the hill by today's standards."

"Trust me. I know you could do it."

"But I don't want to." I'd had enough of living off my looks. One day, I'd prove I was more than a pretty face. But there might be advantages to marrying a businessman; maybe Michael would help me set up a company, even though I hadn't decided what kind of enterprise I might start.

To say the least, his proposal was unconventional. "Shut up and kiss me. We'll talk after our honeymoon."

I laughed. "Honeymoon? What are you talking about? We're not married."

"Let's go to city hall and fix that."

Flattered, I accepted, thinking why not? A man who adored me and a very cushy life were just what I needed. I hadn't met his parents. Of course, he'd never meet mine. Just thinking of Michael in his fine Italian leather shoes stepping on a cow pie at my family's ranch made me cringe. "When am I going to meet your family, Michael?"

"You're not. Mother will flip her wig if I bring a shiksa home."

"A what?"

"A non-Jew. A Gentile."

"If you don't dare bring me home, how will she react when we're married?"

"You let me worry about that. Just pack for a honeymoon trip on a yacht in the Bahamas."

Caught up in the romance of the moment and a little drunk on Champagne, I kissed him with fervor. When he recovered his breath, Michael said, "You're one spicy tomato." I'd hoped for an "I love you."

That night, when Imogene got in, I told her the news. "I don't know what to think about not meeting his family. This is happening so quickly. He's very persuasive. And intense. I hadn't ever heard the word 'shiksa' before, but I could tell from the sound of it that it wasn't a compliment."

"Hmm. Not sure that bodes well. I haven't much knowledge of Jewish culture." Imogene waved her cigarette holder, which held a marijuana cigarette. "Enjoy him as long as it lasts. Go sailing. See what happens. You're only twenty-two and have lots of time if it doesn't work out."

The next afternoon, Michael and I visited City Hall, obtained a license and a judicial waiver, so we could get married without a twenty-four-hour delay.

As we cooled our heels in the lobby waiting to be called, I thought about Imogene's advice. It seemed so jaded. At thirty-six, my aunt was as iconoclastic as ever. When I moved back, she had a long talk with me about her philosophy of life and how she chose to live hers. The succession of lovers, both male and female, and of other races would never be tolerated where I grew up. Mama would faint dead away if she had an inkling of Imogene's romances. After the living I'd crammed into the last six years, I didn't think anything Imogene could do would surprise me, or even get me to raise my eyebrows. She was a force to be reckoned with, as Mama had warned me before my first trip to Manhattan.

"Goldfein and Eaton," a clerk announced. We stood and Michael grabbed my hand and led me into the chambers of the Justice of the Peace. As the officiant intoned the standard spiel, I thought back to saying those same vows to Ben and held back a sob.

Michael squeezed my hands, bringing me back to the present. "Well, do ya or don't ya?"

"I do."

We celebrated with dinner at Sardi's, then went back to his place and made love. It was as quick as our courtship. Michael blamed the booze. The next morning, we boarded a flight to Miami where we had to overnight.

The flight to Nassau left early in the morning. He leaned past me to look out the tiny window in the plane, then at me and said, "The sea is the same color as your eyes."

"Ooh, you're a romantic."

He kissed me. "Look at my inspiration."

"I've never been on a sailboat before."

"Don't worry about it, baby. The captain and crew take care of everything. They drive the boat and make the food and all that. We get to relax and see the sights."

Upon arrival, we were whisked to the marina where a sleek sailing yacht awaited us. The fifty-foot boat, with "Money Honey" in large script across the back end, belonged to his father and was staffed with a captain and crew, including a chef. What reason had Michael given his parents for borrowing the yacht? I doubted he told them he was taking his new and unapproved bride on the trip.

During the lazy sunny Caribbean days, Michael relaxed and became playful, rather than acting the intense businessman. To my great relief, the sex was much improved.

I fell in love with the crystal-clear Caribbean waters and pristine beaches. The fresh sea air left a sheen of salt on my skin. As we sailed through the passages, the sight of hundreds of uninhabited islands made me imagine life à la Swiss Family Robinson. We stopped at several of those tiny islands with white sand beaches and one magical place with pink sand. Michael taught me to snorkel in the warm, shallow waters.

He filled my head with names of the reef inhabitants: triggerfish, creole wrasse, tile fish, fairy basslet, parrot fish, seahorse, trumpetfish, stingray, porcupine fish, butterfly fish. The array of colors amazed me. We feasted on lobster, conch, grouper, and dorado, some of which Michael caught. His athleticism impressed me. At night, after the crew retired to their quarters. Michael and I lay in the rear cockpit, lounging on the cushions, marveling at the stars and constellations, sipping wine.

Was this what heaven was like? The sunny days, the soft sea breeze, scenery out of a movie, and an attentive man. I didn't want this sojourn to end. But banking beckoned to Michael and our lovely time ended after ten days of bliss.

On the flight home, Michael asked, "Why don't you quit your job, baby?"

He didn't have to ask twice.

The day after our return, I woke up at Michael's and stretched. When I cuddled into his side, he pushed me away. Startled, I asked, "What's wrong?"

Sitting up, he all but growled. "Nothing. Got a lot on my mind. Don't get all emotional." He sighed. "I guess you'll have to move your things in. Do you have a lease?"

"No, I live with my aunt." We really didn't know the first thing about each other. His abrupt manner and coldness hurt worse than if he had slapped me.

"Oh. Well, go to work and drop the news on that jerk you work for. Then go to your aunt's place and pack your things. I've got to make some calls."

Without so much as a kiss or a smile, he rose and opened the bathroom door.

"Not going to the office today?"

He turned back and raised an eyebrow, "No. And cool it with the third degree."

My mouth fell open.

What he said next nearly floored me. "Oh, I'll be busy until four or so and can't be interrupted, so don't come back until later."

Who was this stranger? What did he do with the romantic and passionate man on our honeymoon? Quite the let-down after our idyllic interlude in the Bahamas. A chill came over me.

I carried my powder blue suit and cosmetic bag into the hall bath and got ready for work, telling myself to give Michael a break. He didn't mean to cut me off like that. Since he was absent for ten days, he must have a lot of work to catch up on. Once ready, I hopped a cab to Bergdorf Goodman, an hour late for work, but that no longer mattered. Mr. Thomas Evermore would nevermore have any impact on my future.

I strode to his door and flung it open, not waiting for an invitation. He looked up from a pile of papers and frowned. Before he could speak, I announced, "I quit. As of right now. Put that in my permanent file, you pompous jackass."

Looking back over my shoulder, I relished the sight of his open mouth and bulging eyes. I smirked and almost danced out of the store. Elated, I decided to walk home to Imogene's. The sun was warm, the sky a perfect blue as I strode along, head held high. I broke into a chuckle as I recalled the look on Mr. Thomas Evermore's face and drew a few concerned looks from passersby. I looked forward to telling Michael about the incident. Then, remembering his abruptness that morning, I winced and hoped his mood had improved. All that remained was to pack a suitcase with my immediate needs, fill my trunks with the bulk of my wardrobe, and arrange for delivery of the rest of my belongings to Michael's apartment at the Century, just across the park from Imogene.

Two hours later, with the packing progressing at a snail's pace, Imogene sashayed into my room to help me. Together we made short work of filling the three trunks.

"You know, darling, I'm going to miss you." Imogene folded the last of my blouses and sat on the bed.

I looked up from my suitcase and asked, "Really? We don't spend much time together."

"Really. Even though we seem to pass like ships in the night, it's kind of nice to know you're here."

We hugged, and I closed my suitcase. "When did the delivery service say they were coming?"

"Not until tomorrow, I'm afraid."

"Well, I can get by for a few days with what I'm taking over."

"Are you staying for dinner?"

"No, thank you. But I do want to say goodbye to Vandine."

Imogene rolled her eyes. "It's not goodbye. Don't be dramatic."

When I arrived at Michael's place, the doorman tipped his hat but averted his eyes. Odd. I unlocked the door to our apartment and heard a scuttling noise from the bedroom. "Michael?"

Heated whispers reached my ears. Dropping my suitcase, I rushed to the bedroom door and threw it open.

Michael was in bed with a woman, heavily made-up and with unnatural-looking jet-black hair. Quite a bit older than me, she was dressed in black leather from head to foot, which did nothing to hide her chunky figure. She brandished a whip, striking Michael's bare buttocks! The three of us stared at each other, speechless.

My feet were glued to the floor. I couldn't unsee what I'd just seen. Bile rose in my throat. What was this—perversion? How could he do this to me? All I could think was, "Two weeks, two lousy weeks."

Michael broke the silence. "I can explain."

The woman slapped him. "Shut up."

A sneer of her face, she advanced toward me, smacking her whip into her palm. I retreated and stammered, "I'll s-send f-for my things." Backing away from the abomination, I closed the door behind me and left the apartment. Once in the hall, I remembered my suitcase. I couldn't leave it because it held my best perfume and several months' supply of makeup. Very quietly, I turned the key in the lock and tiptoed into the apartment to claim my bag.

I didn't cry. Too shocked. Like a robot, I took the elevator to the lobby and plastered a smile on my face for the doorman, who hailed a cab. He must have known that another woman had gone up to Michael's, and of course, he noted the suitcase I carried. The implication was clear, yet his stoic face gave no sign he'd seen a thing.

At Imogene's, I threw a five at the cabbie, grabbed my bag, and stumbled to the front door. Entering the foyer, I called for her, and she came rushing out of the parlor. "Darling, did you forget something?"

After taking one look at me, she rushed me to the couch and poured me a stiff drink of bourbon. Although I didn't care for bourbon, I took the drink in one huge swallow.

"Tell me."

I did, and as she listened, Imogene, quite the libertine, raised her eyebrows.

"What a cad! But it's better you found out now rather than later. Don't worry about your things. I'll send a big strapping fellow over to retrieve them."

At last, the tears came, running down my cheeks. Imogene tutted. She wasn't one for tears—her own or anyone else's. "There now. No need to cry. He's not worth it. Why don't you head upstairs and draw a nice hot bath? I'll bring your bag up and get you a lovely bath sachet."

I stood, still crying, shaking with my...what? Not grief. Embarrassment or humiliation sounded about right. "Okay. Thank you."

Imogene guided me to the stairs. "I'm staying in tonight, so if you want to talk, I'll be here. Vandine is making her fabulous beef tenderloin for dinner. Come down when you're ready."

"I'm not hungry." I trudged up to my room and started the tub.

Imogene brought in my suitcase and popped a lavender-scented sachet into the bathwater. "Can I get you anything?"

"No, thanks."

"All right. See you later."

Once she left, I stripped and found some tailored cotton pajamas which I took to the bathroom. The sexy negligees I'd packed would stay in the suitcase. No need for them.

As I soaked, cleansing my body, and trying to cleanse my mind of the debauchery I saw, Imogene's advice echoed in my mind: *Enjoy him as long as it lasts. Go sailing. See what happens. You're only twenty-two and have lots of time if it doesn't work out.*

Choking with bitter laughter, I shouted, "See what happens? Oh, I saw all right. As long as it lasts? Two weeks!"

Maybe I was still young, but I felt like a hundred. What was wrong with me? Why did Michael think he could take part in those vile activities after our marriage? Somehow, I didn't think this was the first time he and that harpy had been together. How gullible I was, thinking he cared for me when he wouldn't even take me home to meet his family. Rehashing my disastrous past was pointless, but I did anyway. There I was, a widow and soon-to-be divorcee. My choice of men was seriously flawed. Alain abandoned me. Theodore humiliated me. Ben left me, too. As I recalled my licentiousness in Dallas after the men came home, my face burned. How many men had I slept with? Their faces were a blur, a lineup of horny soldiers and sailors out for a cheap thrill, and I had supplied one, willingly and drunkenly.

While I had cut back on my drinking when I first returned to Manhattan and stayed chaste, it was only a matter of time before my base instincts reemerged and my alcohol consumption rapidly increased. Would I have agreed to marry Michael if I hadn't been drunk on Champagne? I'd asked myself a version of that question more than once.

The dissolution of my sham marriage was effortless. Michael wrangled a quickie divorce in Reno. It seemed all one had to do was establish residence for six weeks in that Nevada city and a divorce would follow. Certain he didn't actually move to Nevada, I avoided Central Park West like the plague. My life became small. Lounging around Imogene's, keeping to the east side of the park, a few phone calls with Milly, making excuses about why I couldn't come out to Scarsdale. I'd neglected Harold during the whirlwind Michael episode. The last time I'd spoken with him was before the wedding. He had called to ask why I'd missed our Friday lunch date.

When I said I'd forgotten, he hung up in a snit. I should apologize but didn't have the energy.

Seven weeks after the debacle, weeks mired in the mud of self-pity, I received a copy of the divorce decree, a nice fat check for my trouble, and a note demanding my "discretion." Once the check cleared, thoughts of starting my own business resurfaced. So far, it was only a dream. I hadn't a clue about how to go about it and reluctantly decided I'd have to get another job for the time being. Restless and frustrated, I wandered into the bathroom, selected nail polish in a pretty shade of rose, and sat at my makeup table. I'd neglected my nails and needed to do something about it.

Imogene flounced into my room—without knocking—and waved a packet of letters in the air. "I have just the thing to take your mind off your troubles. Evelyn writes to me every so often. She relays news about the child and sends a Christmas photograph each year. Thought you might want to take a look at these!"

I gaped at her in horror. "You thought wrong. I do not want to see anything from Evelyn."

Imogene raised her eyebrows. "I didn't realize—"

"Apparently not. That's history. A mistake I'd rather forget, and I have forgotten—thanks to those drugs I was given. It's a blur, a bad dream. So, no, no, no!" I stood and ran into the bathroom, slamming the door and locking it. My hands were shaking, and I'd smeared my manicure.

Imogene knocked on the door.

"Go away!"

"Look, kiddo. I never imagined you'd react like this. It's been five years. Aren't you curious?"

I shrieked. "No! Leave me alone."

"All right. I'm going."

My breathing didn't return to normal for several minutes. I ran the cold water, soaked a washcloth, and patted my face and neck. I couldn't even remember giving birth or seeing the baby. How could I miss what I never had? I didn't want to know if she favored me or Alain or the color of her eyes. I simply didn't want to know.

That evening, I descended the stairs for dinner, composed and with my manicure complete. As I stepped into the foyer, I heard Imogene in the kitchen, talking to Vandine about our "squabble."

"I never thought she cared so much."

Vandine's velvet voice questioned, "Does she care, or does she just wanna forget?"

I flew into the kitchen. "Just stop! Imogene, you have no right. Thank you for your hospitality, but I'll be finding another place to live. I can't stay here any longer."

Before Imogene could respond, I ran back upstairs, snatching up the *New York Times* from the console table in the front hall. I wouldn't consider moving to the Village, as I'd previously done. No, I'd find a little place on the Upper West Side, put the whole damn park between me and Imogene. I gasped. What was I thinking? That was Michael's turf.

Then I came to my senses. I needed to get far away. Both times I lived in Manhattan, disaster tagged after me like a malevolent ghost. I'd go back to Dallas. But not to Neiman Marcus, not to the clothing business. I had a little cushion from my divorce and could take my time in finding the right position.

After only five months in Manhattan, I moved back to Dallas, believing I was escaping the chaos of my life.

It would be years before I realized I was running from myself.

Chapter Eight

DALLAS REDUX-1946-1948

I wasted no time booking my train tickets from New York to Dallas. Wanting to hide from the world, I booked a Pullman. Due to my hasty departure, my three trunks were making the trip with me. The New York Central would get me to Chicago in about seventeen hours, then I'd have to transfer to the Atchison, Topeka, and Santa Fe line for another twenty hours. As I boarded, I hummed the song from the movie *Harvey Girls*, picturing Judy Garland singing the catchy tune, although I much preferred the peppier rendition by the Andrews Sisters.

Because of the explosion and fire at the Baker Hotel a few months ago, I had reserved a deluxe room at the Adolphus. It was uncomfortably close to Neiman Marcus, but I wasn't about to darken their door.

The long journey would give me plenty of time to think. Why was I returning to Dallas? I'd burned my bridges with my former employer and my friend Alice. Simple answer—I had nowhere else to go. Having some degree of familiarity with the city would be helpful, I told myself. For the briefest moment, swallowing my pride and going to the ranch had crossed my mind. But I couldn't face my family, especially since I hadn't attended Mason's memorial service last year. They didn't know about my second marriage and divorce, and I'd keep it that way. Mama wrote what I considered duty letters—short and to the point—filling me in on family news. After Travis returned from the war, he married my old friend Clare.

That girl had set her sights on Travis from the get-go. They built a cottage on the western border of the ranch and were expecting their first child. Still disappointed he'd missed the war, Dylan set out on his own, moving to the mountains of Idaho. Jace, the baby, was sixteen and dedicated to the ranch.

One bridge I didn't want to burn was my friendship with Harold. I recalled his last words to me. "Well, if you decide you have time for an old friend, give me a jingle." I'd hurt him and hadn't taken the time to mend fences. When I got settled, I'd write to him.

Even more than a change in scene, I needed a change of career. With my financial windfall from my brief and horrifying interlude with Michael Goldfein, I was flush with cash, but I couldn't remain idle. With the boom after the war, Dallas was growing. New businesses sprouted up every week, and the opportunities seemed boundless. Faced with the fact I'd be working for someone else—for a while at least—I decided to explore all the possibilities and not jump at the first offer.

During the long, tedious trip, my history played to an audience of one, like a failed B movie. Alcohol had a starring role in each of my personal disasters. Determined to learn from my missteps with men and alcohol, I promised myself I'd exercise restraint in both areas. How hard could it be to have a social life without booze and sex?

For three years, I'd vacillated between holding Ben's memory close and shoving it away. Our marriage was the closest I'd come to living a normal life, and it only had lasted a few fleeting months. Would we have stayed together if he had returned from the war? I believed so. Saddened that his face had faded from my memory, I remained grateful for his gift and pledged I would put it to good use. Someday.

Just thinking about Michael Goldfein was painful. How foolish to be seduced by his superficial charm and the promise of a comfortable life. Lesson learned.

By the time the train rolled into Dallas, almost two days after I had walked out of Imogene's home without a word to her and only a tearful hug with Vandine, I was exhausted. After I checked in the Adolphus and had my trunks brought to my room, I marveled at my sumptuous quarters, with elegant French Provincial furniture and the finest linens. Expensive at twelve dollars and fifty cents a night, I'd better find an apartment as soon as I got a job. I telephoned room service and ordered a club sandwich and a newspaper. I fell asleep reading the want ads.

The next morning, I wrote to Harold. In my letter, I apologized and explained the Michael debacle, purging the story of the unsavory details. He must have written back at once because a warm return message arrived a few days later. "Honey, we all make mistakes. The thing is to learn from them. Keep in touch." Relieved we were good again, a burden lifted from my heart.

During my job search, I exercised great restraint with liquor. I had one slip when I hadn't found a job after two weeks, then got right back on the wagon. It wouldn't do to miss an interview because of a hangover. In the eight weeks it took me to find a job with a future, I about wore out my shoes traipsing all over town and racked up quite the bill at the hotel. But when I landed a dream job, it was worth the shoe leather and money.

I had dressed with care for my interview. A new, collarless suit in a subtle plaid, smart navy pumps, and matching bag. Color was back in shoes and clothes, and I indulged in a shopping spree for the pretty things unavailable during the war.

After exiting the elevator on the fifth floor of the office building that housed the Dallas Advertising League, the receptionist ushered me through a large open space with cubicles around three sides featuring tall partitions that did nothing to guarantee privacy. Rows of desks occupied by furiously typing staff filled the center of the room. Along one side of the huge room were the enclosed private offices of the bigwigs. The receptionist directed me to one of those offices with frosted glass in the upper half of the door. Fancy gold script announced: Brett Owens—Vice President.

She opened the door and waved me in. The poor woman could use a fashion makeover, and if I got the job, I'd share a few tips with her.

I stepped into a bland space, rather utilitarian, but the man who rose to greet me was anything but bland. He was a bit older, maybe late twenties, tall, dark-haired, tall, and wore a black patch over his left eye. The war, I was certain.

"Miss Eaton, please have a seat. I'm Brett Owens. Can I get you a cup of coffee or some water?"

"No, thank you." I sat in a chestnut leather armchair that had seen plenty of use, given the patina on the seat. I gave him my best smile, which was not returned. This man was all business.

"I reviewed your application. Your prior experience was in the fashion world. What do you think qualifies you for a job here?"

Blunt. As I thought about his question, my smile faded. Did he consider me unqualified? "Well, Mr. Owens, my work has always entailed customer service, marketing, and merchandising. I've had several roles in the clothing industry, and my success at previous jobs speaks to my ability. Have you spoken to my references?" Of course, I had omitted Bergdorf Goodman from my application.

He glanced up from his desk where he was perusing papers. What was he looking at? Did he hear a word I said? "You wouldn't be here if I hadn't."

"Oh." That slipped out.

"When can you start?" At last, he smiled.

"Oh!" I smiled back. "I'm available now."

"Come prepared to work, have you? Well, let's get to it."

We did. Brett, as he insisted everyone call him, handed me off to my boss, Harlan Jones. Jones had a military bearing, and I figured he was another veteran. I filled out the usual paperwork and was given material to read about our mission, which was to suppress fraudulent advertising schemes, attract business to Dallas, and improve the results of legitimate advertising. During my modeling years, I'd had some exposure to the ad game and applauded the goals of the DAL.

Once I'd completed the paperwork, Jones led me to a desk where a woman was typing at an astounding clip. "Miss Lauren Eaton, you'll be working with Miss Jeanine Crandall. For now, I'll have her show you the ropes. She works on member events and will get you started."

A petite blonde, Jeanine was about my age and far from a fashion plate in her dun brown shirtwaist dress. Then I caught myself. If I wanted to make friends, I had better curb my criticism of the fashion sense of Dallas' female population. When she popped up from her chair and extended her hand, I smiled.

"Welcome aboard, Lauren!"

"Thank you. I'm happy to be here."

With unflagging energy and enthusiasm, Jeanine shepherded me around the office, introduced me to too many people to count, showed me the break room, and then explained our role in member events. By the end of the day, I'd made a friend and looked forward to planning my first gathering with her.

Glad to end my expensive stay at the Adolphus, I rented a furnished apartment in an elevator building within walking distance of the office. While the space was small, it had good light and was freshly painted in a soft yellow. I would freshen it up with new curtains.

Once I learned the ropes at work, I would explore ideas for striking out on my own. I threw myself into the job, wanting to learn everything about my role and the League. After a few short weeks, Jeanine complimented my efforts, and the stiff and proper Jones added a few words of encouragement too. I rarely caught a glimpse of Brett Owens and wondered why I hoped to. Then I counseled myself to remember my past and avoid entanglements with men.

Three months later, when I received a letter from Imogene, I suspected Vandine encouraged my aunt to write to me. How did she get my address? As I read her note, I was floored by her confession that the Babcock family attorneys tracked me down. She apologized for intruding into my "personal business about the child" and asked for forgiveness. Remembering my aunt's kindness and support, I wrote back, telling her that if she ever visited Dallas to let me know. Reconnecting with Imogene lifted a weight from me I hadn't realized I carried. The estrangement from my immediate family continued, but I did send a brief message with my new address.

Late one evening, I found myself alone in the elevator with Brett. We were the last two people to leave the office. As people did, we studied the numbers above the elevator door as if fascinated. Brett cleared his throat. "Care to join me for a cocktail, Lauren?"

The elevator stopped in the lobby, and I staggered, not only from the cessation of motion but from the question. I gaped at him.

He stood there in his overcoat, briefcase and hat in hand, with an eyebrow raised.

I stared at his eye patch and wondered if he could tell where I was looking. How embarrassing. The gossip in the office was that Brett's wife had run off with another man while he was fighting in the Ardennes Forest in the Battle of the Bulge. He lost an eye at Bastogne and was lucky to escape with his life. He wasn't known to date. A giant of a man, Brett stood at a trim six-foot-four and had broad shoulders. Glossy black wavy hair a little too long. I caught a whiff of Brylcreem. Had to admit, he was quite attractive. It was the eye patch that grabbed attention, making it hard to assess the entire package, but that night, I assessed and liked what I saw.

"Okay." I sounded about fourteen years old, not twenty-three. I thought of myself as quite sophisticated, and there I was acting like a dope. Good Grief!

Brett nodded. "There's a little place I like. We can walk."

"Sure."

We entered the dim room. From what I could see, it was a decent place, nicely decorated. I relaxed a little. Given my indiscretions with alcohol, I had to be careful. Brett took a pint of bourbon and a pint of vodka from his briefcase. "What's your poison?"

Those words would resurface time and again. "I don't care for bourbon."

"Vodka it is. What kind of mixer do you like?"

"Tonic water, please."

He ordered ginger ale and tonic from the waiter. When the setups came, I asked for a light touch of the liquor. Brett grinned. "Heavy hitter?"

My face burned, and I was thankful for the dim lighting.

"Never developed a taste for liquor," I lied. It wouldn't be the last lie I told him.

We chatted about everything but work. I listened to his life story. A city boy, Brett was born and raised in Dallas. He asked me a lot of questions about my childhood on the ranch.

"You get home much?" he asked.

I sipped the vodka and tonic. While gin was my drink of choice, the vodka went down smoothly. After I set the glass on the table, I answered. "No."

"Why not? Mineral Wells is less than a hundred miles from Dallas."

"First off, I don't own a car."

"And second?"

"I moved to New York when I was sixteen, seven years ago. During the war, I was working and couldn't travel." I bit my lip and went silent, hoping I hadn't sounded defensive.

I didn't want him to know I was estranged from my family, but Brett was perceptive. He seemed to understand the topic was difficult for me and changed the subject.

"How'd you like New York? Sixteen is pretty darned young to move away from home."

"I was given a chance to be a fashion model and couldn't pass it up. I lived with my mother's half-sister, Imogene. Even though they were raised together, they're nothing alike. My aunt is a bit bohemian and rather the woman about town. Mama left New York at seventeen for life on the cattle ranch, and the closest Imogene comes to a cow is a rare Porterhouse."

Brett chuckled. "Tell me about this aunt of yours."

Giving a sanitized version of Imogene's wild years as a flapper, I emphasized her love of music and dance. Of course, I omitted what type of music she favored, her scandalous love affairs, and her unwanted intrusion into my ancient mistake, a mistake never shared with the men in my life.

"Sounds like she's quite a character." Judging by his facial expression, even my edited description of Imogene's life caused Brett consternation.

"She is. She stood with me during a challenging time...when I was...having health issues." Opening my eyes wide, as if that would help the lies flow, I continued. "I'm fully recovered."

Brett frowned and took a sip of his drink. "Glad to hear it." He tugged at his shirt collar. He seemed as discomfited as I. Could he tell I was hiding something?

When he offered me another drink, I declined. "It's getting late."

"All right, I'll walk you to your place."

At the entrance to my apartment building, I bid Brett a formal goodnight. He didn't try to kiss me. Before that evening, I never even considered I might want him to. As I climbed into bed, I cautioned myself not to rush into a romantic relationship. Then I had to laugh. Was Brett interested in more than a friendship?

After the way our first evening together ended, I was surprised when he asked me to join him again. Soon, we were seeing each other for a drink every week. He asked me about my time in New York, and I offered him an edited account of my experience as a Powers Girl. I glossed over the reality of being handled like a piece of meat by photographers and designers, emphasizing the fun times with the girls, the unusual assignments. My stories kept him interested. He told me a few things about his time in the army, although without much detail. His face grew serious, and his remaining eye got a faraway look as he gave me a two-minute summary of the battle in the Ardennes. It was clear he had difficulty talking about the war.

After a few weeks, our conversation got more personal. He told me about his marriage, and how devastated he was to receive his "Dear John" letter. They had been married for two years before he enlisted. As he spoke, I watched his face and felt his sadness. My heart melted. Brett didn't seem to have any resentment toward Joan, just a broken heart.

How much should I reveal? I shared about losing Ben at the Battle of Salerno. "We were only married for a few months before he enlisted." When I confessed how I was angry with his decision to enlist despite his legitimate job deferment, I couldn't hide my tears. "His work was vital, but I wasn't." Brett leaned forward, took my hand, and cradled it. His touch sent chills through me.

That night, he walked me home as usual. As we waited for the elevator, he asked me to dinner. Since he hadn't even made a move to kiss me, the invitation was unexpected. What were his intentions? I had vowed to refrain from romance, so the pace of our relationship suited me for the time being. But when he was near, my body told a different tale. I'd become such a proficient liar, I even practiced on myself.

Saturday evening, I selected a black dress with a swirling skirt and plunging back. The demure neckline belied the back of the dress, which always drew male attention. As I spritzed Shalimar on my wrists, I chewed on the fact I hadn't been intimate with a man since Michael. Over a year without sex. I shuddered as the scene of that horrible morning when I found him with that woman replayed in my head. That tawdry betrayal crossed my mind more often than I'd like to admit. Off-putting. But a year. A whole year.

I stared in the mirror. The sexy dress, the Shalimar, the desire for a man—no, Brett—stared right back. On the strength of a dinner invitation, I was already considering sleeping with him. Time to face it. I might be falling for him. And why not? He was everything I—

The doorbell rang, ending my reflection, and I buzzed Brett up and waited for his knock on the door.

He took a dramatic step back and whistled when he saw me. In the elevator, he leaned in and kissed my cheek. "You look gorgeous in that dress."

Did I imagine an unspoken "and out of it?" I shivered. Brett took my wrap and placed it around my shoulders. He was parked right in front of the building. His dark green Buick Super gleamed in the setting sun.

"What a beautiful car, Brett."

"Like it? I sure do." He opened the door for me and rushed around the front of the car to get in the driver's seat. Switching on the ignition, he grinned. "Listen to that engine purr."

Large neon letters on a marquee announced we had arrived at one of Dallas' best restaurants: Town and Country. DeSotos, Cadillacs, and Packards lined up at the valet. Liveried staff handed Brett a claim check for the car and rushed to open the double doors of the restaurant. For a moment, I was reminded of the glamour of Manhattan. Brett tipped the doorman and placed his hand on my back to usher me inside. He seemed different that night, more attentive.

The maître de rushed forward. "Mr. Owens, I have your table ready."

"Thanks, Dominic. This lovely lady is Miss Lauren Eaton. I want to impress her, so send us your best waiter."

A hostess dressed in a stylish black sheath escorted us to our table in the "town" half of the vast dining room. What a cute idea: visually dividing the space into "town" and "country." Although the designer's idea of the country seemed odd—palm trees and beach cabana doors. The town side was elegant, with wallpaper covered in orchids. Even the ceilings were different in each area.

It seemed as if everyone smoked; a haze hung in the air. White linen cloths covered the tables, and the napkins were stenciled with the carriage logo and restaurant name. I hoped the odor of stale cigarettes wouldn't detract from the meal.

A waiter arrived to take our predinner drink order. While hard liquor wasn't available at restaurants in Texas, beer and wine were. I ordered a Champagne cocktail and, as I did at every encounter with Brett, would make sure it lasted all evening. He ordered a bottle of ginger ale to go with the bourbon in his flask.

A white-jacketed chef wheeled the beef cart past our table. Brett explained guests could select their own cut of prime rib, and I wondered if the beef had come from the Eaton ranch. A tiny twinge of guilt made me squirm in my chair, and I focused on the extensive menu to distract myself. The selections rivaled some of the Manhattan restaurants I used to frequent. Brett ordered for us, choosing a double sirloin steak for two with tomato bisque to start and Caesar salad.

The nature of our relationship changed over dinner. Charming and complimentary, Brett endeared himself to me. Maybe I could fix his broken heart. Was I falling in love? If so, it was a gentle, slow tumble, with not a trace of my previous headlong rush into romance.

Was Brett falling for me? If he ever got around to kissing me, I'd know.

The waiter brought our soup. I tried to focus on the company and the meal, but my mind stubbornly took me down another road. If I began a relationship with Brett, I could never tell him about my past. A man of his integrity wouldn't accept my behavior. I'd already presented him with an edited history, full of omissions. If those things ever came to light, then—

My nerveless fingers dropped the spoon and red soup splattered all over the white tablecloth. Embarrassed, I apologized and left the table. In the ladies' room, I locked myself in a cubicle, ignoring the greeting of the attendant. Several minutes later, I emerged and checked my appearance in the mirror. No one would guess my transgressions looking at me.

Brett was waiting for me in the hallway outside the restroom. His concern was touching. I assured him I was okay and eager to finish dinner. Another lie.

When we arrived back at my building, Brett walked me to the elevator. Our eyes locked, then our lips touched. Breathless and electrified, I stepped back. Restraint required.

On Monday, I invited Jeanine to lunch. We had eaten together several times, but our conversations had never advanced to the level of intimacy I had with Milly or Alice. I was glad Jeanine steered the conversation to romance, so I didn't have to. She was dating a fella at the Cotton Exchange, and things were getting serious. "I think he might be getting ready to propose."

Obligatory squeal. "How exciting."

"What about you and Brett?" She tilted her head and smiled. "He's never given the time of day to any other girl in the office, but I guess that's history."

I bit my lip. "I think I'm beginning to fall for him."

"Beginning?" Jeanine giggled.

I felt heat rise to the roots of my mahogany hair. "So, does everyone know?"

"You betcha they do. Those long, lingering, smoldering glances—from both of you—have not gone unnoticed."

"Yikes! I had no idea."

"Don't worry about it. The whole team adores Brett. With the tragedy in his life, he deserves happiness."

We finished our tuna sandwiches and strolled back to the office. I was awfully glad I had confided in Jeanine and pleased to learn my budding romance was accepted by my co-workers. And I reminded myself to keep the relationship in the bud phase for a good, long while. Luckily, Brett seemed in no hurry to rush things.

Our bud blossomed all winter and spring. We weren't intimate yet. I was holding back, maybe to appear virginal. What a stretch. Brett was ardent but respectful of the limits I put on our love.

We went dancing. Brett was skilled, and we meshed perfectly on the dance floor. He took me to the places locals frequented. His favorite was

Louann's, way out of town on Lovers Lane. The place was immense, with indoor and outdoor spaces, and had featured some of the great bands, like Harry James and Glenn Miller. One evening while dancing to "Day by Day," he whispered in my ear, "I love you." Tears stung my eyes. It had been a long time since I heard those words. Without reservation, I decided to give love another chance and open my heart to Brett.

He invited me to dinner at his parents' home in June. Wanting to impress Brett and his family, I baked a pecan pie from scratch, dredging up the old skills I'd used as a girl. When he saw my effort, Brett's face glowed with tenderness. "You made me a pie? Oh, honey, thank you." Then he blushed, perhaps a little embarrassed at his effusiveness, and joked. "Is it any good?"

I chuckled. "Back at the ranch, I was fairly good at baking. It's been a while, but I think it will be edible."

We played the AM radio on the way to the house in Bluffview. An old standard, "I'll Be Seeing You," sung by Bing Crosby. We had our first argument because Brett liked Bing's version, while I preferred Frank Sinatra singing with Tommy Dorsey's band. Well, you couldn't really call it an argument.

As we neared our destination, he noticed me looking at the large homes on generous lots. Since Brett was so down to earth, I was a bit surprised. "Quite the ritzy neighborhood."

"My dad made a pile of dough after the stock market crash. Then he bought this place. I grew up on the south side, kinda hardscrabble at times. So, coming here is like visiting royalty, I always say. Drives my mom crazy. She still misses raising her chickens."

That information was welcome. While I had wealthy relatives and had some high- faluting experiences for a girl from Mineral Wells, those things faded into the past as time went on. I liked nice things and took good care of what I had, but no longer considered myself the acquisitive type.

Brett's parents were delightful. They welcomed me with literally open arms. Mrs. Owens enveloped me in a hug. "Now, Lauren, honey, you call me Edna, none of that Mrs. Owens, ya hear?"

"And please call me Jim, purt near ever'body does." It was easy to see where Brett got his size and good looks.

Throughout the meal, thoughts of my past intruded. Ever since the confrontation with Imogene—almost two years ago—I had been plagued by unwanted memories. What would his folks think of me if they knew of my indiscretions? Although Edna and Jim were lovely and welcoming, my inner turmoil prevented me from enjoying the day. On high alert, I watched my words when answering their questions. By the time my pecan pie was eaten and complimented extravagantly, I had a raging tension headache and asked Brett to take me home. When we got to my place, I told him I'd see him at work on Monday, but he insisted on coming up and nursing me. In my heart, I knew I didn't deserve this good man. He brought me an aspirin, a glass of water, and a washcloth wrapped around ice cubes.

As I lay on the couch with the cold pack on my forehead, he got down on one knee and drew a jeweler's box from his pocket. "Lauren, will you do me the honor of becoming my wife?"

I didn't hesitate. "Yes."

It would be different this time, I told myself.

Chapter Nine

DALLAS DISASTER-1949-1952

With newfound restraint, I insisted on a lengthy engagement and set the wedding date for March 1949. Brett expressed his eagerness to meet my family. I explained it was calving season, and they couldn't leave the ranch, but didn't tell him that was why I selected the date. Then I lied about Imogene, telling him she would be on an ocean liner heading to Europe. Even though I'd forgiven her, I couldn't imagine her flamboyant presence at my wedding. Who knew what she might say after a few cocktails or who she'd show up with?

I wrote to Harold with the news. His return letter was full of details about his work, the warden, and Tom, but he wouldn't be able to attend the wedding. His closing thought gave me pause. "Third time's the charm."

Well, it had better be. I had taken it slow, gotten to really know Brett. And everything I learned made me love him more. He was close to his family, generous in giving his time to The Buckner Orphans' Home, to say nothing of the tenderness with which he treated me. My only misgiving: me.

Our nuptials took place at city hall. Brett picked me up that morning. I wore a cream-colored suit with a rose blouse. When he saw me, the look on his face brought tears to my eyes. "You're so beautiful. What did I do to deserve you?"

The justice of the peace recited the traditional vows, and I teared up again. As he kissed me, the words "for better or for worse" echoed in my head.

Fifty people, most of whom I hadn't met, attended the low-key reception at his parents' home. Brett's younger sister Carlene, husband Gary, two rambunctious boys, and a little toddler girl drove in from Oklahoma City. Brett picked up the child and doted on her, but when he asked if I wanted to hold her, I shook my head. With trembling lips, I excused myself and rushed to the restroom. I stayed there until I thought my absence would be noted, then pasted on a smile and returned to the festivities. Although my smile felt fake to me, it seemed to pass muster.

We didn't take a honeymoon trip. Brett promised one later, after he opened his own advertising agency. That bit of news came out of left field. I was proud of his ambition but wondered why this was the first I'd heard of his plans.

As farcical as it was, I had refrained from consummating our relationship until our wedding night. I felt like a fraud. But, as I dressed in a white negligee, I found myself pretending I was a virginal bride, offering myself to my one and only husband. If only it were true.

Brett and I spent hours exploring each other's bodies. With tenderness, I kissed his battle wounds. He was gentle with me. When I caressed his eye patch, he grasped my hand and placed it on his heart. Then we joined together, and I was certain I had found the man I would cherish forever.

Brett's lease was up, so he moved into my apartment, which was closer to the office. During the next few months, I started to believe I could live a normal life.

I should have known it couldn't last.

Our first year of marriage flew by. We created a warm nest of a life, with Brett helping with the housework and taking me out to dinner regularly. When he gave me a bottle of Arpège for our one-year anniversary, I tossed out the Shalimar and made the Lavin perfume my scent.

At work, our paths seldom crossed. Brett was the Vice President of Community Outreach, while I worked in member events. Apparently, I was happier in my position than he was in his. When he had confided his plans for starting his own agency, I wondered if there would be a place for me in his future endeavor or if he'd want me to remain at the League. Aghast at my thoughts, I reminded myself of my own ambitions. Had I become subservient? Had I forgotten I wanted to learn the intricacies of the business so I could start my own venture? Not wanting to rock the boat, I didn't say a word to him about my reservations.

Our lives changed because of Brett's plan; we saved every spare penny, no longer dined out, only went to an occasional movie. Rather than stopping at our favorite bar after work, cocktail hour moved to our apartment. Brett could hold his liquor. In fact, a drink or two didn't seem to affect him at all, and he seldom had a third. As the weeks passed, I developed a tolerance for vodka, which I preferred to gin. After a while, I noticed we were going through more fifths of vodka than bourbon. I took to hiding the empties in the under-sink cabinet, so I could dispose of them when Brett wasn't home. I also stashed a couple of full bottles there.

Our usual evening routine consisted of cocktail hour, a hastily assembled meal, and working on the business plan.

"How 'bout a refill, Lauren?"

"Sure thing, honey." I got up and staggered slightly. Glancing at Brett to see if he noticed, I was relieved he was engrossed in writing his business proposal. In the kitchen, I filled my glass with vodka, adding only a splash of tonic.

After handing him the bourbon and ginger, I stood at his shoulder. "How's it going, darling?"

Brett put down his pen and sighed. "Slow, honey, real slow. I'm short several thousand in startup costs. Rent. Furniture. Office equipment. Looks like my venture will have to wait another year or two."

Hmmm. "My venture" rather than "our venture." I thought about offering some of my money but didn't. The settlement from Michael was gone, spent at the Adolphus and buying a wardrobe of new postwar fashions. That left only the nest egg I'd sworn not to touch. Of course,

Brett didn't know about that money. Add that nugget to the list of things I'd never told him.

I patted his shoulder. "Guess you'll have to wait until the time is right. In the meantime, I'm really excited about the Kudo's College project. Aren't you?"

Brett drained half his bourbon and then answered. "I've got mixed feelings. In my opinion, it seems a little sophomoric. I mean, giving diplomas to industry leaders is just too cute. Sure, we should recognize their contributions to putting Dallas on the map, but maybe in a different way. Why do Doak Walker, Stanley Marcus, and Margo Jones need to be named president of an imaginary college?"

Well, that burst my bubble. I felt my brows contract and relaxed my face so my irritation didn't show. "Darling, I disagree. I think it's quite original and fun, as well as in complete harmony with our goals. Really, don't be a stick-in-the-mud. Jeanine and I are thrilled to be part of the project."

He smiled and drew my hand to his chest. "If you like it, I like it. I want you to be happy."

I melted.

"There's that smile. Come on, let's hit the hay."

That was the night I got pregnant.

When I told Brett about the baby, he whooped and picked me up in his arms. "That right there is the best news ever! Have you called your folks? I can't wait to tell mine."

"Yes. Phoned them this morning. They're thrilled." What was another lie at this point?

The thought of bearing another child sent me to a dark place. Even though I was moved by Brett's delight and enthusiasm, my spirits plummeted. Ten years had passed since I gave birth and, in that time, I'd had little contact with children. In fact, I avoided them. Yet, there were moments when I wondered about a mahogany-haired girl living in Boston. Although I shut down those thoughts fast, the speculation was never far from my mind now that I was expecting.

Self-doubt congealed. What kind of mother would I make? As soon as my brothers could walk, Mama left their upbringing to Daddy. Since she never knew her own mother and was raised by nannies, what did Mama know about raising a daughter? She sure didn't do a blue-ribbon job with me. Even after a decade, I was too ashamed to face Daddy and my brothers. What did they think of me?

Knowing I would lose my figure bothered me. Did that make me shallow? Unsuited for motherhood? Since the end of the war, the country experienced a bumper crop of pregnant women. They were everywhere, as if a spree of reproduction overcame the nation. One could barely navigate the sidewalks through the gauntlet of buggies and prams. To top it off, just the thought of wearing unflattering maternity clothing for months depressed me.

Would our child favor me or Brett? What if it was a boy? I had been too young to help Mama with the daily care of my younger brothers, so I had no experience whatsoever.

Ambivalence about my marriage, motherhood, and my career became my reality.

The first three months of my pregnancy were miserable. I lost weight, couldn't keep food down. I wasn't even showing. Then, the morning sickness stopped, and a flutter in my belly forced me to face the fact there was a baby inside me. Seemingly overnight, my abdomen grew rounded. Nothing in my wardrobe fit, so I went shopping for maternity clothes at Sears, Roebuck. Cheap things that I'd give away after the child arrived.

During the fifth month, while at work writing on the blackboard at a planning meeting, I bent over in agony, clutching my abdomen and screaming. My beige skirt blossomed with blood. The last thing I remembered was collapsing on the floor. Then I woke in a sterile room hooked up to machines and tubes.

Jeanine was there, but my husband wasn't. "Where's Brett?"

"Don't you remember? He had a big presentation and business dinner across town."

Emotionally numb, I wondered if he even knew. But at that point, my focus was on the loss and the physical discomfort.

The nurse came in and took my vital signs.

"I'm in a lot of pain. When will it stop?"

Looking through my chart, the nurse said, "I can bring you a shot."

"Well, what are you waiting for? Get it!"

When she returned with the syringe and administered the medication, I floated away, and barely heard her say, "The doctor will be in soon."

In hospital time, "soon" meant five hours. Bleary-eyed, I came to and saw the doctor standing at the foot of my bed. "Mrs. Owens, I'm sorry for your loss. We had to perform surgery to stop the bleeding." He looked at his feet. "Unfortunately, we had to remove your uterus. You won't be able to have children, I'm afraid."

He was afraid? How should *I* feel? His words grabbed me by the throat. I struggled to raise my head. My abdomen felt like I'd been pummeled by Joe Louis. Lifting the sheet to inspect my body, I about fainted. The doctor had no explanation to offer about why I'd lost the baby, but I had a couple ideas. Was something inside damaged during my first pregnancy, or should I blame the drinking?

I buzzed for the nurse. When she stuck her head in the door, I demanded, "Let me out of here." Visions of vodka danced through my head. A gallon of my magic potion would be just the ticket.

"Ma'am, I'm afraid I can't do that. Your doctor will determine when you can be discharged."

I sat up and tried to get out of bed. As soon as I became vertical, my head swam, and my vision went black. I fell to the floor, and the nurse rushed to my side, calling for help. A stinging injection of some magic elixir took me away—for a while.

When I woke, my mouth tasted foul, and my abdomen still throbbed. Brett arrived bearing flowers and candy. His face told me he knew.

"Honey, I'm so sorry. So very sorry." Was that a tear dripping down his cheek?

My utter failure as a woman tormented me. Brett had been over the moon about parenthood, but after the surgery, I couldn't make his dream come true. With sudden insight, what I had to do became clear—letting him go would be best for him.

I learned quickly that if I became agitated, a nurse would bring a dose of release in her syringe. After a week or so, the ruse no longer worked, and I found myself craving vodka so desperately my hair hurt. I begged the doctor to discharge me, but that didn't happen for five long days.

Brett brought me home and tenderly helped me into pajamas and to bed. His kindness did nothing but irritate me. As he left again for the office, he promised to return as soon as his meetings were over.

When I was certain he was gone, I dressed and went out for a bottle of vodka but left the store with three. I wanted to mainline it, to get the sensation I had in those few moments after the injections. I had chased that feeling for years, and this time, I was determined to catch it.

While waiting for clearance to return to work, I continued to guzzle vodka and did my best to hide it from Brett. Six weeks after the miscarriage, I had my final visit with the doctor. "You've healed nicely. If I do say so myself, I did a great job suturing the incision. That scar will fade over time. So, you're good to go back to your job." He stood and stuck my chart under his arm. "Mrs. Owens, once again, let me express how sorry I am for the loss of your son."

"A boy?"

"Didn't Mr. Owens tell you?"

"No, no, he didn't." As I walked home, I pondered the doctor's comments. Healing nicely? A scar that would fade. Maybe on the outside. And why hadn't the doctor told *me* at the time it was a boy? Anger flared. Why hadn't Brett told me? Wallowing in my own private hell, I stopped at a liquor store in a neighborhood where they didn't know me.

With my still-expanded waistline, I had to use a rubber band to close the button on my skirts, but I was happy to be back in my regular clothes. Tears threatened to fall as I packed up my maternity wear. After I donated everything, banishing all reminders of the loss, I finished an entire fifth of vodka in one sitting.

At the office, everything annoyed me, like I was one big, exposed nerve. My heart wasn't in my work, and Jeanine's passion for our project and constant chatter grated on me. As she rambled on about Kudo's College, I rolled my eyes and snapped at her. "Just stop babbling, will ya? You're giving me a headache."

Her only answer was a hurt look.

I plodded through my duties, trying to dredge up a little of my old enthusiasm for my project. Maybe the problem was that the job cut into my drinking. By the time I arrived home, hands shaking, my craving for a drink was off the charts.

Cocktail hour resumed. Brett pinched pennies and mooned over his business plan while I snuck an extra vodka. Our sex life dwindled into oblivion. We never talked anymore unless it was about his sacred project. By tacit agreement, the topic of the miscarriage was taboo.

Then one night after arriving home from work, Brett turned to me and put his hands on my shoulders. Our eyes met, and wordlessly, we rushed to the bedroom, bourbon and vodka forgotten for once. And it was good. As I lay in his arms, my mind traveled to fantasy land. Could I make a go of our marriage? No. I couldn't allow the seduction of making love to cloud my thinking.

After our breathing returned to normal, Brett said, "Honey, I found a whole slew of empty vodka bottles under the sink. You know I like my bourbon but not to excess. When we met, you said you'd never developed a taste for liquor. Well, boy howdy, you sure do have one now."

My body tightened, and my temper flared, but I cautioned myself to relax and listen. "You're right." The words squeaked past my vocal cords.

Brett exhaled. "I didn't know how you'd take hearing this."

"I'm listening." Might just have to nominate myself for an acting award.

"Good. Today I met with a fella who declined a cocktail before lunch. When I asked him why, he told me he was an alcoholic but stopped drinking with the help of an organization called Alcoholics Anonymous."

"And?" I burrowed into him, relishing the closeness of his body. How I'd missed making love to him. And I knew I'd miss him after our divorce. I stifled a gasp. Realizing that the idea of letting Brett go had solidified into a plan, I vowed to find an attorney.

"These folks have a meeting downtown at 912½ Main. I'd like for us to go to a meeting tomorrow night."

"Okay," I whispered. If that's what it took to appease him until I executed my plan, I'd attend the stupid meeting.

The following evening, Brett and I walked over to the AA place. I recoiled at the door to the smoke-filled room. A woman rushed forward. "Welcome. I'm Ester E. Is this your first meeting?"

I couldn't speak. Brett nodded and said, "Sure is. We're here to see what y'all are about. Met a man who says he frequents this place."

Ester gestured toward the rows of folding chairs. "Please have a seat. We'll get underway in a bit." Her smile lit her face. Given her elegant appearance, I found it hard to believe she had a problem with alcohol.

Taking a seat in the back row, I kept my eyes down and clutched my hands in my lap. During the meeting, I had a hard time focusing on what was being said, but the sense of community in that room got through to me.

After the meeting, Ester approached me. "I do hope you'll come back."

Avoiding her gaze, I mumbled something and turned to leave. Outside, I took great gulps of smoke-free air. A minute later, Brett followed and grabbed my shoulder, turning me to face him.

"What was that? You were rude."

"Rude? I could hardly breathe for all the smoke."

Brett's lips twisted in disbelief. "Yeah right. Did you hear a word they said in there?"

"Take me home."

He handed me a book. "That nice lady wanted you to have this. Please read it. Give it a chance."

I accepted the book but didn't read it until years later.

Over the next two months, I oversaw the dissolution of my marriage, watching my plan unfold like a cheesy melodrama. The people in AA said they were powerless over alcohol. I was powerless to stop my mission of unraveling Brett's love for me. Never considered how losing another marriage would affect him. Never considered him at all. The fabric of lies I'd told him was industrial strength. I wallowed in my self-inflicted morass of pain and couldn't get the losses I'd suffered out of my head. Reminded myself that I knew from the beginning I didn't deserve this good man. Why didn't he see how much better off he'd be without me?

When Brett suggested we go to another AA meeting, I snarled at him. "Will you just give it a rest?" After that, he walked on eggshells around me. I ignored him. At work, I avoided him, and Jeanine noticed. "Trouble in paradise?"

I snorted. "Paradise? You know damn well my life has been hell since I lost the baby."

She patted my shoulder. "Sorry, hon. Too flip. I know you're hurting. What're ya gonna do?"

I touched a tissue to my eyes. "I don't know yet."

"You were so in love. When misfortune strikes, you need to support and comfort each other."

"Right. Support and comfort. I'm sick of the hangdog looks and sighs. I've about had it." Jeanine knew nothing of my checkered past or my plan to liberate Brett.

After consulting an attorney, I'd learned there weren't many grounds for divorce in Texas. Adultery, insanity, a felony conviction, or being separated for ten years didn't apply. A rather amorphous reason listed excesses, outrages, or cruelty that made living together impossible. Bingo. While I was the one who was outrageous and excessive, I filed against Brett, knowing I could work it so he wouldn't fight the legal action.

The day he was served, Brett came to my workstation. Outwardly, he appeared calm, but his bunched jaw and clenched hands indicated otherwise. "Lauren, please come to my office." Not wanting to cause a scene, I stood and followed him. He didn't slam the door, which I took as a good sign.

"Are you determined to end our marriage?" He spoke formally, standing to his full height.

"I think it's for the best. Don't you?"

"No."

"What?"

"No, Lauren. I don't think it's for the best. But if this is what you want, I won't fight it."

"Excellent." That comment wasn't necessary, but I said it anyway, telling myself I was being cruel to be kind in the long run.

"Brett, we'll have to make plans when we get home from work."

He turned his back, and I slunk away.

That evening, I fixed us strong drinks of our favorite poison, and we sat at the kitchen table. Not mincing words, I began. "I want you to pack your belongings and leave. Go to a hotel."

Brett's face bloomed with anger, turning an ugly shade of purple. He chugged his bourbon and ginger and banged the glass on the table. "Why don't *you* pack up instead?"

"Come on. You moved into my place, remember? Besides, I have ten times the things you do. Be practical. We still have ten months on our lease. Once the legalities are over, I'll move out, and you can have the apartment to compensate you for your trouble."

Brett put his face in his hands. "My *trouble*? God, you're cold. Where is the woman I married?"

I sipped my vodka and tonic. "You have no idea who you married."

He glanced up. "What does that mean?"

Time to stick the knife in. And twist. "You know nothing about me."

"Oh, really? After three years of marriage? Please."

I tossed my head. "If you knew my story, you'd hightail it out of here like the devil was chasing you."

He snorted. "Try me."

"All right. When I was sixteen, I got pregnant and had a baby out of wedlock. A daughter. I gave her away to family."

Brett's face went ashen. "You're lying."

"No. I'm not."

"I don't know if I can forgive you. Not for bearing a child, but for not telling me."

I smirked. "Not seeking your forgiveness." I folded my arms across my chest so he couldn't see my shaking hands.

Brett nodded slowly. "I get what you're doing. You really do want out. Okay. Your wish is granted." He got up from the table and went to our bedroom. I heard him banging around in the closet. While I waited, I refilled my drink.

Fifteen minutes passed. Brett trudged to the apartment door, lugging two suitcases. He turned and said, "All right then. Guess I'll be seeing you."

I leapt to my feet. "No. You won't. I'll make damn sure of that!"

Instead of resigning from my job, I just stopped going to the office. How could I show my face after what I'd done? Jeanine called to commiserate, but I cut off her sympathy. "Look, I just want to forget the last three years, so let me."

"What're you gonna do? How about we meet for lunch?"

"Sorry. No. I have to stay in this lousy town for a few months until our divorce is granted, but I'm cutting all ties."

"Wow. Message received. Call me if you change your mind."

"I won't." I hung up the phone and poured a drink.

For the next weeks, I cut down on my drinking. I figured tapering the daily amount I consumed would make it easier. It didn't. The cravings were still there, and I overindulged a time or two or three. I stopped counting. But after a month of abstention and sprees, I made enough progress to confine my drinking to the weekends.

To keep myself occupied while I waited for the divorce decree, I took a new job at Safeway grocery store's regional office, looking for something to inspire me to start my own business. I knew none of my friends or business acquaintances would think to look for me in the world of groceries—a bonus. Strategically, I stopped drinking by five in the afternoon on Sunday, so I could show up sober each Monday. It seemed to work. I rebuffed overtures of friendship from the women in the office and refused all offers of dates from the males.

Although my job was writing the weekly ads, by asking the right questions, I became familiar with the operation of a grocery store. It got me thinking I could do a better job. By the time my divorce decree came through, I had settled on my new career and new city.

I bought my first car, a 1952 Ford Deluxe in Alpine Blue. Since I rarely drove, I decided on the Fordomatic transmission, so I didn't have to worry about shifting gears on the hills in Austin, Texas.

Chapter Ten

A REINVENTION-AUSTIN-1952-1965

As I motored past the city limits of Dallas, I clenched my jaw and ignored the tears tracking down my cheeks. The guilt for how I treated Brett pierced my heart, but there was no going back. I'd done the right thing in setting him free. He could still find a woman to give him a child.

Besides changing cities and careers, I was pledging myself to a no-frills, down-to-earth life. Wasn't it about time to face my failures and mistakes and try something different? But sobriety had to come first. I had accumulated twelve hard-fought days without a drink. A good start.

My former boss at Safeway had recommended the Austin Motel to me. Never having been to the state Capitol and being an inexperienced driver, I was nervous and kept the Humble Oil roadmap open in my lap. As I entered the city, I followed the signs for highway 81 and crossed the river. Then I saw a towering red neon sign—a vaguely phallic but nonetheless welcome beacon—as I puttered down Congress Avenue. I pulled in the lot, turned off the ignition, and lay my head against the steering wheel in relief. At the check-in counter, I asked for a second-floor room away from the pool, and then brought in my suitcases. The accommodations were clean and neat but a far cry from the luxury hotels I used to frequent. The décor appalled me, way too much orange and plaid, but my stay would be short.

After I unpacked, I dropped to the bed as the reality of my new life hit me. Alone in a strange town, not knowing a soul. No friends—not that I intended to make any, at least not until I had stopped drinking permanently. I wanted a fresh start, after all, so there was no use feeling sorry for myself.

Although exhausted, I tossed and turned in the unfamiliar bed, wondering if I'd ever fall asleep. The sound of laughing people passing my door startled me awake, as daylight made the bright orange curtains glow. After a quick breakfast, I picked up a paper and scoured the ads for apartments to rent. A listing for a one-bedroom on Seventh Street, just off Congress, looked like the best bet, so I called for an appointment to see it. Cheap at $35.00 a month, my new digs included a parking spot in the lot behind the building. The furnishings weren't fancy, but certainly adequate. I signed a lease for a year and moved in the next day.

Before I left Dallas, I had pared down my wardrobe from the extravagant excess I'd accumulated during my youthful modeling days. At twenty-eight, I was more practical, so the evening gowns, high heels, and silly hats were history. I bought good quality, versatile pieces and maintained them. All my worldly possessions fit in two suitcases and two boxes, one of jazz and blues records and one of keepsakes. The old 78 format discs contained but one song, so I started buying those new albums that featured several. When I moved, I'd abandoned my record player, so I splurged on a Lafayette Playall that accommodated all three speeds, even though I didn't buy 45s. The console was too dear, but I could swing the tabletop model. It cost me a month's rent, but the music helped ease my loneliness.

Once settled in, I set up an account at a bank. When I handed over the check for my nest egg, still untouched and supplemented by interest, the banker gave me a look of respect, which I relished. Eventually, I'd put it to use in my own venture. I kept telling myself that, but my dream seemed out of reach. As I exited the building, it occurred to me the only time I thought about Ben was when I moved my money from one bank to another. My sweet husband, dead and gone for nine years. The grief had dissipated long ago; it was almost as if our marriage had never happened. Callous, but that didn't make it any less true.

I shut off that line of thinking and got on to the next order of business—a job. While reading the newspaper, I saw ads for a grocery store I'd never heard of, H-E-B. There was a location on Red River and East Sixth, not far from my flat, so I put in an application. Soon, I was behind the checkout counter. Not content to languish there, I offered to help with other duties, eager to learn the grocery game from the ground up.

For the most part, my life was a model of moderation. Despite knowing I'd never attain my goals unless I was sober, still I drank to excess on the occasional weekend, usually when I violated my vow not to think of Brett. Had he found someone new? That thought opened the floodgates to every memory I wanted to forget. I had no friends, so it was just me, vodka, and a splash of tonic. With mournful blues standards keeping me company, I isolated in my apartment.

A year after the move, I started dating or, more accurately, had one-night stands. Was I surprised when that behavior led to an increase in my alcohol intake? No.

After one of those "lost evenings," as I called them, one of my co-workers, Mabel, pulled me aside in the employee locker room on a Monday morning.

"Lookin' a little rough today. Big weekend?" Mabel put her hands on her chunky hips and raised her eyebrows.

"What do you mean?"

She leaned in so close, I could see every pore on her round face. "If I can tell you're hungover, the customers can too. Have you tried AA?" she whispered.

I recoiled, remembering the one meeting Brett had dragged me to. "I'm fine, had a sleepless night."

My tone of voice must have rattled Mabel. She raised her hands and stepped back. "Maybe it's none of my beeswax, just tryin' to help. My husband's a changed man after joining."

"Good for him," I snapped. I'd make certain to avoid Mabel in the future.

As I walked home from work that afternoon, I determined that if the aftereffects of my drinking were apparent to others, I'd better give the self-help program another try. I found a meeting south of the river, far from my neighborhood and job. The Bouldin group met in a house, a smoke-filled house. On my first visit, I was struck by a home truth that rocked me. A man named Joe talked about how he'd moved to a new town when his drinking got out of control and consequences smacked him down. "Learned the problem with a geographical cure was wherever I ran, I took myself with me."

In shock, I realized I'd done the same thing—several times. Would the move to Austin be my last geographical cure? While I wasn't ready to embrace AA, whenever I had a stinker of a hangover, I'd drop in. Sitting in the smoky room, chugging burnt coffee, I watched the clock tick away the minutes as members recited the same bromides. "So grateful for the program, keep coming back, it's alcohol-ism, not wasm, feelings aren't facts, tell it to your sponsor or you'll tell it to the bartender, you're as sick as your secrets." I heard the words but didn't take them to heart. My pattern was to duck into a meeting after it started and to leave before it ended. That allowed me to avoid pesky human interaction.

I'd had such high hopes for my future when I arrived in Austin four years ago. Was it possible to live the same year over and over? All but indistinguishable from each other, 1952 through 1956 passed in a blur. So deep in a rut, I couldn't see a way out, my life contracted, became small. Work, the occasional "lost evening," trying to sober up on Sunday. Although lonely, the fear of letting anyone get close to me was worth the isolation. Would I ever be stable enough to start a business?

Very little from that time stood out in my mind except for one incident a year or two after I moved to town. Austin, like most places, was racially segregated, but the neighborhood on East Sixth Street where I worked catered to the diverse population of the area. One afternoon at my checkout line, I heard two Negro women talking about the Victory Grill where they had seen B. B. King, Bobby "Blue" Bland, and Big Joe Turner perform.

I couldn't help but jump into the conversation. "I love 'Shake, Rattle, and Roll.' Where is this Victory Grill?"

The two ladies exchanged a knowing look. The younger one said, "It's across East Avenue, on 11th Street. Just a few blocks but a world away if you get my meaning."

"Not sure I do."

"White folk don't venture down that way. 'Nuff said."

"Where can a white person hear some blues then?"

"You might try the radio. 1260 AM. Tony Von has a show at four in the afternoon on weekdays and two on Saturdays. Gotta ask, what's a white girl like you know 'bout the blues?"

I totaled her order, collected the money, and made change. "When I lived in New York City, I went to a club where whites and Negroes mingle. Café Society, they call it. Big Joe Turner played there until he moved to Los Angeles and got famous."

"Well, they ain't no such thing in this town. But I'll be darned, appears you do know your stuff."

The younger woman waited while I served her friend. I watched them leave, wondering at the state of race relations. Even though I had my record collection, it was good to know where to find the latest music on the radio. I also found Dr. Hepcat on KVET.

When H-E-B opened its first supermarket on South Congress in 1957, I jumped at the chance to move to the larger store. Since it was only a short drive over the river, I didn't bother moving to south Austin. If I ever managed to start my own shop, it would be near the University. While my goal was alive and breathing in my mind, achieving it was still out of reach. I tried all sorts of things to curb my alcohol intake, even taking up crocheting to keep my hands busy. After three days, that idea died in a tangle of yarn. Another ploy was reading. If I was holding a book, how could I hold a drink? I soon proved that strategy laughable. None of my tactics worked for long. After weeks of abstention, when a painful memory intruded, or I watched my life trickle away with nothing to show for it, I always broke my vow and rushed to the liquor store.

After only five months at the supermarket, an opening for an assistant shift supervisor was posted. I applied and was granted an interview.

Nervous as a cat in a room full of rocking chairs, I entered the office and sat across from the manager, Andrew Tolliver.

"Miss Eaton, since you transferred here, your performance has been exemplary. I notice you had a few attendance issues when you were at the Sixth Street location but haven't missed a day here. Good for you."

"Thank you. And I appreciate you for considering me for the job. I'm interested in learning more about operations. The innovations here at H-E-B are most impressive. The strategy of using local sources puts us head and shoulders above the competition." Was I laying it on too thick?

Given his wide smile, those words struck a chord with Tolliver. "I like your attitude, Miss Eaton. You'll begin your orientation on Monday."

At last, some forward progress in my life. I curbed my drinking, going longer without an episode, never missing a day or coming in late.

During my training, I learned as much as I could about store operations: the ordering process, scheduling deliveries, and other details vital to the grocery game. Coupled with the corporate experience I'd garnered from the job at Safeway, that new knowledge reignited hope that I'd soon be ready to strike out on my own.

One Saturday, I ventured to the Texas Book Store on The Drag and made a fabulous discovery: Joe Pilates' *Return to Life through Contrology*. How did this book end up in Austin? I knew there wasn't a Pilates studio in town because I'd looked. Elated with my find, I rushed back to my apartment and reviewed all thirty-four floor exercises demonstrated by Joe himself. At a minimum, I did the Hundred every day.

With my higher salary, I was able to afford a television. On the evening of October 2nd, 1958, I sat on the couch with a cup of tea. Playhouse 90 came on the set. A somber Sterling Hayden introduced "The Days of Wine and Roses." Thinking it was a romance, I almost got up to turn it off. But it starred Cliff Robertson, an actor who reminded me of Brett, so I stayed put.

It was a romance all right, a love story about alcohol. Despite my reluctance to watch, the acting and plot kept me glued to the television. Not exactly my tale, but close enough to give me chills. Robertson played Joe, an ad man, who speaks about his journey to sobriety at an AA meeting. Kirsten, portrayed by Piper Laurie, refused to admit she was an alcoholic and continued to drink, disregarding the pleas of her husband. When she walked out the door in the final scene, abandoning her child, Joe prayed for serenity. I broke down, reminded of how I left Brett. Where was he and what was he doing? Was he married? A father? Whatever his situation, I was certain he was happier than he'd been with me. I switched off the television and dug out my old 78 of Frank Sinatra singing "I'll Be Seeing You" and played it once. Then I smashed it to pieces.

That night I cried myself to sleep, lamenting the way I had treated Brett. But the thing I regretted most was that I couldn't wait for the first sip of vodka and tonic the next evening.

Even though I had such an intense reaction to the teleplay, nothing changed for three years. I labored through the days, like a hamster on a wheel, and with as little self-reflection. Through sheer grit, I performed well at my job, never giving anyone a chance to fault my work. Although I backslid on occasion, the length of time between drinking binges steadily increased. There were men too, none of them worth a bucket of warm spit, but did I deserve better?

On Christmas Eve 1960, after a bad spree, I tried a new AA group near my apartment. While there, I locked eyes with a man. Instant connection. We got up and left in the middle of the meeting, and went to his place, where he had a bottle. The next morning, I snuck out while he was still asleep.

Something had to change. If anyone had told me I'd still be a slave to alcohol and working for someone else eight years after arriving in Austin, I wouldn't have believed it. Yet, there I was, spinning my wheels in the sandpit of addiction. Then, one summer night, fate kicked me in the ass and propelled me to a new way of life.

I got serious about AA when I had to, and I had to. In June 1961, I hit what I fervently hoped was my bottom. An off-duty cop saved me from a slobbering drunk who had attempted to have his way with me behind the Continental Club on South Congress. To my shame, he wasn't the man I started the evening with but a stranger. Shaken, I rose from my knees and leaned against the back wall of the bar, sobering up fast.

The last thing I remembered was stopping for a drink with my date, Jeff, at the Driskill hotel bar. He suggested we go hear some music, and I agreed. Guess I was already pretty drunk by then. As I swabbed my skinned knees with a wet towel my cop savior brought me, I tried to recall what happened inside the club.

My attacker was in handcuffs in the back of the squad car that had responded to the scene. With my alcohol-sodden brain banging around in my skull, I struggled to answer the beat cop's questions. When he told me if I wanted to press assault charges, there would be a trial and publicity, I declined. That couldn't happen. I'd lose my job, be publicly humiliated, and forced to move again. Bile rose in my throat. I loved Austin and didn't think I had another reinvention or geographical cure in me. I'd run from myself for far too long. No, I told the officer, I don't want to get involved, figuring they had him on drunk and disorderly without my help.

When the squad car left, my hero introduced himself. "Roy Martinez, at your service, ma'am."

I closed my eyes. *Ma'am?* I probably reeked of vodka. What did I look like after the night I had? And I'd been doing so well. Hadn't had anything to drink in three weeks. How did I let myself fall again? Luckily, I didn't have to go to work until Monday, so I had two full days to sober up.

"Hi, Roy. Can't quite bring myself to say nice to meet you, given the circumstances. I have no idea what happened to my date. Where is he?"

"Hmm, you don't remember?"

I hung my head. "Guess not."

"If you're blackout drinking, then you're in trouble. I'm a friend of Bill."

"AA?" Unable to meet his eyes, I studied my shredded nylons.

"You betcha. Been sober five beautiful years. You sure you wanna know what happened in there?" His chin jerked toward the door of the club.

"Better tell me." I stiffened my spine, prepared to hear an ugly tale.

"You got up from your table, leaving your date, and sat on another fella's lap. Your lips were glued to his for a good, long time." He shrugged. "The guy you came in with up and left. Then you and the other fella—the one on his way to the station—went out the back door."

I groaned. "I'm so embarrassed."

"Yep, not a good thing. Ever done this before?"

My head shook in denial, and I immediately stopped and gripped it with both hands. "Not...not to this extent."

"I got the feeling things might go south, so I followed y'all."

"Oh. Lucky you did."

"Yeah, it was." Roy looked at his watch. "I gotta get on home. You need a lift?"

"Yes. Or I could take the bus."

"Don't do that." He handed me my purse. "Come on. My car is down about a block."

On the drive, Roy told me about his AA group. I confessed I'd gone to a few meetings, although not at that location. "It didn't work for me."

"Well, doesn't sound like you worked the program. Sitting in a couple of meetings won't do it. Read the literature and work the steps with a sponsor. Can't just stick your toe in. You gotta take the plunge. Commit."

My updo had fallen out of the clips and hung in my face. I shoved the curls behind my ears. "I've heard people call it a cult."

Roy snorted. "It ain't. That I can tell you." As he drove, I watched his profile. His black hair gleamed in the ambient light. When he pulled up to my apartment building and turned to me. I read compassion in his huge liquid eyes. Placing his hand on my arm, he said, "Let me take you to a meeting tomorrow."

I broke down in tears and nodded. He handed me his handkerchief and patted my shoulder. "Gonna pick you up in front of your building at eleven-thirty. Okay?"

"Yes, I'll be there."

The next morning, I woke at ten with a foul taste in my mouth. I stood under an ice-cold shower—as if I could freeze my problems. I really didn't want to look in the mirror, and when I raised my head to do so, found I'd been right to hesitate.

My under-eyes looked bruised. The road map of shame, with many side streets, showed in the whites of my eyes. I shuddered. My stomach revolted, and I vomited dark bile into the sink.

How could I be ready in an hour and a half? I'd have to face not only Roy but also a roomful of earnest, clean-living people who might be under mass hypnosis. No thanks. I gasped aloud. Was I sabotaging myself? After last night's incident, I knew I needed help. Brushing my teeth until my gums bled, I rinsed with full-strength Listerine and relished the sting. There'd be plenty of pain ahead, and I might as well get used to it.

I toweled my hair and noticed a few gray hairs. Only thirty-seven and gray hair. Time was marching on and taking my youth with it. Carefully applying makeup, I used all my old modeling tricks. It helped, but I still looked "rode hard and put up wet," as my daddy would say. A pang of regret doubled me over, but I had no inclination to set things right with my family.

The inheritance from Ben was all I had left. Twenty years of interest had increased the sum handsomely, but I was no closer to bringing my idea to fruition than when I first conceived the idea of becoming an independent businesswoman. Without a plan and dependent on working, I had to do everything to keep my job. So far, my weekend binges hadn't been noticed, but after this latest fiasco, how much longer could that last?

I grappled with the decision of what to wear. Finally, I chose the yellow plaid gingham shirtwaist with a Peter Pan collar, my most conservative dress, and added black heels and a clutch bag. Once more, I checked my appearance in the mirror and pitied the sad visage staring back at me.

Half my life ago, I was a fresh young thing on my way to an exciting modeling career in Manhattan, never suspecting the long string of calamities and tragedies that would follow. Those events had trampled my spirit, taken a toll on my mind, and etched lines around my eyes. But it was futile to start down that road. Once I began, I could wallow in tragedy for days, reliving my losses. Ragged sobs shook my body, and I ran into the bathroom for a handful of tissue. My emotions were close to the surface. I'd tamped them down for years, pretending to be indifferent.

Thinking back to the AA meetings I'd attended, I couldn't think of anything that helped me. But, with each fall from grace, the shame increasingly weighed on me. One thing was clear—the boozing couldn't continue.

I locked the apartment and took the elevator to the lobby. Taking a deep breath, I pushed through the door to the street. There Roy stood, leaning against the fender of a powder-blue Nash convertible. Probably the same car he drove last night, but I had no recollection of it. When he saw me, he grinned, and I reflected on how gentlemanly he was, not presuming to ask for my phone number. In my heels, I was eye-to-eye with Roy. He wasn't as tall as I preferred my men. I caught myself. Roy had done nothing to indicate he had the slightest romantic interest in me, and with the way I looked these days, it was mighty presumptuous to think about it. Humbled, I had to remember that I'd fallen far and landed hard.

"Good morning!" I strove to keep my voice upbeat despite my throbbing headache.

Roy opened the passenger door, and I climbed into the compact car. He hustled to the driver's side and slid behind the wheel, heading south on Congress. Ten minutes later, he pulled into a church parking lot and ran around to open my door.

I unfolded myself, taking his huge brown hand to help me out of the low seat, my hand white as paper in his. Because of Roy's military bearing, I wondered if he'd served in the war. Too many personal questions about him when I needed to concentrate on getting sober. If I could.

Alcohol had stalked me for years. I lied to myself and everyone in my life about my drinking, pushed people away when they got close. After the visit to Scarsdale, I dropped Milly like a hot skillet. And I hadn't written to Harold in months. My real issues started after the birth. The reason I couldn't remember much about that time was because of the drugs I was given. Morphine and scopolamine kept me in a daze for almost two weeks after the not-so-blessed event. My comeuppance.

As I walked beside Roy into the meeting, I stumbled, shaken by the realization that the child I bore was now older than I had been when I gave birth.

Roy caught my elbow. "You all right?"

I manufactured a smile and nodded. "A little misstep." My whole life was a series of little—and big—missteps.

We took the stairs to a dimly lit hallway and followed the cloud of smoke and the smell of burnt coffee to the meeting. When we entered the room, several men clapped Roy on the shoulder or shook his hand. I kept my eyes averted, not caring to be introduced. Roy got the message and guided us to seats in a row of folding chairs. My hands were cold and quivering, even though the room was toasty. I sat on them.

Staring straight ahead at the huge posters on the wall proclaiming the Twelve Steps and Twelve Traditions, the words blurred. My stomach growled, and I was certain everyone in the room heard it. Clenching my jaw, I hoped I would survive the next hour.

A booming male voice startled me. "My name is Jimmy, and I'm an alcoholic."

I sighed, opened my eyes, took my hands out from under my bottom, and settled in.

Listening to the testimony of the other drunks, I watched the minutes tick by on the clock. Slightly different versions of stories I'd heard before, reminders of my own experiences, all shoved in my face. After a while, my stomach calmed, and my shoulders came down from around my ears. Then Roy raised his hand.

"I'm Roy, and I meet the membership requirement."

"Hi, Roy," the blended voices answered.

"Through the grace of God, I've been sober five years, two months, and four days, but who's counting?"

A typical introduction, but there were plenty of chuckles and whistles, as if they were hearing it for the first time.

"I'm grateful all y'all for saving my life. I was on a real downward spiral, lost my marriage, almost lost my job, when a friend of Bill introduced me to this program. It took me a while, but I finally got it. After reading the Big Book, I recognized myself and wholeheartedly worked the steps. That's why I'm here today and why I'm sober."

"Thanks, Roy," the crowd chanted.

I put a dollar in the basket, but that was the extent of my participation.

Relieved the meeting was over, I stood. Roy joined me, and we walked through the gauntlet of Roy's chums. Again, I remained aloof.

When we got to the car, Roy asked, "Want to grab a bite to eat?"

I tasted bile. "Thanks, but I'm not hungry."

"Oh, come on, you gotta eat. Did ya have any breakfast?"

"Well, no..."

"Then let's get us a burger at Hut's."

I loved Hut's burgers and fries. "Okay."

Over our meal, Roy talked about his job. He no longer rode in a patrol car. "They kicked me upstairs."

"Good for you." I grabbed another fry.

He sipped his vanilla malt. "I guess so. At least over on east Seventh, I can get me some good Mexican food at lunch."

I made small talk about my favorite restaurants, blues music, and my job at H-E-B.

Roy was attentive and shared a few war stories about his time on the mean streets of Austin. We laughed and chatted like old friends, so I was surprised when he asked for my phone number. I gave it to him and wondered if he would become more than a friend.

Back in my apartment, I rummaged through a box I hadn't unpacked since I arrived in town and pulled out a blue book, the long-ignored Big Book, the Bible of AA. I commenced reading.

Two weeks later, a little shaky, a little sweaty, and very much craving a quart of vodka, I slunk into a Bouldin AA meeting. The hankering was so intense, I might even have considered gin or bourbon. That day, I heard something that broke through my wall of resistance. A gray-haired woman named Helen told her story.

"Through the grace of God, I've remained sober for fifteen years. I have learned to accept that I am, and will always be, an alcoholic. If I pick up a drink, I'll be right back where I was when I crashed my car into the rear end of a school bus." Her voice thickened. "In a drunken stupor. So lucky that no children were on the bus, and the driver escaped with a few scratches. Oh, how I hated myself that day. A friend brought me to my first AA meeting, and I heard something that resonated. 'Let us love you until you can love yourself.' This program has truly been a new beginning for me."

"Thanks, Helen," I said with fervor. Until you can love yourself. Was self-hatred my problem?

After the meeting, I approached her. "Can we go somewhere to talk?"

Her gaze pierced me, as if she could see into my soul. "Sure, let's walk over to that new cafe on Barton Springs."

After ordering two coffees, we sat on the back patio. My hands shook so badly, coffee spilled all over the table. I planned to ask Helen to be my sponsor. The conventional wisdom was to find someone who had what you wanted, and I wanted her serenity, gentleness, kindness, and her fifteen years of freedom from alcohol.

I told her the truth. "Listening to you today, I realized I hate myself...for so many things. When I lived in Dallas, I went to a meeting in 1952, but never returned. A lovely woman gave me a Big Book, but I never even opened it until recently." I confessed my periodic drinking binges to her. She was kind, non-judgmental, easy to confide in. Why had I feared a sponsor would be pushy and overbearing?

"Lauren, I'll sponsor you on one condition. Read the book in its entirety, then get back to me."

At that point, reading a book was a small price to pay. "I'll start tonight."

When I told Roy I was going to meetings at Bouldin, he stopped by when his schedule permitted. He was an attractive and viral man, but I was aware that AA counseled against romantic involvements for the first year of sobriety. Unless all my instincts about the opposite sex had died, I knew he was interested in me.

But I never got a chance to know if a relationship with him was possible. In October, I turned on the evening news after work and learned Roy was shot dead when he responded to a call for an officer down at a bank robbery. He'd been about to leave the office for the day but instead headed to the scene.

My first thought—run to the liquor store and buy a big bottle of vodka—but I did the smart thing and called Helen. I told her about Roy and how I was desperate for a drink.

"I'll be there in fifteen minutes. Whatever you do, don't pick up."

"There's nothing in the apartment."

"Promise me you won't leave."

I closed my eyes and imagined the fizz as I poured tonic into a tall glass of vodka. My fingernails dug into my palms. "Promise."

For the next quarter-hour, I paced, turned on the television, then shut it off. When the bell rang, I stumbled in my haste to open the door. Helen took one look at me, put her arm around me, and led me to the couch. We sat, and I started babbling. "All I can think about is vodka. I can almost taste it." I grabbed Helen's hands and squeezed so hard, she winced. "Roy and I were just friends, but I believe we could have been something more. Now I'll never know. I mean, I was attracted, and I'm fairly sure he was, but we never—"

"Lauren, slow down. If you drink, you'll be right back where you were when you stopped. You might have quit for a few weeks, but the disease is lying in wait, ready to take you to places you'll regret—and might not come back from."

"But vodka is how I always coped. I know it will kill me if I keep it up, but it's so hard." I buried my face in my hands.

"Have you finished reading the Big Book?"

"Yes."

"Did you see yourself in the pages?"

I squared my shoulders and met her eyes. "Sure did. What comes next?"

Helen smiled. "It's time for you to start working the program, dear. We'll meet every week and do the steps. Have you taken step one? Before you answer, remember this is the one step which must be taken without reservation."

I took that first step, admitted I was powerless over alcohol and my life had become unmanageable. And I never looked back. Well, at times I did look back longingly on the release and oblivion drinking gave me but didn't act on it.

Helen and I attended Roy's funeral and the reception at his home group afterward. As we drove into the cemetery, I was stunned by the huge police presence, with squad cars from all over the state of Texas. The press contingent included reporters from San Antonio. Much pomp and circumstance. The color guard consisted of over a dozen men.

I didn't know Roy's family but identified them from their prominence at the graveside. Didn't feel it appropriate to introduce myself. Had Roy even mentioned me to them? The service took almost two hours. Wearing a somber black suit, the last remnant of my Dallas work wardrobe, I cried my way through most of it. When the bagpipes played "Amazing Grace," I dissolved into a puddle of grief. Helen grasped my hand and squeezed, and I leaned into her. We stood in camaraderie with the AA crowd, hanging back from the family and police attendees.

After the interment, it took thirty minutes to clear the traffic jam and head to the AA reception. The place was packed with people sharing their memories of Roy, drinking coffee, and consuming store-bought cookies and cakes. We didn't stay long.

A month of sobriety grew to two, then three, as I tackled the Twelve Steps—one per month. In July 1962, I got hung up on Step Nine. Helen counseled me about making amends to my family and Brett.

"Direct amends, personally addressing your wrongs with those you've hurt, are recommended. But if doing so would injure them or others, indirect amends are acceptable," Helen said.

I wasn't familiar with the concept. "What are indirect amends?"

"Well, another way to call them is living amends by adhering to the principles of the program."

"I can do that." Inside, I breathed a sigh of relief I wouldn't have to get in touch with Brett and my family at that point in my journey. Maybe I would someday.

"After you've made your amends, you will live in Steps Ten, Eleven, and Twelve. Learn to admit when you are wrong and make immediate amends. Maintain your conscious contact with God. And once you are ready, give back to AA by helping others."

As I took the program to heart, Helen became my touchstone and guiding light. I was immensely grateful for her compassion and wisdom. Would I ever be fit to sponsor another woman? There were many personal flaws I had to address before I dared take a fragile, newly sober alcoholic under my wing.

My routine shrank to work, AA, and work. Management took notice and hinted I might be in the running for a store manager position in the future. With my confidence boosted, I decided I was ready to chart my own way.

Rather than spending my weekends going through a fifth or two of vodka, I started to draft a business plan. From my research, I learned the Austin population had grown by fifty percent since I arrived. With the burgeoning growth, there was room for another player in the grocery game. In a mere two years, I'd be forty, and I wanted to be up and running by then.

But something was missing. Men. I missed the companionship of a man. To be honest, I missed sex. It had been a while, a long lonely while, so I started dating again. But I didn't want to date anyone in AA. Was that shallow? Truly, I couldn't face the embarrassment of being in a meeting with a man I had ended a relationship with. And a no-strings affair was all I was looking for; I'd never consider marriage again, not after what I did to Brett. My first two marriages resulted in carnage, although not through any fault of mine. However, I was grievously guilty of the demise of my third marriage. I couldn't fathom telling a man about my past, but I ached for companionship, and I eventually found an irresistible man, or several, with whom I had brief affairs.

Brief being the operative word. Harley proposed marriage each time we made love. I laughed it off. After the third time, with much regret, I had to cut him out of my life. Cal invited me to meet his family after an idyllic two-month interlude. I declined and moved on to Wade.

On New Year's Eve, I turned down a date from Wade, knowing there would be alcohol involved at any holiday celebration. It pained me to do so because he was a gorgeous hunk of a man, a former NFL football player. Instead, Helen and I went to see the new movie, "Days of Wine and Roses." I couldn't decide which version I hated more, the one on television four years ago or the movie. The cinematic take wasn't my and Brett's story, just as the teleplay hadn't been, but it dredged up images of my life with him. That was torture, even ten years later. My eyes burned, but I refused to cry.

As we left the theater, Helen asked, "Hit a little too close to home?"

Unable to speak, I nodded and left it at that.

A year later, I couldn't call myself happy, but I was sober. H-E-B recognized my accomplishments and offered me a promotion to manager. When I turned it down, I don't know who was more surprised—me or them. Then I got serious about planning my venture. Visions of a boutique grocery shop near the U. T. campus danced through my mind, and I pursued that idea. I found an empty storefront a few blocks south of the university and jumped on it. Construction took seven months. While reviewing my bank balance, I discovered I could cover the buildout, first year's rent, and other start-up costs, but was short several thousand dollars for inventory. Disaster. In a panic, I called Helen, who referred me to Carol, an AA friend, who was a lawyer specializing in small businesses. I scheduled an appointment with her and presented my dilemma. She suggested I form a cooperative and take a few investors to provide the rest of the capital for my opening expenses. Although I was disappointed, I decided that was my only option.

In May 1965, I cut the ribbon on Cornucopia, my food store. After all, I'd finally achieved my dream: financial independence and a business of my own. Shouldn't I be happy?

Chapter Eleven

THE GHOST OF LAUREN'S PAST-AUSTIN-1985

In the twenty years since I opened my food store, Cornucopia, I'd spent thousands of hours at bureaucratic tasks. I dreaded tax time with its piles of thankless paperwork. Although I had a great bookkeeper, preparing the final returns was up to me.

That Wednesday, a week before the monthly deadline, Jolie, my day manager, rapped on the office door. I had asked not to be disturbed—a standing order when busy with taxes. "Come in." Under my breath, I muttered, "This better be important."

Jolie stepped into my office, retro, horn-rimmed glasses giving her the look of a studious waif. A recent UT graduate, she appeared nervous—as she should be.

"Yes?"

"Sorry to bother you, but there's a man asking for you."

"A man."

"Yes. Tall, old guy with a patch over one eye."

I dropped my pencil and gasped.

"Miss Eaton, are you okay?"

Not wanting Jolie to see my shock, I spun my chair to face the credenza behind me and shuffled folders. "Of course, I'm fine. You know I'm terribly busy. Did you at least get his name?"

"Um, no."

"Well, find out who he is and what he wants." As soon as I heard the door close, I got up and rushed into the restroom. Staring at myself in the mirror, I wondered how Brett had tracked me down. I needed to pull myself together before I saw him. Tears welled. Guilt congealed. Goosebumps chilled my arms. After several deep breaths, I found my backbone. Luckily, I kept a full array of makeup and facial products in the cabinet. At my advanced age, I couldn't afford not to, although I congratulated myself on my ability to lie about my age with impunity. No one would guess I'd just turned sixty-one. But Brett knew. He knew a lot about me. Why had he shown up after all these years?

After repairing my makeup, I returned to my desk. Jolie knocked, and I told her to come in. With her hands shoved in her Cornucopia apron pockets, she shifted from one foot to the other. I almost felt sorry for her. "Miss Eaton, his name is Brett Owens, and he's really persistent."

Brett strode into my office as if he owned the place. "Yep, I'm nothin' if not persistent."

I didn't answer him. "Jolie, thank you. Please close the door behind you."

My nails bit into the palms of my clenched hands. "Why are you here, Brett?"

"No 'hello, how are you?'"

"Don't push me."

He took a step forward. "I saw the write-up on Cornucopia in the *Dallas Morning News*. Congratulations on buyin' out your investors."

I softened a tad. "Thank you. It was time. When I first opened, I had the funds to do it all—except to buy inventory. I relied on a few friends. Over the years, through attrition, only five co-op members remained. They were very understanding about me taking over control." Then I realized his intention was to disarm me with flattery, and I changed my tune. "So, you drove down to Austin to congratulate me in person?"

"Yep."

"Well, as I said, thank you. If that's all…" I stood and gestured toward the door.

"Cut me a break, will ya? Been on the road for hours. I'd like a chance to talk."

"About what?"

"You're not blowing me off, Lauren."

"Watch me." Could he see my heart trying to escape the confines of my chest? I willed my face to remain serene. Inside, I wilted like a neglected plant while struggling to maintain a veneer of calm.

Brett shook his head and smiled. "Nope. I'm stayin' put. I'll just make myself comfortable in this here leather chair." He settled his big frame in the guest chair.

How brazen. I imagined his next move: leaning back and putting his feet on my desk. "It's tax time, and I'm elbow-deep in my return." Although his hair had turned to silver, I'd have recognized him anywhere. He'd aged well, remained trim, jaw still firm.

"I'll wait. Ain't you gonna offer refreshments? That coffee smells mighty good."

"You're infuriating!"

"Don't mean to be. Got it in my head I want to reconnect with you. Did you know you're the love of my life?"

His smile pierced me—and shamed me—as I recalled the circumstances of our break-up. My chance to make direct amends to him stared me in the face, yet I couldn't do it. Knowing he could always read my emotions, I turned away to pour two cups of coffee.

"I don't believe that for a minute, Brett. It's been thirty-three years. Haven't you remarried?"

"Nope. Have you?"

"No."

"See, right off, we got something in common. You're looking mighty fine, too. How long you been sober?"

"How do you know I'm sober?"

"You couldn't run a successful business if you were drinking. I know that for a fact. I tried and failed. Been sober for fifteen years."

"How wonderful! Congratulations." I handed him the coffee and sat down, keeping the desk between us. "Twenty-four years. 1961."

"Got me beat. Always did get the better of me. Damn, it's good to see you. Gotta ask, when you left me, did ya head to Austin straight off?"

"Yes." Determined to cut his visit short, I played the ice queen.

He nodded and sipped the coffee. "So, you've been two hundred miles away this whole time?"

I decided not to respond. My mind searched for a way to end the encounter. Rudeness wasn't working.

Brett charged ahead with his inquisition. "Let me do the math. You got sober in sixty-one, so it took nine years?"

"Yes, about that long, but it finally stuck. A hard-fought battle, but when I hit bottom, there was no mistaking it."

"My story's a little different. I continued drinking until 1970. One day, I took stock of my consumption, which was steadily increasing. A visit to the doctor showed elevated liver enzymes, and that good old GP read me the riot act. Quit cold turkey. Had the shakes for about a week, but that was the extent of it. And of course, I went back to the rooms."

"So, you're a member of AA?"

"Yes, ma'am. Couldn't do without my group."

"They still meet downtown?" Why was I prolonging his visit?

"Yeah, but now I go to the Suburban group, a little farther north."

"Austin has good AA. I stop by a few different meetings around town, but I favor Westlake." I pointedly looked at my watch. "Brett, it's been nice chatting, but I have to get back to my taxes. Have a safe trip."

Brett stood and placed his empty coffee cup on my desk. "No plans to return to Dallas right yet."

Heat shot up my neck, and I cursed how easily I blushed. "No? What are your plans?"

"Already told you. To reconnect with you. I felt a compulsion to see you again. Call me crazy."

"Okay, you're crazy."

Brett laughed, then turned serious. "I've never forgotten you. You know I didn't want the divorce. I let you go 'cause that's what you wanted. Been missing you since you left. Every. Damn. Day."

His words rocked me. I never thought I'd see him again, and I never imagined he'd want to see me after the shabby way I treated him.

"Too much, too fast." Oops, didn't mean to say that part out loud. He had me shook. "I'm not sure I'm inclined to get reacquainted. I like my life just as it is."

"Give me a chance." Brett was too proud to plead, but he was darned close to it.

"What's that mean?"

"Let me take you to dinner. I made reservations Friday night at Jeffrey's."

"Pretty sure of yourself."

"Not really. Just hopin'." He grinned, and I saw the man I fell in love with almost forty years ago.

I blinked away the vision. By design, love wasn't a feature in my life and hadn't been for a long time. But after his gesture, I didn't have the heart to shut him down. "I do have to eat."

"Reservation's at seven. Can I pick you up?"

"No. I'll meet you there."

"Suit yourself. I'll see myself out."

He strode to the door and turned back to face me. "I'll be seeing you."

Those words.

No sooner had he left, Jolie came knocking.

"Miss Eaton, is everything okay?"

"Everything's fine."

"Mr. Owens sure seemed a lot happier when he left than when he got here."

"Yes, he did." I raised my eyebrows.

Jolie blushed. "Sorry."

"It's all right. Mr. Owens is an old friend from a past life."

"Got it. I'll make sure they're no more interruptions this afternoon."

"Thanks, dear."

As soon as she closed the door, I grabbed the phone and dialed Jane. Why was my first inclination to call her rather than Helen? I'd have to examine that choice later.

I tapped my foot as Jane's phone rang three times. At last, she answered. "It's Lauren. We need to talk. I've just had a ghost from a past life descend on me."

"Whatever do you mean?"

"His name is Brett Owens. He was my third husband."

"Third? How many times have you been married?"

"Three. I said I'd tell you my story one day. Looks like the time has come. I think you're ready. After all, you're almost done with your Ph.D. in clinical psychology. You can handle it, but what you might not be able to handle is the checkered past of your AA sponsor."

"No, you're wrong about that. You taught me well. We all have feet of clay and should never place anyone in AA on a pedestal, for they are sure to fall."

"Truer words... Let's get lunch tomorrow. Are you available?"

"No. Come here. I'm still typing my dissertation and don't have time to go out. Around ten?"

"Yes. I'll be there. Can I bring you something from Sweetish Hill?"

"No! I never know when morning sickness will strike. These early weeks have been hellacious, but I've cornered the market on saltines, so I'm good."

Promptly at ten the next morning, I rang the bell at Jane's home. The door opened, and she waved me inside. Jane's new kitten, Delilah, pawed Jane's legs, and she bent to pick up the tiny fluffball.

My nose wrinkled despite my efforts to keep a pleasant facial expression. "You know I'm not partial to animals. But that right there is the cutest little thing I've ever seen."

"Want to hold her?"

"Not on your life. Silk and kitten claws do not mix. I'll admire her from afar. How are you faring with the grief process? I know how much you loved Tallulah." Even though I didn't understand the bond, I sympathized with my friend.

Jane cuddled the baby Persian and sighed. Her voice thick, she said, "I'll never forget her. So grateful she passed quietly, in her sleep." She shrugged. "I'm coping. When Joshua brought Miss Delilah home two days after Lulah...died, I thought I wasn't ready, but look at this baby. Who could resist?"

Instead of answering, I changed the subject. "Lead me to where you're gonna shrink my head."

Jane chuckled. "No head-shrinking. Promise. I've set up on the sun porch."

We entered the glass-enclosed room overlooking the Pennybacker Bridge and Lake Austin. In the spring, the backyard's downhill slope would be awash in color from the flowering trees, but nothing was blooming in December.

I took off my velvet wrap, and Jane took it. "This is gorgeous." She peeked at the tag. "Norma Kamali? Nice. You're such a fashion plate."

I settled on the chintz-covered loveseat and sighed. The room always elicited a sense of peace. The light-drenched space and muted colors of the décor soothed my soul.

Jane sat on the chair to my left. I had half-expected her to sit behind her desk or ask me to lie on the couch. She placed Delilah on the floor, and the kitten curled up in a basket under the coffee table. "Thank you for trusting me to help with your dilemma. But I must clarify something."

"Clarify to your heart's content."

"I can't treat you in a professional capacity. It's not ethical to work with friends. You might consider seeing an objective stranger."

"Considered and dismissed. Anything else?"

"Aren't you concerned our personal relationship will get in the way?"

"No. Ain't gonna happen."

"Okay. Just so you understand you're not a patient. Why don't we have some discussions and probe the issues together, informally?"

"However you want to call it, I'm game."

As Jane settled back in her chair, she exhaled. "Okay. Good. We'll make it work."

"Sure will. Sorry you got your panties twisted."

"Let's get serious. Tell me about Brett or start wherever you'd like. Maybe some background would be good. I know next to nothing about your life before we met. Goodness, it's almost ten years ago." Her brow wrinkled. Perhaps she suspected there was more tragedy in my past than three shattered marriages.

"Well, I can't deny it. I admit I've been a bit secretive. Did I ever tell you I grew up on a cattle ranch outside Mineral Wells?"

Jane's eyes widened. "Cattle ranch! No, I had no idea. I always thought you were putting on the country, as so many Austinites do."

"Nope. I come by it honest. Had to work hard to improve my elocution and diction when I lived in Manhattan, but once I got back to Texas, my natural speech pattern bubbled to the surface."

"Manhattan?"

"Yes, Jane. Manhattan. You'll hear all about it. Where should I begin?"

"I'm intrigued by the cattle ranch. Why don't you start there?"

Although I shouldn't be, I was apprehensive. I trusted Jane. Nevertheless, while I gathered my thoughts, I pleated the skirt of my silk kimono dress—a nervous habit. "Okay, I suppose I have to go there, as the kids say."

An hour later, I had spilled my story from my early family life to the 1940 Fort Worth Stock Show to landing in Manhattan, where I had studied to be a model with John Robert Powers.

"Wow!" Jane said. "My mind is blown. Not very professional, I'm afraid. Guess I'm identifying too much, but we both left home at sixteen."

We sat in silence for a long two minutes. Then Jane rose and said, "I need a little break. Meet me in the kitchen, and I'll find us something to eat."

I watched Jane leave, with the kitten toddling behind her like a baby duck after its mama. Shuddering, I lay my head in my hands. Wait until Jane hears the next installment.

Before I followed her to the kitchen, I practiced a deep breathing exercise. Then, confident what Jane called my "patented veneer of cool" was in place, I found her rifling through the cabinets. "Whatever are you lookin' for?"

Jane glanced at me. "I have the strangest urge for a tuna fish sandwich. And I don't even care for tuna, so there isn't any. I'm searching for something edible." She opened the refrigerator and rummaged around. "Ah, sliced ham. Want a sandwich?"

"No, I'll pass, but you go ahead. I wouldn't say no to a cup of tea."

Jane pointed at a cabinet. "In there. Take your pick. I have several varieties."

After selecting Earl Grey, I did a double-take when I saw her tea kettle. "What the heck is this?"

"Oh, do you like it? It's a new design. The blue handle doesn't get hot, and the cute little red bird is such fun."

"As long as it does the job." I filled the kettle and found cups.

While Jane scarfed her sandwich, I stepped to the bay window and admired the view. Even at this time of year, boaters were enjoying a day on Lake Austin. The bird whistled, and I made two cups of tea.

Jane patted her mouth with a paper towel. "I was famished. No morning sickness today. Let's take our drinks and get back to work."

We made our way to the sunroom and settled into our respective seats. Delilah followed us and settled again in her basket. Looking refreshed, Jane took the lead. "I was astonished to learn your name was actually Ruby."

Guilt hit me like a hammer blow. "I butted heads with Mama about that for years. Just sorry I never understood why they named me Ruby until I was in my forties."

"Tell me."

"My daddy told me how thrilled they were when I was born after having two sons. He said, 'A little girl. More precious than rubies.' And Mama smiled. 'Proverbs 3:15. Let's name her Ruby.'" I reached for a tissue from the end table. Didn't want to cry, but that story always got the best of me. "At that advanced age, I wasn't about to start using the name, but I do wish I hadn't been so ornery about it as a child."

Jane nodded. "We all have regrets." Her faraway look made me think she was reflecting on some of her own. "Ready to continue?"

"You ready for more true confessions?"

"Sure am." Jane propped up her feet on an ottoman.

Another hour passed. I told my story without emotion, speaking quietly and quickly. Once, I glanced at Jane and saw her shock. My pregnancy, Alain's abandonment, the hazy birth, the adoption, Mama's visit to New

York, the start of my drinking, and the affair with Theodore, which led to my departure for Dallas. It was a lot for anyone to absorb. I hoped she'd been truthful about not putting me on a pedestal. My clay feet were crumbling.

With her hands cradling her not-yet-noticeable pregnant belly, Jane asked. "Did you ever see your daughter after the adoption?"

"No."

"I guess you don't care to elaborate."

"Got that right." My eyes stung, but I controlled myself.

Jane seemed to take the hint and changed her tack. "So, then you moved to Dallas? At seventeen?"

"I sure did. Imogene set me up with Neiman-Marcus. I started my job on the day after Pearl Harbor. As you might imagine, the fashion world changed dramatically after the war began."

Jane nodded. "The rationing."

"Yes. Still, I had a busy social life, went dancing every weekend. One night when Tommy Dorsey was in town at the Baker Hotel, I met Ben, my first husband."

Jane held up her hands. "Hold on a minute. I know you're in a hurry, but we're moving too fast, and I need to backtrack a bit—to the birth. Twilight sleep was a horrific practice, yet it lasted into the sixties. Like Medieval torture, but with modern pharmaceuticals. Thank God it's not used any longer. What do you remember about your hospitalization?"

"Little to nothing. I lost time, drifting in and out of consciousness with each injection. Didn't understand why my wrists were red and chafed. I was in the hospital for ten days and have only a vague recollection of seeing my dau—the baby. And of meeting Clark and Evelyn. After forty-five years, even those memories have faded."

"Of course. So, you never held your daughter, never bonded?"

I shook my head. "The social worker said that would delay my recovery. Truthfully, I don't remember wanting to."

"How do you feel about that now?"

Looking out the window, I replied, "I feel nothing. Does that make me a monster?"

"It makes you human. How could you possibly form an attachment with the drugs and the societal norms of the time?"

"Thank you for that, Jane."

"I have a question about your relationship with your mother. Seems like there was friction between you when you were a teen, but when she told you she would have sent you to a home for unwed mothers, things deteriorated. Did you ever mend fences?"

"I didn't expect that question."

"And that was not an answer. Surely you can see why it's relevant."

I sat silently, wondering at Jane's motive for raising the question. Was it because of her own issues regarding her mother?

Jane must have read my mind. "Sorry, Lauren. You know the difficulties I had with my mother, but I'm not asking for that reason. That would be countertransference or double-secret projection, or some other violation of psychological protocol. Can't do that!" She smiled widely while I wondered what on earth she'd just said.

I decided to go ahead and answer straightforwardly. "During the war, travel was difficult, so I had a ready excuse for why I didn't visit. Then, my life devolved into a series of unfortunate events caused by my alcoholism. The last thing on my mind was family ties or family *anything*. After I had meaningful sobriety and the co-op was successful, I returned to the ranch in 1970."

"Thirty years with no contact?"

"Thereabouts. Although we wrote from time to time, had a few phone calls." I felt my brow furrow and at once relaxed my facial muscles. "I doubted they'd want to see their widowed, divorced, childless, alcoholic daughter. Would any parent?"

"That's a pretty harsh put-down of yourself. Tell me about your reunion."

I stood and walked to the windows overlooking the lake. With my back to Jane, I spoke. "I'd been thinking of getting in touch, to make direct amends at long last, when Jace called me from the ranch and told me Mama was dying. And she was asking for me." A sob escaped from my tight throat. I returned to the loveseat and plucked several tissues from the box on the table.

"Did you visit her?"

I skewered Jane with a glance. Was she recalling her own mother's death, the mother she hadn't seen after leaving home at sixteen? Jane never got the closure I did. A shiver chilled me. "Yes, I went home, I mean back."

Jane patiently waited for me to continue. She just might make a decent therapist. Her focus on my family life made me uncomfortable. Was it normal to leave your childhood home and not look back? Probably not. Then again, Jane had done the same thing.

When I gathered myself, I said, "Driving up the gravel lane gave me chills. The old barn and pastures looked the same, but the house had a fresh coat of paint. My daddy met me at the door, his face lined with grief. He never said a word about our estrangement, just hugged me. At the age of forty-six, I felt like his little girl again, although I cringed inside, aware that he knew about my ancient mistake. But it didn't affect the way he treated me."

"Still the apple of his eye?" Jane asked.

I couldn't help but smile. "I doubt it, but I'd like to think so." A mental switch flipped, and I was back at the ranch. "The old place had different furniture and drapes, but even those were a bit shabby. As we climbed the stairs, so many emotions swirled about me—like ghosts. For a moment, I sensed the presence of my brother Mason, who never came back from the war. Then I entered the bedroom while Daddy waited outside."

Despite not wanting to cry, tears slid down my cheeks. I gasped and bent over, resting my head on my arms, ashamed of the emotional display. "Mama was unrecognizable. She barely made a bump under the covers. When she was young, she had the most luxuriant strawberry-blond hair, but it had turned white—and sparse. That was so hard to see."

Recovering a bit, I sat up. "But her eyes were the same, that amazing emerald color. They bored into me, questioning." I studied Jane. "I could tell she was wondering if I had forgiven her. So, I rushed to the bed, kneeling beside her, and told her I had."

Jane nodded slowly. "Wow. I'm glad you had the chance."

Sighing, I continued. "I stayed two days. We had our moment, and for that, I am grateful. At dawn on the final day, something told me to go to her room. I climbed right into the bed with her, held her close, and told her how sorry I was. I confessed that my life had gone off the rails for a long time, but I was doing well now. She patted my hand and hushed me. I don't think she was capable of speech at that point. For an hour, she rested in my arms. Then I heard her struggling for breath. I called for Daddy, and he and my brothers rushed in. A few minutes later, she was gone."

Silence descended. Regret sat in my throat like a lump I couldn't swallow. My "therapist" was giving me space, I figured. "I do want to get through this saga today, but if you have questions, let me have them."

"Just a couple if you're up for it."

I lifted my chin. "Shoot."

"You said you stayed two days. Did you go to the funeral?"

I shredded the tissues in my hand. "I did not."

Jane's astonished look gave me notice I'd better explain. "Don't judge me. While my daddy was kind, my brothers were another story, cold and remote." I shivered. "Like the South Pole. I shouldn't have been surprised because I hadn't gone to Mason's memorial service, but it was clear I wasn't welcome."

"Have you stayed in touch with them?"

"Only my daddy. We still write, and I call him from time to time. Travis runs the place now. He married my old friend Clare, and she treated me like a pariah too. Let me tell you, that hurt." I met Jane's eyes.

"I'm sure it did."

"Jace built himself a little cottage on the ranch, and he works the cattle with Travis. Dylan moved out of state long ago, although he returned for the funeral just as I was leaving."

Jane looked uncomfortable and shifted in her chair. "Change of subject—I'm curious about Alain. Did you ever hear from him again? Find out what happened to him?"

"No."

"That's it? A one-word answer? We're not going to make much progress if you shut down like that."

"I have nothing to add. I was a child. With the war, what could I have done?"

"And after?"

My mouth trembled. "I only knew his name and didn't even know how to spell 'Morseau.' Still not sure."

Jane flushed. "Oh. I see. Didn't mean to harangue you. Just wondered if you ever had any closure."

"Well, now you don't have to wonder." I stared past her shoulder.

"Looks like I touched a nerve."

"Not a nerve, just an old, old wound that scarred over a long time ago."

"Lauren, that wound is still tender, even after all these years."

"Until last night, it wasn't. Then Brett walked back into my life, and my checkered past reared its ugly head. I need to decide what to do about him. You could have knocked me over with a feather when he turned up out of the blue yesterday, after everything I put him through."

"We'll talk about Brett in a minute. Forgive me, but I'm intrigued by your story—and Aunt Imogene. She sounds like quite the character. Are you still in touch?"

"Once in a while, I get a phone call when she's home in Manhattan. And then there are the postcards she sends as she travels the world, often with her latest lover." A smile tugged at the corners of my mouth. "At seventy-six, she's still a pistol."

"From what you told me, she sure sounds unconventional."

"You don't know the half of it. But Imogene treated me well, despite her flamboyance and occasional lack of thinking through her actions. And she has a good heart. When I lived in New York, I witnessed the strong bond she and Vandine shared."

"Tell me more."

"From what I saw, Vandine was more like a mother than a housekeeper. Her daughter Pearl was just a little older than Imogene, and the girls grew up much like sisters."

Jane's eyebrows shot up. "Manhattan wasn't the Jim Crow South, but race relations were still difficult in those years, weren't they?"

"Maybe elsewhere, but not in the Babcock house. When Pearl graduated high school, Imogene prevailed upon her father to pay for Pearl's business college. She became a great success, opening a women's clothing shop in Harlem. Over time, they had three locations and employed dozens of women. The two still travel together. In fact, I think they're on a Mediterranean cruise as we speak."

"I see what you mean about Vandine—and Pearl—being family."

"Yes. In 1974, Vandine passed away at the age of ninety, and Imogene was inconsolable. She and Pearl had nursed her for days, one of them always at her bedside. They both lost a mother."

Silence fell again. The theme of motherhood was inescapable and fraught with significance for both of us.

Jane spoke first. "One more question. I was fascinated by your relationship with Harold. Did you stay in touch after you left Manhattan?"

"Oh, yes. He was a dear friend throughout the years. I lost touch during the worst of my alcoholism, but we always reconnected. I sent him an airline ticket to come to Austin for the opening of the co-op. We had a marvelous visit, but that was the last time I saw him. His partner Tom wrote to me a few months later to tell me Harold had passed away. By the time the letter arrived, it was too late to go to the funeral." I clutched the tissues, willing myself not to break down again. "He meant a lot to me. His humor and sunny disposition never faltered when I needed him most. He was a joy to know."

Delilah broke the spell of my recollection, yowling like a tiny jungle beast. Jane struggled to her feet. "Oh, it's past Delilah's lunchtime."

I stood and stretched my spine.

Jane groaned. "I wish I could stretch like that. I'm just starting to show, and already I'm feeling awkward."

"You're showing? Where? And you awkward? I highly doubt it."

Jane snorted. "Watch me. I've been bumping into everything in sight."

I glanced at my watch. "We haven't even touched on the subject of Brett. There are years of trials and tribulations I have to unload before you help me decide what to do about tomorrow."

"Can you bring me up to speed in an hour or so? Let me feed this little bitty girl." Jane picked up the kitten. "Come on. After all that talking, you might need some nourishment."

"Well, you're right about that."

In the kitchen, Jane opened a can of smelly cat food and scooped a portion into a tiny dish. Delilah followed her to the laundry room, where the kitten ate her meals. Jane returned, breezed up to the sink, and washed her hands. "What can I get you?"

"A yogurt, if you have it."

"Sure do. Plain or vanilla?"

"Plain."

Jane handed me the carton and a spoon. "I have some grape Crystal Light. Want a glass?"

"Grape? Well, I'll try it."

"If it's good enough for Linda Evans, it's good enough for me. No sugar."

I shuddered. "I've seen the commercials. Aerobics, leotards, and leg warmers. I'm sure it's absolutely delicious."

She poured us two tall glasses, and we settled at the breakfast room table.

Between bites, I relayed the next part of my saga: the years in Dallas, my too-short marriage to Ben, how I devolved into a drunken, promiscuous woman, and Imogene's suggestion I return to Manhattan.

Jane listened, and her face revealed a deep empathy for my history. I expected nothing less.

"I had a very brief, very foolish marriage to Michael Goldfein. The denouement was a shock. Found him in bed with a dominatrix right after returning from our honeymoon. He got a Nevada divorce, and I got a juicy check."

Jane's eyes widened. "A dominatrix? How old were you at that point?"

"Twenty-four."

"What then?"

"I took the train back to Dallas after a mere five months in Manhattan. No real reason except I knew the city. I met Brett at my job at the Dallas Advertising League."

"And sparks flew?"

I laughed. "Nothing like you and Joshua. Actually, not at all—at first. I had sworn off romance and was trying to curtail my drinking, so, un-characteristically, I took it slow. But, from the start, I lied to Brett. Lies of omission and plenty of the other kind." I bit my lip. "I was never honest with him."

"When did you marry?"

"1949. I'd known him for two years by then. We worked together, but Brett had ambitions to open his own advertising shop. I wasn't sure there was a place for me, or even if I wanted one. I had my nest egg and planned to have my own business one day too. Never told Brett about the money, never offered to help him."

"Why not?"

"Good question. Maybe because I was holding back. Since all I did was lie and drink too much, my heart told me I didn't deserve him. And let me tell you, Brett was a drinker too. He could really put away the bourbon and ginger, but he never missed work or seemed to have a hangover. Our nightly cocktail hour rolled off his back while I circled the drain. Then I got pregnant."

Jane couldn't hide her shock. "Oh, Lauren. What happened?"

I pushed my empty yogurt cup aside. "I lost the baby at five months. And they removed my uterus." The words fell like bitter tears.

We sat in silence. Jane's hand cradled her belly in a protective gesture. I could imagine what was going through her mind.

"I'm so very sorry."

"Water under the bridge." My vision blurred. "Brett had been so excited about the baby. I knew I had to let him go—for his own good."

Jane smacked the table and glared at me. "What?"

"Actually, I drove him away." Unable to withstand Jane's glower, I hung my head. "He resisted, wanted to stay with me, but after my failure as a woman, after all my lies, it was apparent I was incapable of maintaining a marriage."

"Lauren, that's just plain wrong. I'm shocked."

"You sound judgmental. I didn't expect that."

"Judgmental? Where was *your* judgment? Don't you see that what you did was so hurtful, so unnecessary, so cruel, so, so...selfish! I can't believe he came to see you after what you did."

"Neither can I." My heart hurt from Jane's disapproval. I didn't have a clay foot left to stand on. "What should I do? We have a dinner date tomorrow."

"Let's go back to my office." Jane stood and led me and Delilah to the sunroom. We seated ourselves, and I poured out the rest of my story. How

I changed careers, moved to Austin, and after much struggle, achieved lasting sobriety in 1961.

Once more, silence descended. Just to have something to do, I fiddled with my bracelets. "There's something I've wondered about. Did the morphine turn on some synapses in my brain that led to my alcohol addiction? I don't think I really craved liquor until after...the twilight sleep."

Jane's clipped voice didn't hold a shred of warmth. "Neurobiology isn't my field, but I've read some recent articles about research in this area. A discarded theory from the seventies is receiving attention. But let's be practical. Would the cause of your addiction matter for our purposes? After becoming sober, you need to focus on today and your behaviors. Although, at some point, we should talk about your proclivity for burning bridges."

Darned if she didn't sound like a college professor. "You're right. I had a heck of a journey for twenty years, but I'm sober and want to stay that way."

"Yes, and we do that through rigorous honesty, exactly as you pointed out to me just last year!" Jane grimaced, then rose. With that zinger, she hurried from the room. "Another potty break." Delilah didn't follow but padded over to me and meowed.

Frozen in fear for my silk dress, I held the kitten at bay, waiting for Jane to return and rescue me. A few minutes later, Jane entered the room and saw my dilemma. She smirked, swooping up Delilah. "Come here, baby. Leave Lauren alone."

Wondering if Jane would ever respect me again, I stood and gathered my bag and wrap. "Well?"

"Well, what?"

"Do I keep my dinner date?"

"I think it's only fair to Brett that you do. One meal doesn't commit you to anything. I know you have regrets about how you treated him, so this is a perfect opportunity to make amends."

The truth of Jane's words struck me like a blow to the solar plexus and reinforced the necessity of making direct amends. "I'm aware, but what I did was so egregious, I'm not sure where to start. The situation—and the man—has me rattled."

"Tough stuff." Jane's lips twisted.

"Yes. I'll think on what to say to him. Pray on it."

"Report back."

"Sure will. Now get back to that dissertation. It ain't gonna type itself."

Chapter Twelve

THE BRETT DILEMMA

While dressing for dinner with Brett, my emotions got the better of me. As I applied a last spritz of Arpège, my image blurred in the mirror. Brett had given me a bottle of Lavin scent on our first anniversary, and I'd used it ever since. An omen? Tears threatened. After a few calming breaths, I hurried to repair my makeup. Didn't know if I was crying out of misplaced self-pity or for the harm I'd caused him. Was Jane right? Was I a selfish fool for leaving him? Table that thought. If I went down that rabbit hole, I'd never survive our dinner.

I had amends to make. When I first worked the steps with Helen all those years ago, my indirect amends to Brett consisted of treating the men in my life with honesty. But I had to wonder, was it honesty or just a function of being emotionally unavailable? Where did that come from? Was I finally gaining insight into why I was alone at the tender age of sixty-one?

That evening, I would sit across from the man I'd grievously harmed. My lies were legion. If I confessed it all, how would he react? I wasn't certain how to approach it and had mixed feelings about atoning for my sins in public. Funny how I used a religious connotation to couch my thoughts. Except for funerals, I hadn't set foot in a church since my youth in Mineral Wells. Not that I didn't have a deep belief in God, I just lacked the patience for the interpretation of His Word by fallible humans. And I knew how fallible humans were—I was looking at one in the mirror.

Once satisfied I had the tears under control, I drove to Jeffrey's, one of Austin's premier restaurants. The valet took my car, and I threw my shoulders back and strode into the restaurant. Brett's face broke out into a huge smile when he saw me. His right eye glistened, the other hidden behind the black patch.

My throat clutched. I moved forward into his arms, couldn't help myself. After a hug, Brett stepped back and gripped my hands. "You're gorgeous. Always were a looker."

I knew my cheeks were red and not only from the compliment. The strength of Brett's embrace primed my muscle memory and a few other memories too. "Thank you."

We were seated at a corner table and presented with menus. "What would you like to drink?" the waiter asked.

"Club soda with lime," I answered.

"Make that two." If the waiter was disappointed we didn't order alcoholic beverages, he didn't show it.

Brett set his menu aside. "Glad you came. Wasn't sure you'd show up."

"I wasn't either, but here I am."

An uncomfortable silence descended. Guess we were each waiting for the other to speak, and I wasn't about to start. Gazing across the table became awkward, so I busied myself with my napkin. The waiter returned with our drinks and to take our order. Could he sense the tension coming off me in waves?

Certainly, Brett did. "Can you come back in a minute?" he asked the waiter, who nodded and receded into the dim room.

Brett reached for my hand, and I let him take it. "Darlin', just relax and enjoy the meal. If you ain't in the mood to talk, we can do that later. Now, have you figured out what you want to eat? 'Cause I'm starving."

Despite my misgivings, my lips formed a smile. I started with a Caesar salad, and Brett chose the *foie gras*. For the entrée, I selected the scallops while Brett decided on the ribeye. I passed on the dinner rolls, but Brett dug in.

During the first course, I made small talk about Austin and how much I enjoyed living there. Brett listened as if I were revealing the secrets of the sages.

He took the last bite of *foie gras* and patted his mouth with the napkin. "Got me a little apartment downtown, right around the corner from the Paramount Theatre."

"You rented an apartment?" Aware that my voice rose in disbelief, I forked a bite of salad into my mouth to shut myself up.

Brett picked up on my astonishment. "Why're you surprised? Told you I had no plans to go back to Dallas. Sold my business, sold my house, kept my truck, and I'm gonna enjoy gettin' to learn my way around this town. Might could be I know someone who can give me a tour."

I swallowed my well-chewed mouthful and stared at him. His grin lit up his face and dragged me back to a time when he filled my world. "Who?

The smile fell from his face, and he hung his head, staring down at his plate.

I'd hurt him—again. "Sorry, Brett. That was plain mean."

He raised his head, and I found myself looking into his right eye like I used to. When we first met, it took a few embarrassing interactions before I mastered meeting his gaze and not staring at the patch. Falling back into old habits felt natural. It felt right.

His steak arrived, preceded by a waft of deliciousness. He coaxed me to take a bite.

After I finished a tiny piece, I said, "Excellent."

Brett ate with enthusiasm. With my stomach in knots, I picked at my food. He noticed and stopped eating. "Somethin' wrong with the scallops?"

"No, darling." I dropped my fork, realizing my slip. Brett's only reaction was a smile.

Grateful Brett didn't comment, I took a bite of the delicious seafood. Why was I falling back into our old ways so quickly? It seemed absurd to feel so comfortable with him after all those years.

We finished our entrees in strained—at least on my part—silence. Once the waiter had cleared our plates and brought dessert menus, Brett asked if I wanted coffee.

"Decaf, please."

Brett held up two fingers. The waiter nodded and left. I pretended to study the dessert menu until the waiter returned with two steaming cups. "I'll give you folks a little time to decide on dessert."

"Thanks," Brett answered. He reached for my hand. "What're you doin' tomorrow?"

"No plans." I wasn't about to let him know I had to complete my taxes because of him. I'd never confess my inability to focus on much of anything since he walked into my office two days ago.

He picked up his coffee cup. "How 'bout that tour?"

"What do you want to see?"

"Your place."

Despite my inner turmoil, I chuckled. "Does that line work for you?"

"Don't know. Never tried it before." He ducked his head and hid his smile.

I glanced around the restaurant. "Well, this is your lucky day."

He sat up straight, eyebrows raised. "Really?"

"We need to talk. But not here. Follow me home."

"What about dessert?

"Really?" I shook my head and grinned.

"Check, please."

On the drive to my place in Zilker, I had a few minutes to evaluate the evening. Did Brett think I was going to sleep with him? Had I been suggestive? Not that I wasn't horny. It had been a while. Six months ago, my latest lover, Max, moved to Boise, Idaho, of all places. So, I was vulnerable.

Brett's gigantic F 250 truck stayed on my tail across the river and up Barton Boulevard. I turned onto Spofford and pulled into the drive, my ex-husband right behind me.

When we entered my mid-century home and I flipped the light switch, Brett whistled. The slate floors, vaulted ceiling, and soaring stone fireplace always impressed my guests.

We stepped through the dining room into the living space. "Is that a pool out there?" Brett tipped his head toward the floor-to-ceiling glass doors.

The lighted pool glowed an inviting aqua, but this time of year, it was too chilly to take a dip. Not that I intended to do so.

"Sure is."

"Looks long enough to do laps. You swim?"

"Sure do."

Brett raised an eyebrow. "Woman of few words. Remember, *you* said we needed to talk. So, talk."

In return, I raised my own eyebrows and gestured at the couch. He sat and patted the cushion to his right.

I settled in the leather chair across from him and watched his face reflect his disappointment. "Would you like some water or tea?"

"Nope. I'm fine."

Unable to meet his gaze, I began. "Brett, I owe you amends." Then I ran right out of steam.

"That you do." My heart tugged at his rueful half-smile. "Why'd you leave? Broke my heart, you know."

With my eyes stinging, I plowed ahead with my oft-rehearsed speech. "I failed you as a woman—"

Brett jumped to his feet. "Hold it right there! That's not true. We could've gone on, made it work." He knelt on the floor before me and took hold of my hands.

I shook my head, choking back tears. "Maybe, but I didn't think so at the time. I've made other...mistakes besides bearing a child. I just couldn't bear to tell you. And then there was the drinking."

He released my hands, took out his handkerchief, and handed it to me. "Might need another one for me." Then he stood, pulled me to my feet, and led me to the couch to sit beside him.

For once, I let him lead me. "Words can't express how sorry I am for what I did. I ran from my problems instead of facing them. You'd think I'd be more mature at twenty-eight, but there you go."

His arm cradled me, and I sank into the warmth and comfort of his body. "It takes what it takes, as they say in AA."

We sat like that for several minutes. I broke the connection because the intimacy was too easy, too fast. Then I thought back to what I told Brett at the store. Did I really like my life the way it was?

In my heart, I knew my amends were not complete, but my mind jumped to the obvious question: did I want to start over, renew our bond? My body said "yes," but my brain said, "slow down." After my session with Jane, I wondered if I was even capable of a real relationship.

"I'm going to make some mint tea. Want a cup?"

"Sure. I'd even drink mint tea if I can drink it with you." His grin stretched his cheeks.

I rose and headed for the kitchen. "Be right back."

"Let me help." Brett trailed me and stood close while I filled the kettle. I had hoped to have a minute to figure out a way to end the evening because I sorely needed to regroup and consider my next move.

When the tea was ready, he took his cup to the kitchen table. I sat across from him.

He sipped and puckered his lips. "Delightful."

I laughed. "You don't have to drink it."

"Good."

"Thank you for a lovely dinner, Brett."

"You're very welcome, my love."

I dropped my cup, and hot liquid flowed across the table and onto the floor. "Stop it! I'm not your love." Rushing to the counter, I grabbed towels from a drawer and mopped up the table.

"I'll give you a hand." Brett grabbed a towel and blotted the floor. I snatched it from him, stalked to the laundry room, and threw them all in the washer. When I turned back, he blocked my way.

I folded my arms and hissed at him. "Please move."

"Nope."

"Brett, I mean it. Let me through. And I would like you to leave."

He stepped toward me but didn't touch me.

Did I want him to? I was torn.

"You sure about that?"

I couldn't look him in the eye. "Yes, I'm sure."

"No tour?"

"No tour."

"All right, then. I'll go." He turned to leave, then glanced back over his shoulder. "But I'm not givin' up on us."

With that, he strode to the front door. I trailed him at a distance and threw the deadbolt after he'd gone. Then I sank to the floor in a puddle of guilt, self-reproach, and regret.

The next morning, I woke from a fitful sleep with a headache. Was it too late to rekindle the relationship I'd had with Brett? Most likely. But I was surprised at the tug I felt when I embraced him, and, if I was truthful, it was a whole lot more than a tug. Loneliness plagued me. When I considered my affairs over the years, I couldn't name a man I truly missed. Every relationship had been superficial. Only about the sex. Why was that? Had I been missing Brett the whole time? I recalled thinking of him when I watched the teleplay and, years later, the movie *Days of Wine and Roses.* Like the men in the films, he tried to help me with my drinking. If I wandered down the path of what might have been had I stayed, I would go mad. How could I be sober for twenty-four years and as clueless as I apparently was?

I stumbled into the bathroom and avoided my image in the mirror as I brushed my teeth. When I made eye contact with the fool in the looking glass, I hung my head.

"Suck it up, buttercup," I mumbled and dressed for work. I'd make a pot of coffee when I got to the store.

I grabbed my bag and opened the door to find Brett's truck angled across the driveway. I wanted to retreat inside and crawl back into bed but realized how ridiculous that would be. Boundaries needed to be set, and I was the woman to set them. Storming outside with the intention of berating him, I approached the cab of the gigantic vehicle.

He rolled down his driver-side window and offered me a cup of coffee from Flipnotics, my favorite coffee spot.

Outraged, I almost slapped it out of his hand but restrained myself and refused to take it from him. "Move. Your. Truck."

Brett shook his head and withdrew his offering. "Yes, ma'am."

I stalked back to my car, in no mood to deal with him after my sleepless night and gnawing guilt. As I drove across the river, I vacillated between anger and acknowledging the absurdity of the situation. When I checked the rearview mirror, his truck loomed, and I floored my car. My emotions were all over the place, and I believed Brett sensed my vulnerability.

The wheels of my Mercedes squealed as I pulled into the alley behind Cornucopia. I slammed the gearshift into park and bolted into the back door before Brett could get out of his truck. If he knocked, I wouldn't let him in, and I prayed he wouldn't enter the store and cause a scene. What were we? A couple of teenagers?

I got right to work making coffee and dug into the tax filing but couldn't concentrate. Hadn't been able to focus since Brett resurfaced in my life, and that was why I had to work on a Saturday. My ears were tuned to pick up the rumble of his voice, and I had to admit I was kind of disappointed when he didn't appear.

Just before noon, I finished the taxes, put on my jacket, and headed out to an AA meeting.

The meeting brought me no peace. I sat through it and tried to listen but couldn't bring myself to share. I drove home dissatisfied, far from serene, and hungry.

Rummaging in the fridge, I found a yogurt that hadn't expired and sat down to a lonely meal. For someone who owned a food store, my shelves were bare.

The phone rang, and I leapt to answer it.

Jane said, "I thought I told you to report back about your date with Brett."

"Hello to you too."

"Hello. Well?"

"We had dinner and came back to my place."

"What? Don't tell me—"

I gasped. "Oh, no, nothing like that. I didn't want to make amends in public. Our evening ended when I kicked him out for being forward."

"Really? How forward?" Jane's voice held a smile.

"He wants us to try again, but I just don't think I have it in me. Not that I'm not horny as hell with Max moving away."

"Lauren, I don't think it's about horniness. You never remarried after Brett. And in all the time I've known you, you never let a man get close. To me, Brett's return seems like Kismet. Whether you knew it or not, you were waiting for him to come back to you."

"Oh, posh!" How did she do that—get inside my innermost thoughts?

Jane chuckled. "Don't discount the possibility. Surely, it's crossed your mind."

I almost dropped the phone. "Well, yes."

"I knew it!"

"You don't have to sound so smug."

"I'm not smug. Just think you might want to consider Brett's offer. Have you been to a meeting lately?"

"Actually, I just got back from one." I sank into a kitchen chair. "Didn't get any serenity, so I'm going to the six o'clock at Westlake. Want to join me? We can grab a bite afterward."

"Don't mention eating. I've had morning sickness all day. So, my dinner will be a few saltines if I can stomach them. Joshua has been hovering. He needs some attention. Raincheck?"

"Sure." I hung up, disappointed. Then I called my sponsor, Helen. It was high time I did.

I told her about Brett's shocking reappearance in my life and how I was thunderstruck, unable to cope, at a loss, and various other cliches.

"Are you done?" Helen's dry voice told me she was singularly unimpressed with my news.

"I guess so," I said.

"Well, you definitely need a meeting. Pick me up at 5:45. I'm in the mood for Mexican. How about Trudy's?"

"Sounds good."

At the age of eighty-five, Helen no longer drove in the evening but picking her up was no burden after all she'd done for me over the years. Lately, she appeared frail and had started to use a cane for walking. It hurt to see her decline, and I dreaded the day I would lose her. On the way to her apartment, I got a case of nerves, knowing she'd hold me to account for my past treatment of Brett—and my recent treatment too.

Pulling into the drive, I beeped the horn, then got out and opened the car door for Helen. She lowered herself slowly into the low-slung seat, refusing my assistance. "I'm not dead yet, Lauren. Go on and get in."

As always, I obeyed her. Helen knew my history—most of it, anyway—since she had been my sponsor since I got sober in 1961. I wracked my brain for how detailed I'd been when I told her about leaving Brett. Probably not very. "Rigorous honesty," a guidepost for AA members, appeared on my mental marquee as if to mock me. Then I sobbed aloud.

"Better tell me what happened."

I confessed my callousness and ill-treatment of Brett, fully disclosing every detail.

Helen listened and refrained from comment until we neared our destination. "You have work to do."

When we pulled into the parking lot at Westlake, several members, who had been waiting on the porch, wandered over to my car. Concern could be seen on the faces of those who knew Helen. Big, burly Murray, a young newcomer to the program, helped Helen alight without her objection. She had a soft spot for him.

As the clock closed in on the hour, we took seats near the front of the room. The comforting ambiance and familiar setting helped me relax.

Then Brett strode in and sat next to me. My jaw dropped. How could he? I brought myself up short. Deep breaths, I told myself, deep breaths. I ignored him, and he didn't intrude.

The meeting began with the usual readings. That night I concentrated on every word of "How It Works." Had I completely given myself to the program? Even after twenty-four years of sobriety, I felt like a fraud. I hadn't had a drink of alcohol in all that time, but my feeble amends and lack of honesty about my past behavior were gnawing at my soul.

Helen nudged me in the ribs when the meeting opened for members to speak. "Not tonight. Brett's here!" I whispered. She leaned past me to take a look, then patted my hand.

"My name is Brett, and I'm an alcoholic. Through the grace of God, I've been sober for fifteen years."

"Hi, Brett," the crowd intoned.

"Hi, y'all. First time here. I recently moved to town from Dallas. Like what I've heard so far, so I'll be darkening all y'all's door again. That's it."

"Thanks, Brett."

During Brett's comments, I remained silent. Then a memory intruded, and I almost laughed. At a recent meeting, a female newcomer had grumped, "My ex is messing with my serenity." While no one messes with one's serenity unless one allows it, I understood her sentiment.

At the meeting's close, I pointedly turned away from Brett and nudged Helen to the other side of the room to join the circle for the final prayer.

"Dang," Brett muttered. But he didn't follow.

That left me standing across from him as we recited the "Our Father." I stared at my boots but felt his eye on me. With our joined hands bobbing up and down, we chanted, "Keep coming back. It works if you work it!"

For sure, I knew I had to keep coming back because, as Helen informed me, I had work to do.

Brett shouldered his way through the crowd and greeted me. "Well, hey there, Lauren. Good to see you. And who is this lovely lady with you?"

Helen's eyes crinkled with pleasure. "I'm Helen, Lauren's sponsor. Welcome to our group. I hope we'll be seeing a lot more of you."

"Count on it."

"We're going out for dinner. Would you like to join us?" Helen beamed at Brett and ignored me.

I stiffened at Helen's invitation, but before I could say anything, Brett accepted with a hearty, "You bet."

Struggling to appear unruffled, I nodded. "You can follow my car. We're headed over to Trudy's."

I had a few choice words for Helen, and the drive would give me a chance to vent. But, before I could say anything, Helen said, "Don't even start. Being kind and accepting of newcomers is the AA way. My, my, Brett sure is a big, strapping, handsome fellow. And that patch gives him a rather swashbuckling air. I look forward to getting to know him."

"Swashbuckling?"

"Yes, quite dashing."

I had to laugh. "Sounds like you're describing Errol Flynn. Still a fan?"

Helen shot me a sideways glance. "Plenty sassy tonight."

"I will be as gracious as can be. Just watch."

"Oh, I'll be watching."

"I bet you will," I muttered, hoping she didn't hear.

"I heard that."

We parked in the nearly full lot and watched as Brett maneuvered his big truck into a parking space.

"Might as well walk in together," Helen said.

There was a short wait, and I buried my nose in the latest *Austin Chronicle* for fifteen minutes. Brett and Helen chatted like they'd known each other for years.

"What's good here, Helen?" Brett asked.

"I always have the fish tacos, but the enchiladas and fajitas are good too."

"Gettin' mighty hungry, I have to confess."

Not wanting to engage, I kept silent.

A minute later, the hostess called our party, and we were escorted to a booth. Helen slid in and patted the seat for Brett to sit next to her, leaving me to stare at him for the whole meal. I felt like a child being manipulated into an unwanted social situation.

Brett smiled and took his menu. "Got any specials tonight?" he asked the waitress. She rattled off several items and said, "Let me give y'all a minute to decide. What do y'all want to drink?" Katy, as her name tag read, wrote down our order for three unleaded coffees and strolled away.

Chips and salsa appeared shortly after, along with three steaming mugs of decaf. Brett and Helen helped themselves to the chips, but I'd lost my appetite. Knowing I'd best improve my attitude if I wanted to get through the evening's torture, I smiled and said, "I know what I'm having. Have you two decided?"

The waitress wandered back to the table and took our order for three fish taco dinners, and after she left, silence fell like a shroud.

Even though I tried, I couldn't think of a neutral topic of conversation. My brain was otherwise occupied, living in the land of might-have-beens and what-the-hells. I'd planned to have Helen to myself, so there I sat, like a tongue-tied fool.

Brett munched on chips and nodded his approval. "Good salsa."

"At my age, I have to go easy. A little goes a long way," Helen said.

"How long have you known Lauren?" Brett asked. "I only ask because she seems to have misplaced her voice."

Helen patted Brett's arm and chuckled. "You're right about that. Very unlike our Lauren."

Although I cringed inside, I maintained a neutral expression. *Our Lauren? God grant me the serenity—*

"I first met our Lauren at an AA meeting at the Bouldin group. She was newly sober and sorely in need of a sponsor," Helen said.

"And you've been her sponsor ever since?"

"I sure have."

Brett's brow creased. "Then you know our history."

"Well, I thought I did." Helen pursed her lips.

"Hmmm." Brett glanced at me and rubbed his chin. I widened my eyes and sipped my coffee.

Almost as a reprieve, our food arrived. The sooner we ate, the sooner I could get home. Unfortunately, Helen was a slow eater and always had dessert.

Though I should have been hungry, and the fish tacos were superb as usual, I could barely swallow. I'd get a to-go container and hope for the best when I reheated them.

Helen asked Brett about his Dallas AA group. When he told her the story of our first AA meeting, I wanted to sink into the ground. "Excuse me." I dashed to the restroom. How long could I stay there before they came looking? After freshening my lipstick and tucking a few stray curls into my updo, I lifted my chin and marched back to the booth of doom.

Brett and Helen had finished their meals. The waitress came to clear the table, and I asked for a to-go box. "Sure. What can I get y'all for dessert?"

"Just decaf for me," I said.

Helen and Brett decided to share a sopapilla sundae. I almost groaned out loud and promised myself I'd stop back—alone—and order one.

Checking my watch, I was surprised to find it was only eight-thirty. I sat back and watched the bustle of the busy restaurant, mentally ticking off the minutes and surreptitiously stealing a glance at my wrist to check the time. Did the minute hand even move?

The lavish sundae arrived, and my two tablemates oohed and aahed as they shared the dish. I knew I was acting like a sulky teenager but couldn't help it. On some level, I was surprised neither Brett nor Helen pushed more about my lack of participation that evening. It seemed they were letting me stew in my own juices, and stewing I was.

A strained goodbye to Brett in the parking lot left me guilt-ridden, and I dreaded the ride home to Helen's. She started in on me as soon as I shut the car door. "You acted like a petulant child tonight."

"Well, I felt petulant. I wanted to talk to you about this...this...Brett debacle, and you go ahead and invite him to join us. So, I was frosted. Still am."

"Your lack of graciousness and empathy is unlike you."

Helen's words hit their target. She was right. And I was wrong. Damn, that was hard to admit. Maybe I had put myself on my own pedestal, thought too much of myself, but that didn't negate the fact Brett had me struggling for equilibrium. I visualized alternately pulling him close, then shoving him away. I was a mess.

"Are you going to respond or give me the silent treatment too?" Helen's tart voice ended my reverie.

"You're right."

"You don't have to sound so grudging. Humility won't kill you."

"Are you sure?"

Helen chuckled. "Come in for a cup of tea. We'll have that talk."

Driving home, I thought about Helen's wise counsel. She acknowledged my confusion and pain but held me to account. I would have to make direct amends to Brett. The "how" was my dilemma. I pulled into the drive, relieved there was no Ford F250 Supercab on the street. Or was I a tad bit disappointed?

Sunday morning, I dressed in leotard and tights but no legwarmers, leaving them to that *Flashdance* girl, Jane Fonda, and all those perky Crystal Light aerobics people. In my studio, I rolled out my mat and started with The Hundred but had a hard time with The Boomerang and The Shoulder Bridge for some reason. After a good forty-five-minute workout, I staggered into a steaming shower and let the water rinse my sweat away.

It took thirty minutes to dress in a slim sheath and apply makeup before I was ready to face the world—and Brett. Very telling that I strived to look my best before seeing him. At least, I thought I'd be seeing him at the noon meeting. In the kitchen, I brewed a mug of Earl Grey tea and sat at the table overlooking the pool. A slice of rye toast sufficed as a late breakfast. I read a few pages in *As Bill Sees It* to pass the time. At eleven-forty, I left the house and saw his truck behind my car in the driveway.

Hiding my smile, I approached his vehicle. He hopped out and said, "Need a ride to the meetin'?"

"Yes, thank you. I was hoping to see you."

At my words, his face broke out in a grin. "You just made my day." Brett hustled around the front of the truck and opened the door for me. Luckily, there was a step up into the cab.

Before firing up the engine, Brett asked, "Can I buy you lunch after the meeting?"

"That would be lovely."

Brett made the turn onto Barton Springs Road. "I gotta ask, why the change in attitude? Did Helen work you over?"

"Yes, she sure did. Still smarting."

He reached over and patted my hand. "Well, whatever happened, I'm darned glad for your company."

"There's a lot I have to tell you about my past. I seriously doubt you'll want to have anything to do with me after you hear it."

"Ain't gonna happen. The way I look at it, we both have a past, but it's the future that matters. And I'd like to spend the future with you."

Luckily, giving directions saved me from a response. "Turn left on the street after the next light."

Relieved that we'd arrived in the parking lot and our heart-to-heart would have to wait, I reflected that even that short exchange had taken a lot out of me. I watched Brett come around to my door to help me out. We walked into the meeting together, and the buzz of interest from those in attendance made me want to turn right around and leave.

Brett had no such concern, nodding and saying "hey," to just about everyone there. As we took seats near the middle of the room, I steeled my spine.

Murray shared, telling the group about the recovery ranch where he'd achieved sobriety. "Thanks to the good people at the ranch, I got me sixty days sober and real proud of it. And I'm giving back. Every Sunday, I drive out there to volunteer. If anyone is interested in helping out, just let me know."

With Brett present, I decided not to share—again—and listened to each speaker share their experience, strength, and hope. Personally, I had a lot of experience, not much intestinal fortitude given my Brett dilemma, and hoped I would make the right decision about a future with him.

After the final prayer, we joined the other members outside for a little "meeting after the meeting." We begged off an invitation to a group lunch at El Arroyo, or "the Ditch," as locals called it, and headed to Omelettry West on Lake Austin Boulevard.

"They serve breakfast all day, and I'm in the mood for an omelet," I said.

"Whatever you want is fine with me."

Delighted that we snagged the last spot in the small lot, we put our names on the waiting list. Twenty minutes passed quickly as we perused the personal ads in the *Chronicle*, always a source of free entertainment, especially the "Shot in the Dark" section. When we were finally seated and had ordered cheese omelets, the aroma of coffee enticed me to skip my usual Hibiscus iced tea.

"One of these days, I'll take you to Kerbey Lane for pancakes," I said before realizing the implication.

But Brett didn't miss it. Was it possible for him to look any happier? Maybe I better start paying attention to my gut reaction to him. He rubbed his hands together. "Can't wait. Love me some pancakes."

The waiter returned with our omelets, and we chatted amicably while we ate.

"They got some good chow in this town." Brett nodded his appreciation of the food. "By the way, can I get your phone number? It's a little weird to keep showin' up at your house."

"Yes, it is." I dug in my purse for a pen and wrote my number on a napkin.

Brett glanced at the paper and smiled, tucking it in his shirt pocket. "Got my line hooked up, so here's mine." He jotted his number on another napkin and handed it to me. "Don't lose it, now."

I merely nodded and smiled. Once again, I was all over the map on how I felt about him. The very idea I presumed to give other AA members advice stunned me. Recalling how sure I had been when I counseled Jane about facing her past a year ago made me feel like a phony. Hoping none of my uncertainty showed on my face, I finished my lunch.

I insisted on paying for the meal. Brett had been generous, and I wanted him to know I had means. And that I was independent—even if I might not turn out to be.

On the drive home, he asked about the recovery ranch he'd heard mentioned at the meeting. "You know, I wouldn't mind gettin' involved with that. Whereabouts did that fella say it was located?"

"It's about twenty miles south on I-35, but you really should talk to Murray about it. He knows all the details."

"I'll do that."

He pulled into the driveway and turned to me. "When will I see you again?"

"I'm not sure, Brett. I've got a business to run."

"Well, ya gotta eat lunch. Can I pick you up tomorrow?"

I shook my head. "I don't normally eat out every meal. I'm about restauranted out."

Brett frowned. "You're in retreat from me. I can feel it."

"Look, I don't know where this is going, so I've got some thinking to do. Please give me some time."

His mouth turned down. "How much time you need?"

Unable to meet his gaze, I said, "I'm not sure."

"Okay, then." He got out of the truck and came around to let me out. "We haven't had that talk about our pasts. Give me a ring when you're ready. But for now, I'm gonna back off just like you want." His puppy-dog look didn't pierce my armor, and I didn't ask him in. Once inside, I peeked through the blinds, watching his slumped posture as he got in the Ford and drove off. I planned to follow the advice I gave others and write down my thoughts to get some clarity.

Chapter Thirteen

TRAPPED-DINNER AT JANE'S

Sunday evening, I sat in my home office with a cup of tea gone cold, crumpled pages covered with scribbles from my restless and incoherent mind littering the desk and floor. Glancing at the clock, I noted I'd been at the frustrating task for five hours.

With no resolution to the Brett dilemma despite the pro and con lists and introspection, I gave up and got ready for bed. My emotions tumbled, spinning from sadness over my long-ago losses to fear of a future with—or one without—Brett and everything in between. I knew sleep would be elusive, so I picked up the Big Book from my nightstand and read until my eyes fluttered shut.

At 4:05 a.m., I woke from a dream—really a nightmare. Grasping at the wisps of my vision, I shuddered. I had been lying in my coffin wearing my newest Flora Kung silk—the gold one with huge pink hibiscus flowers—with Brett sobbing over my corpse. What deep neurosis did that reveal? Throwing back the covers, I rose and scrounged through my dresser for my swimsuit. It was preposterously cold to dive into the unheated pool, but I did it anyway. Maybe I wanted to feel alive, maybe I wanted to punish myself, maybe I just needed the exercise. I lasted a whole seven minutes. Spent and chilled, I grabbed onto the edge and, with the last of my strength, scrambled up the pool steps and padded into the house to take a hot shower.

Three hours later, I sat at the kitchen table watching the clock hands inch toward 8:00 a.m., when I could decently phone Jane. I dialed her number and breathed a sigh of relief when she answered.

"Good morning, Jane. Can we meet today?"

"Aren't you working?"

"Yes, but I could go in late or leave early."

Joshua's baritone rumbled in the background. "Give me a minute. My hubby is just leaving." I heard a thunk as Jane put the phone down, then listened to their sweet farewell.

A few seconds later, Jane said, "I have an appointment with my advisor at two, but I could run by the store afterward, say about four, four-thirty?"

"That would be wonderful. I've got plenty to keep me occupied, such as the employee holiday schedule. Christmas is just a couple of weeks away."

"See you this afternoon, then." After we hung up, thoughts of Jane and Joshua's happiness ran through my mind. Could Brett and I have that connection again?

At the office, I removed my wrap, put on a pot of coffee, and got right to work on allocating time off. What a relief to have something other than Brett to think about. Christmas fell on a Wednesday, and of course, Cornucopia would be closed, but the numerous requests for holiday leave before and after both Christmas and New Year's presented a problem.

I made a grid of the days and sorted the employees' wishes by longevity. Jolie had asked for an entire week off to visit family in Galveston. Perhaps I could prevail on my evening manager, Shondra, to cover Jolie's hours. Shondra's folks lived in town, and a bonus might sweeten the deal.

While waiting for Jane, I also finished the schedule for January and ordered stock. Satisfied with what I'd accomplished, I stopped by the deli next store for a quick bite. Back at Cornucopia, I shopped for myself, packing a cooler with needed supplies for my larder.

At four-fifteen, Jane knocked on the open office door. When she removed her coat, she revealed a purple jersey drop-waisted dress probably meant to disguise her non-existent belly.

"That dress will last you all the way through your pregnancy. You're swimming in it."

Jane's face reddened. "Have you seen what they call 'maternity wear' these days?"

I nodded. "I'm aware. It's hard to stay fashionable."

My friend sank into one of the guest chairs and sighed. "I can't wait to be done with school."

"I don't blame you. What's next in the process?"

"My advisor scheduled my oral defense before the committee on January 15th. At this point, it's anticlimactic because I know my material backward and forward and sideways." Jane suppressed a yawn, then said, "Typing and retyping the darn thing imprinted every word in my brain. When I close my eyes, I see the pages on my eyelids. How I wish I'd hired someone to do the typing. Live and learn."

Her last words struck a note with me. I'd sure lived, but what had I learned?

With a heavy sigh, Jane said, "The finish line is so close. I just hope there are only minor corrections. I want that award letter before the baby comes." Despite a weak smile, she appeared tired and wan.

"You're looking a bit peaked, so I won't keep you."

"Thanks. Why did you want to see me?"

"I'm stuck."

Jane's brow creased. "How can I help?"

"Before I figure out what to do about Brett, you should have the full picture, so you'll understand my position. Please listen while I spin you the rest of my tale."

"I can do that."

"Would you like some juice or a snack?"

"Just some tea, if you have it."

Once Jane was settled with a mug of hot hibiscus tea, I began. "During the worst of my drinking in Austin, I had quite a few affairs, always short-term, some of which I don't remember."

"I see."

"Not sure you do. Because I couldn't get pregnant, I went a little wild." I told Jane what I could recall about the fifties. In my mind's eye, I flashed on a series of men's faces, all blurry, generic, forgettable. The brief periods of sobriety, the binges, the remorse. Jane refrained from commenting through my confession.

"Really, Jane, it's amazing I'd stayed gainfully employed during those years. My strategy of confining my drinking to the weekends—most of the time—no doubt saved me."

Jane sipped her tea and nodded. Had I rendered her speechless?

"One blessing in those years was my love of music. My fascination started when Imogene introduced me to jazz and blues as a teenager, but I really immersed myself in the scene in Austin."

"You know I'm a rock 'n' roll girl, but I'd adore hearing all about it."

"In the early fifties, Austin was very segregated. UT started admitting black students in 1956, and then things changed when white kids began to frequent the clubs on the East Side. Even though I was in my thirties, I was right there with them. Blues Boy Hubbard at Charlies' Playhouse. Ike and Tina Turner at the Victory Grill."

"Wow! Even I know those names. You saw some of the greats."

"Oh yes, I remember B.B. King and Bobby 'Blue' Bland also played there. Those artists toured all over the South. Can you believe they called it the 'Chitlin' Circuit?'"

Jane's eyes widened. "Well, that wouldn't fly today. Fascinating stuff. And now I know where you got your knowledge of the blues."

I nodded. "Up close and personal is the best way to learn. The energy at those clubs was amazing. Best times I ever had. But the drinking and the promiscuity continued." Guilt bloomed. "It's so shameful to remember."

"Hold that thought. I've got to use the facilities." Jane stood and rushed to my private bathroom.

When she returned, she handed me her empty mug. "I'd love more tea, but better not." She pursed her lips. "If I remember correctly, you once told me you had more notches on your bedpost than the legendary thirteenth-stepper Vaughn."

My face burned as I recalled that statement. "Well, who's counting? After I got sober in 1961, I waited a while before I tried romance again. Kept myself to myself."

"That must have been hard."

"Don't you know it. And when I finally took a lover, I made sure to keep him at a distance. No promises. No strings. Also, I swore I'd never date a man in AA."

Jane tilted her head as she resettled herself in the chair. "Why's that?"

"There was an incident...no, never mind."

"Are you kidding me? Spill."

I looked everywhere but at Jane. "Sometime in the late fifties, sorry, can't be any more precise than that, I tried a different AA group near my apartment. A very handsome man caught my eye. We left in the middle of the meeting and went to his place. He brought out a bottle, and we drank until we passed out. I have no memory of what might have transpired, although I can guess since I woke up naked."

"Oh."

"Yeah. Took me weeks to recover from the shame. Never showed my face there again."

Jane's brow furrowed. "And that ancient—sorry—night's holding you back from seeing Brett?"

"Precisely." I rose and began to pace.

"I think you're just making excuses, using your self-imposed prohibition to push him away."

"Do you now?" I turned to face her.

"Yeah, I do." Jane stood and shrugged into her coat. "Look, the past is the past. Why dwell on it? Don't you think Brett had a sex life after you left?"

Thunderstruck by her words, I realized she was right. "Of course. He must have."

Jane rolled her eyes. "Do you think you two are going to rehash every affair? You need to let all that go if you're going to move on." She headed to the door, then turned back. "I'm exhausted and need to get home. I'd like to meet Brett. Why don't you two come over for dinner this Saturday?"

"What? Why?"

Jane grinned. "Just come around seven."

When I arrived home that evening, I busied myself with the groceries, laundry, a failed attempt at meditation, anything to delay picking up the telephone to call Brett. Finally, all out of distractions, I dialed his number, and he picked up on the first ring.

"Hi, Brett."

"Lauren? That was quick. Couldn't resist my charm, could ya."

Playing along, I chuckled. "You got me."

"I'm so glad you called. Does this mean I have a—"

"Don't jump the gun. I'm calling to invite you to dinner on Saturday."

"You don't have to ask twice."

"Let me finish. My friend Jane and her husband Joshua invited us to their home."

"Who are these folks?"

"Jane is a close friend. I've been her sponsor for years."

"Is her husband in the program too?"

"No. He's a normie but quite supportive. He doesn't keep alcohol in the house. I hope you like beef stroganoff because it's the only thing Jane can cook."

"Love it."

"Well, good. Come by to pick me up around 6:45?"

"Will do. How about lunch one day this week? Or breakfast. Or dinner. Or a snack. Or coffee."

"Quit while you're ahead. See you Saturday." I hung up before he could say another word.

Then I called Helen.

"I'm on my way out, Lauren."

"Just wanted to let you know Brett and I are having dinner at Jane's on Saturday."

Helen chuckled. "And that's what you called about? You're sure in a tizzy over that man. Get your head straight, dear. He won't wait around forever."

With that she hung up, leaving me slightly stunned as I realized she was right.

The week passed too quickly. Saturday morning, I did Pilates for an hour and a half. After I finished, I was exhausted but still tense and figured I would be until that night's dinner was over. In the afternoon, I drove to the florist on Lamar to buy flowers for Jane. Although it was the Christmas season and the shop was full of them, I refused to buy a Poinsettia and settled on a bouquet of gardenias. Once home, I soaked in a tub infused with lavender for an hour, then obsessed about what to wear. Although I'd always been partial to silk, after that nightmare last week featuring my new Flora Kung, I shuddered at the thought of wearing it. Instead, I chose the black velvet Norma Kamali. It had a nice round collar, long sleeves, and was anything but flirtatious.

Should I have warned Brett that we would be under the microscope of not one but two mental health professionals? No, he'd figure it out soon enough. And I'd enjoy watching it.

My nerves gave me fumble fingers, and I couldn't manage my usual updo, so I gave up and wore my hair down. The doorbell chimed just as I was finishing my makeup, and I jumped about a foot.

Forcing myself to walk slowly, I headed to the foyer. When I opened the door, Brett stood there with a huge Poinsettia and an equally large grin.

"Stopped by the florist to get this for our hosts."

"Oh, no. I bought gardenias for Jane."

Brett's smile faded. "Then this is for you. Where do you want it?"

I gestured to the sunroom, just off the living room. "It should do well in there."

Brett placed the plant on the floor and hustled back to the foyer. "Every time I see you, you take my breath away, darlin'."

"A little under-dressed ain't you?"

He glanced down at his jeans and boots. "Ya think so? We're not going to a fancy restaurant. I got a sports coat in the car."

"That'll do."

I reached for my black velvet wrap on the console, and Brett rushed to snug it around me. With the bouquet of gardenias in hand, I embarked on unknown waters.

Ten silent minutes later, Brett parked in the drive at Jane's home. "Nice neighborhood."

"Yes, it is." If I didn't get my nerves under control, my conversation would be as stilted and lackluster as it was since I answered the door.

Brett came around to help me out of his truck and put his arm around me as we approached the house. I didn't pull away.

Joshua answered the door, holding the kitten in his left hand. "Hey, Lauren, get on in here." With a smile, he extended his right hand and said, "You must be Brett."

After the men shook hands and expressed what a pleasure it was to meet each other, Joshua said, "Jane's putting the finishing touches on the stroganoff."

I shrugged out of my wrap, and Joshua reached for it. "Let me take that for you. Just have to put Delilah down." He cradled the kitten as if it were made of porcelain.

Brett held out his hands. "Here, let me take her. Sure is a cute little thing. Listen to her purr."

Our host relinquished the kitten and took my wrap. Girding myself to spend the evening with three cat lovers, I asked, "So, it's true. We're having Jane's specialty?"

Joshua grinned. "Ever since I complimented her on the stroganoff, she makes it every chance she gets. I'm hoping one of these days, she'll learn a new recipe."

We entered the kitchen, and I presented the bouquet to Jane, who buried her nose in the blooms. "Love this scent. Thank you." She turned to Joshua. "Honey, can you put these in water?"

"Sure thing, babe."

I introduced Brett to Jane. "So happy to meet you, Brett. I see you've met Delilah. You can put her on the floor. Hope you like beef stroganoff."

"Sure do. And I brought my appetite."

In the adjacent dining room, Joshua placed the vase of gardenias on the sideboard and poured chilled water into Jane's Lalique crystal goblets.

"Anyone care for a soft drink?" After getting no takers, he rejoined us in the kitchen and drained the noodles while Jane ladled the main dish onto a platter. I carried the salad, Brett brought the rolls to the dining room, and our hosts joined us.

With a gracious gesture, Jane showed us to our seats. She placed Brett and me side by side, with the men facing each other and the women the same. The meal—and inquisition—commenced.

Joshua took the conversational lead. "I hear you're from Dallas, Brett."

"Born and raised. The only time I left was to fight in World War Two."

"Is that how you lost your eye?" Joshua wasn't afraid to address Brett's infirmity.

"Yep. Bastogne. Lost my eye and first wife in that war. 'Dear John' letter caught up to me while I was still in the field hospital."

"Oh, I didn't know." With reddened cheeks, Joshua cast a questioning glance at Jane, as if to ask why she hadn't given him a heads-up.

Jane shook her head and kicked me under the table. Her frown let me know she would have appreciated knowing Brett's story earlier. With my black velvet pump, I nudged back and shrugged.

Joshua leaned forward, apparently determined to keep the conversation moving. "What brings you to Austin?" It looked like Jane hadn't filled her husband in on my dilemma and the ensuing drama.

Brett put down his fork. "Why, the lovely woman sitting right beside me. Lauren's my second wife, and I'm here to reclaim her."

"You make me sound like a lost package." I knew my tone was tart but didn't even try to modulate it.

"Perhaps another topic?" Jane's pained expression registered with me. Regret bloomed. I didn't want to ruin her dinner party.

Casting a disapproving glance at Brett, I said, "Let's not discuss ancient history. Why don't you tell them about your work at the recovery ranch?"

Brett nodded and extolled the accomplishments of the group of men who ran the project. "Finest group of fellas you'll ever meet. Real glad to be a part of it."

"Whereabouts is it?" Jane asked as she passed the rolls.

"Just past Buda, down the interstate. I plan to run out there two, three times a week. I gotta tell you, Jane, this dinner is mighty tasty."

"Thank you, Brett. What do you do at the ranch?"

"Only been there once. Right now, I'm choppin' cedar to clear land for another bunkhouse. Then we can start building."

Joshua chimed in. "That ought to keep you in shape."

"Oh, believe me, I felt every muscle the next day, but it's a good cause, and there sure is a need." Brett took another helping of the entrée. "Lauren didn't tell me much about y'all. How do you pay the bills, Joshua?"

"I'm a psychiatrist specializing in mood disorders."

"Hmm. Interesting." Brett turned to Jane. "Lauren tells me you're finishing up a degree."

"Yes, I'm going to defend my dissertation in January."

"That's darned impressive. What's your topic?"

"Women in recovery, with an emphasis on family history."

Brett directed a sidelong look my way. I smirked and picked up the salad bowl. "Anyone care for more of this delicious salad? Jane, this is the perfect complement to the stroganoff. Very inventive—spinach and strawberries. What kind of dressing is this?"

"Strawberry poppyseed. I'll give you the recipe later. For now, I'd like to learn more about our guest." Jane smiled at Brett. "Lauren tells me you sold your business and your house. I guess that means you plan to stay in Austin."

"Yes indeed."

Well, that ruined my digestion.

Brett buttered another roll. "I'd like to hear about your dissertation."

Perhaps I should have set some ground rules for this gathering, or declined the invitation, or maybe I should relax and enjoy the meal. I faked interest and followed the conversation about Jane's oral defense. With that topic exhausted, silence fell, and our host and hostess looked at each other in consternation.

In a fit of compassion, I bailed out the conversation. "How's your pregnancy going?"

Brett exclaimed, "You're pregnant? I couldn't even tell."

Jane blushed. "It's still early days. I'm not due until late June. This week the morning sickness has abated somewhat. I've read it goes away in the second trimester, so I'm hoping it won't be a worry when I meet with the committee."

Joshua patted Jane's hand. "You'll do wonderfully. I'm really impressed with your dissertation and your typing."

"My typing? Well, after thirty tries, I'm now a pro. Honey, I should have listened to you and hired the job out."

"You finished, and that's what counts." Joshua's tenderness toward Jane was lovely to see.

"Thanks for bearing with me through the process." Jane's voice exuded appreciation. "And for your sage advice."

The couple beamed at each other. True love. Had I ever experienced it? I think I did with Ben so long ago but certainly not with Michael. How I wanted to believe in the headiness of mutual adoration. Had I thrown away the real thing when I left Brett? I turned and caught him watching Jane and Joshua with a wistful expression. He glanced at me, and his smile pierced my armor and my heart. As we finished dinner, I floundered, lost in thoughts of my past failed romances, and I couldn't imagine where Brett's head was at.

Joshua cleared his throat, and everyone turned to him. "I hope you saved room for dessert. Sweetish Hill's finest Italian Crème cake awaits."

Brett insisted on helping Joshua clear the table. While Jane put on a pot of decaf, I brought the dessert plates to the table. How soon after the cake could I end the evening?

A tiny meow caught Brett's attention. "What's the matter, lil bit?" He knelt and reached under the table for Delilah. The kitten relaxed and purred at his touch. Why hadn't I realized Brett was fond of cats? After thirty-three years apart, what did I really know about him?

Facing the history of my ruinous personal life was mighty disconcerting, especially at a dinner party. I needed to regroup. At the age of sixty-one, all I had to show was a grocery store—the total product of all that time. In my heart, I knew I was missing out on so much in life by not allowing a man to get close to me.

While Joshua poured coffee, Jane cut the cake into too-big slices. I picked at my serving and sipped the decaf.

Brett asked Joshua, "Who do you like in the NFC? Think Dallas can win against the Rams?"

"I don't follow professional football, just the college teams."

"Which team?"

"Sooners. I'm from Oklahoma."

"Different conference from the Longhorns."

Jane rolled her eyes and forked a huge bite of cake. "Football."

Grinning, Joshua asked, "And what would you like to discuss, babe?"

"Anything else. Baby names."

My stomach dropped. I excused myself and hurried to the powder room. Jane's pregnancy brought up the saddest event in my history. I was happy for her but watching her go through the process triggered painful memories, memories I thought I'd entombed forever.

When I was seventeen, I refused to even think of names for the baby I birthed. For the first time, I wondered what Evelyn had named my daughter. Staring in the mirror, I tried to picture what that forty-something woman would look like. Had she married? Did she have children? Gracious, I might be a grandmother. Overcome with emotion, I let out a cry, then clamped my hands over my mouth. Where was my "patented veneer of cool?" I thought I was made of sterner stuff.

A knock on the door let me know my outburst had been heard.

"You all right in there?" Brett called.

"Yes. Fine. Just stubbed my toe." Great. Another lie. "Be out in a minute."

I ran my hands under the tap, dried off, took a deep breath, and opened the door. Brett stood there with a question on his face. "Did you really stub your toe?"

Warmth rose in my face, and I knew I was red with embarrassment. "No."

"Was it the baby names that got you spooked?"

I could only nod.

He stepped forward and enveloped me in his arms.

I mumbled into his chest. "I'm happy for her and Joshua, but it brings back our loss. Thought I was past it but apparently not."

"I understand. Even now, I wonder about him, what he might have become."

Pulling away, I gazed at him. "Why didn't you tell me it was a boy?"

Brett's brows drew together. "You didn't know?"

I shook my head. "Not until my six-week post-op checkup."

"Honey, we never talked about it. I remember thinking the topic was off-limits."

Sighing, I took his hand. "It was. And it shouldn't have been." The clatter of dishes brought me back to the dinner party. "Goodness, what will they think of us disappearing like this? We better get back."

"Yeah, you're right."

When we entered the dining room, Jane and Joshua exchanged a look. "Would you like more decaf?" our hostess asked.

"No, thanks. Brett and I are heading out. The meal was delicious." I clutched Brett's hand as I spoke.

Jane glanced at our entwined hands and met my eyes. "So soon?"

Brett cleared his throat. "It was a wonderful evening. Good food and good company. Thank you."

Pushing back from the table, Joshua stood. "Let us see you out." He helped Jane out of her chair.

As we said our goodbyes at the door, I whispered to Jane. "Call me tomorrow. I'll be at home."

The ride back to my place was silent. As he pulled into the drive, Brett asked if I was going to an AA meeting the next day.

"No. I have a few things I'd like to do around the house."

"Need any help?"

"Thanks, but no." My hands clenched and unclenched. I was itching to get out of the truck and burrow into my bed.

"Gonna invite me in?"

I scooted around to face him and took his hands. "Not tonight. My emotions are getting the best of me. Tell you what, I'll call you in a few days, and we'll have that talk."

"All right. But I'm holding you to that. If I don't get a call, I'll hunt you down."

"You won't have to."

Brett helped me out of the truck and walked me to the door. We kissed, and I almost changed my mind about letting him in.

Jane called at 8:30 on Sunday morning, waking me from a dream-filled sleep, featuring, of all things, visions of Brett's and my wedding—and not the one in 1949. Bleary-eyed, I snatched at the bedside phone. "It's your nickel."

"Haven't heard that one in a while. Too early?" Jane asked with a chuckle.

"No. I'm just waking up. My astral body is still out at my wedding to Brett."

"What? Don't tell me. Is he still there? Can you talk or should I try you later?"

"No, he's not here." I sat up and propped the pillows behind my back.

"Joshua and I really like him. We are hoping and praying you get back together."

I yawned. "Might could be we're headed that way."

Jane squealed like a high-school girl. "I'm so happy for you. This is the best news."

"Don't get ahead of yourself. I said might—still have some thinking to do. I'm going to call Helen and see if we can get together."

"That sounds like a good idea."

"Yeah. And here I thought I liked my life just the way it was."

"And now you don't?"

"Bingo."

"Talk later."

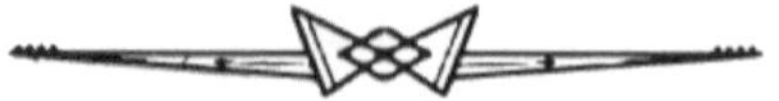

On the way to Helen's, I stopped at Sweetish Hill and bought a selection of pastries, including her favorite—chocolate croissants. Not that I thought the treat would make her go easy on me.

We sat at her kitchen table, a place where I'd bared my soul many times. After our croissants and tea, Helen said, "What's on your mind?"

"Amends. I still haven't had the talk with Brett."

"Why not? No one can do it for you. I haven't seen you this shook up since 1961. How much longer are you going to live this way?" Helen refilled her teacup and mine and peered at me.

I wilted under her steely gaze, felt like a wayward child. And I knew she could keep up that intimidating stare for hours if need be. "As you know. we had dinner with Jane and Joshua last night."

"And?"

That conversational detour didn't take. "They liked Brett."

"So do I, and so do you. Why is this so hard for you?"

"Thirty-three years. How can I fix that?"

Helen leaned forward. "You can't, and you don't have to."

That truth was a big, fat cosmic slap in the face.

Chapter Fourteen

AND THEN WE DANCED

When I got home from Helen's, I watered my plants and fixed a salad for dinner. Rather than going to a meeting, I read a few pages in the *Twelve and Twelve*, seeking inspiration for making direct amends. My mind wandered, returning to the kiss Brett and I shared—a passionate kiss that awakened long-ago memories. With a sigh, I trudged into my exercise room and tried to meditate. No luck. It was ridiculous to keep living in uncertainty, so I bit the bullet and grabbed the phone and dialed.

No answer. Brett was probably at a meeting. Maybe I should have gone too. Two hours later, I called his number again.

When he picked up, I blurted, "I'm ready."

At first, he was silent. Then his voice shook as he said, "So am I. I'll be there in ten minutes."

"No. Tomorrow. How does a steak dinner sound?"

"You're the main attraction, but I won't say 'no' to a steak. What time?"

"Seven."

"All right, darlin'. Until then."

As I replaced the receiver, my hand trembled, and tears threatened. How I wished I could see the expression on Brett's face.

Monday dawned with blinding sun, a welcome respite from the gloom of the past few days. After I showered, I rushed to Cornucopia, touched base with Jolie, posted the holiday schedule, and headed back south of the river to Hudson's Meat Market for Angus ribeyes.

When I arrived home, I rummaged in the cabinet for a shallow platter, seasoned the meat with pepper, brown sugar, and salt, rubbing in the dry ingredients. Then I drizzled each side with Worcestershire sauce, wrapped the plate in plastic, and stuck it in the refrigerator. Made a mental note to remove it about half an hour before placing the meat on a hot grill.

The only side dishes I planned were lemon roasted asparagus and baked potatoes. If Brett wanted dessert, I had vanilla Blue Bell in the freezer.

How was I going to fill the hours until seven? A Pilates session, a toasty warm bath, and food prep brought me to five o'clock. I applied a green clay face mask and lay in bed until it was set. At six, I started awake, surprised that I'd fallen asleep. Barely had enough time to rinse off the facial, get dressed, and do hair and makeup.

Six-thirty and I rushed to the kitchen to take the steaks out of the fridge and preheat the oven for the vegetables. Back in the bathroom, a wide-eyed, panicked woman stared at me from the mirror. That wouldn't do at all. I began to recite the Serenity Prayer over and over until my breathing slowed. With my makeup done, I searched the closet for the perfect dress. Baby-pink silk with turquoise leaves, buttery yellow and lavender flowers, from my favorite designer of the moment, Flora Kung. Nightmare be damned—this dress was a hot ticket. The side-wrap style with three-quarter sleeves, wide draped collar, and sexy slit skirt made me feel like a million bucks. I knew Brett would love it. Givenchy heels in turquoise completed the look. Despite the attack of nerves, I did a decent job of containing my curls in an updo.

With five minutes to spare, I returned to the kitchen, put the potatoes in the oven, and readied the asparagus. When the bell rang, I took a few calming breaths and answered the door.

Brett handed me a bouquet of red roses, which I placed on the console table. "Va va voom! That dress."

Unable to control the urge, I threw my arms around his neck. With the energy of a twenty-something, he picked me up and twirled me in the air, leaving me breathless.

When I landed on solid ground, he kissed me until I felt like I was floating. Reluctantly breaking away, I said, "Whoa, there. Dinner is in the works. We'll eat in the kitchen, where it's cozier."

"Whatever you say."

"How are you with a grill?"

"Try me."

Roses in hand, I led him to the kitchen, motioned to the platter of meat, and pointed him at the patio. "It's propane. Let me know if you need help. Vegetables will be ready in about half an hour. Can I bring you a cup of coffee or tea?"

"Don't think I can stomach that mint tea, even for you, but coffee would be good."

"Just started a pot. I'll bring it to you in a bit."

He ducked his head and smiled.

While Brett grilled, I placed the roses in a vase, set the table and checked on the potatoes and asparagus. My heart raced in anticipation of the talk we'd be having later. With all my years of experience guiding recovering women through their amends, I knew what I had to do, but my nerves were twanging nonetheless.

I poured a cup of coffee and took it out to Brett. He placed it on the cart next to the grill and reached for me.

With a laugh, I eluded his grasp. "Save it for later. Now, drink your coffee."

"The steaks are just about ready."

"Great. I'll dish up the vegetables."

Brett called after me. "Baby, you look just as good goin' as comin'."

With a smile, I entered the kitchen. A few minutes later, the patio door opened, and Brett came in, holding the platter with sizzling, savory meat. "If I do say so myself, these here are done to perfection."

"Come on and sit. Everything else is ready."

During the meal, we made desultory conversation about the food, Brett's activities at the recovery ranch, and the store.

After his last bite of steak, Brett asked, "What are your plans for Christmas, darlin'?"

"Helen hosts an open house for AA members without any nearby family. I go every year. It's a potluck. Want to come with me?"

Brett's face broke out in a smile. "Sure would. What're ya bringing?"

"Hmm. I haven't decided yet."

"I'll help you cook if you'd like."

Our eyes met, and my heart opened. With my pig-headed denial, it was hard to admit I'd been wrong to leave this good man. By a veritable miracle, he'd come back to me. I gulped, dreading what came next. "If you're interested in dessert, I have some vanilla ice cream."

"Ice cream, you say. I do hope it's Blue Bell."

"Of course."

"You havin' some?"

"No. Maybe later."

"Okay. I'll wait too. I'm good at waiting."

"Yes, you are." With a forced smile, I rose from the table and picked up my plate.

Brett stood and took it from me. "No, ma'am. I'm doing the clean-up. Just relax and I'll join you in the living room for that talk."

Unable to get words past my constricted throat, I nodded. Then, I fled to my bedroom and got down on my knees, praying for guidance and humility, for the strength to face my flaws and repair the damage I'd done to Brett. Why was this so difficult? In a way, I felt broken, but in another way, I felt whole at long last. After a few minutes, I took a deep breath, whispered the Serenity Prayer once more, and stepped into the hallway.

"There you are! Come sit." Brett patted the seat beside him.

I settled next to him. "It's time I take an unflinching look at how I've lived my life, and frankly, I'm terrified." My eyes burned, and I was afraid I'd start blubbering. "Right now, I don't like myself very much, and the regrets are piled sky-high."

With his brow furrowed, he reached for my hand. "Regrets?"

"Too many to name."

"About me?"

Unable to meet his eyes, I nodded.

"My only regret is that I let you go, that I didn't fight harder for you."

Despite my trepidation, a smile tugged at the corners of my mouth. "That's sweet, but the way I was back then, it wouldn't have mattered. I was determined to leave."

Brett brought my hand to his lips and kissed it. With that gesture, tears tracked down my cheeks.

"Hey, honey. It's all right. We're here together now." He handed me his handkerchief, and I dabbed my eyes.

When I composed myself, I confessed it all, from my affair with Alain to the adoption of my daughter by the Boston Babcocks. The estrangement from my family, the colossal mistake of marrying Michael Goldfein, the geographical cures, the binges, the men, everything. I recited the horror of my past without making eye contact. Brett's body tensed at certain passages; he grunted a time or two, but he never interrupted me. At last, all out of transgressions, I leaned against his shoulder.

With his arm around me, Brett kissed my forehead. "Feel better?"

I wrapped my arms around him. "Yes, surprisingly, yes." After a minute, I asked, "Do you hate me?"

"No, I could never hate you, sweetheart. In fact, I love you, have from the start and nothing will ever change that truth." His voice brimmed with emotion.

Those words, spoken with deep conviction, touched me in a place I didn't know still existed and reinforced my decision to let Brett back into my life. We sat nestled together for an hour or more. At eleven, Brett yawned. "I better head out."

"No, you're staying."

Exhausted from the unloaded and processed emotional baggage, we washed up and climbed into bed, holding each other, kissing until we fell asleep in each other's arms. Around five a.m., we woke and made love. At our age, it was different, slower, sweeter, but just as, if not more, satisfying.

"How I've missed you, Lauren."

"Oh honey, me too. Welcome home."

"Really? This isn't some dream or hallucination, is it? 'Cause if it is, I don't wanna wake up—ever."

I snuggled closer, drifting back to sleep.

A few hours later, I woke to the aroma of coffee and smiled. I hurried my morning ablutions and joined Brett in the kitchen.

As I entered the warmth of the room, Brett was flipping hotcakes on the griddle. "Hope you like these. Guess you don't have any bacon."

"I don't usually buy it."

"I'll make sure to bring some by." He held out a plate piled high with pancakes.

Accepting the dish, I said, "Looks yummy. Did you find the syrup?"

"Nope. Ya got some?"

I put my plate down, opened the pantry, and found the maple syrup. "I use the real thing, not that blasted artificial-flavored stuff."

"Good to know. Let's eat." He brought his own plate to the table, then grabbed the coffee pot and poured.

After I sampled the food, I said, "These are delicious. I didn't know you could cook."

"Well, after you left, I had to learn to feed myself."

My heart sank, but there was no reproach in his voice. It was a mere statement of fact. I'd best remember not to overreact to every mention of the past. After last night, we had moved on.

And I was more than ready.

"Honey, you said you had some chores to do today, so I'll head out after I finish the dishes."

"No rush."

Brett smiled. "That's nice to hear."

"It's nice to say." Heat rose, and I knew my cheeks were red.

After the meal, I returned to my bedroom to shower and dress for the day. It occurred to me that Brett didn't have a change of clothes and might want to return home. I stepped into the living room and found him rummaging through my stereo cabinet.

He glanced up. "You have quite a collection. I'm intrigued by the selection of blues artists. Who's your favorite?"

"I have to say Bobby 'Blue' Bland. He's got a new album, *Members Only*. I also have his 1962 album, *Here's The Man*. It has one of my favorite songs. 'Turn On Your Lovelight.'"

Brett nodded. "Good choice. Just so you know, I'm pretty sure your lovelight got turned on this morning."

Was I blushing again?

"I like Muddy and B.B. a lot. Seen them a time or two in Deep Ellum. Hey, your turntable plays 78s, I see."

"Yes, being a sentimental fool, I kept a few. They're on the bottom shelf."

Kneeling on the floor, Brett rifled through the old vinyl. "Lots of old big-band stuff we used to dance to. Benny Goodman, Tommy Dorsey, Harry James. Good memories." He grinned and selected a 78. "You came around."

Perplexed, I sat next to him. "What do you mean?"

He held up his find, "I'll Be Seeing You," the Bing Crosby rendition. "You used to prefer the way Frank Sinatra performed our song."

I blinked back tears as I recalled the night I destroyed Sinatra's record after watching "The Days of Wine and Roses" teleplay. I had spent hours wallowing in regret and misery over Brett. Back then, still in the throes of alcoholism, it never occurred to me to make things right with him. The following day, I'd gone to the store and bought Brett's favorite Bing Crosby version, although I never had played it.

Brett removed the disc from the paper sleeve and placed it on the turntable. He stood and helped me to my feet. Our eyes locked. When he pulled me close, I caught sight of both my past and my future in his loving face.

And then we danced.

The End

Acknowledgments

Writing can be a lonely and myopic pursuit. That is why my critique groups are so important to me. The Kerrville Writers Association, Medina Wordsmiths, and the Women's Fiction Writers Association have all contributed to my growth as a writer.

I'd like to thank my beta readers: Tom McEachin, Ann Bishop, Vicki Brower, Vicki George, Carol Milberger, Susan Hull, Martha Dickens, and Elise Harbour. Your comments and suggestions were instrumental in crafting the final product.

Joanne Kukanza Easley

A retired registered nurse with experience in both the cold, clinical operating room and the emotionally fraught world of psychiatric hospitals, Joanne lives on a small ranch in the Texas Hill Country, where she writes fiction about complicated, twentieth-century women. Her multi-award winning debut, *Sweet Jane,* released in March, 2020, was named the adult fiction winner at the Texas Author Project and shortlisted for the Sarton Award and Eric Hoffer Award, among others. *Just One Look*, Joanne's second novel, was a May 2022 Pulpwood Queen Book Club Pick. *I'll Be Seeing You,* her third novel, features characters from *Sweet Jane*. Her prize-winning short stories and poetry have appeared in several anthologies.

Sweet Jane

A drunken mother makes childhood ugly. Jane runs away at sixteen, determined to leave her fraught upbringing in the rearview. Vowing never to return, she hitchhikes to California, right on time for the Summer of Love. Seventeen years later, she looks good on paper: married, grad school, sober, but her carefully constructed life is crumbling. When Mama dies, Jane returns for the funeral, leaving her husband in the dark about her history. Seeing her childhood home and significant people from her youth catapults Jane back to the events that made her the woman she is. She faces down her past and the ghosts that shaped her family. A stunning discovery helps Jane see her problems through a new lens.

Just One Look

In 1965 Chicago, thirteen-year-old Dani Marek declares she's in love, and you best believe it. This is no crush, and for six blissful years she fills her hope chest with linens, dinnerware, and dreams of an idyllic future with John. When he is killed in action in Viet Nam, Dani's world shatters. She launches a one-woman vendetta against the men she seeks out in Rush Street's singles bars. Her goal: break as many hearts as she can. Dani's ill-conceived vengeance leads her to a loveless marriage that ends in tragedy. At twenty-four, she's left a widow with a baby, a small fortune, and a ghost—make that two. Set in the turbulent Sixties and Seventies, *Just One Look* explores one woman's tumultuous journey through grief, denial, and letting go.

www.ingramcontent.com/pod-product-compliance
Lightning Source LLC
Chambersburg PA
CBHW031525310726
48971CB00008B/2349